Any Landing You Walk Away From...

A flight attendant's fictionalized account of her career

during 1980s deregulation

DAWN O'HARRA

PARISIANPHOENIX.COM
angel@parisianphoenix.com
parisianphoenixpublishing.substack.com
@parisianphoenixpublishing
/parisan-phoenix-publishing
/parisianphoenixpublishing
@parisianphoenix
/parisianphoenix.bsky.social
parisian phoenix
PUBLISHING

PART ONE:

Chasing a Dream, June 1981

CHAPTER ONE

May watched from the office window as a small Cessna 152 pulled off the runway and taxied toward the hangar. As soon as the airplane stopped and its engine shut down, a short, stocky young man of nineteen or twenty opened the door on the left side of the aircraft, half stepping, half falling out of the plane. His lean, wiry, and much older instructor emerged from the door on the right, a friendly, patient grin spread across his sun-tanned face.

"Okay, young feller. You did better this time," the older man said. He signed the young man's log book and returned it to him. "I'll see you at the same time tomorrow."

The younger man smiled broadly and headed to his parked car. May opened the office door and met the older man as he entered.

"How did the lesson go, Orrie?" she asked.

He shrugged. "Oh, he wasn't too bad, I guess. I'm still alive. Lord knows, I've seen a lot worse. Needs practice. Just like you, young lady."

She sighed. "I know. Believe me, I'd like to be up there every minute, but I just don't have the money."

The old pilot's eyes crinkled up as he gave her an encouraging smile. "You'll get there. You just keep at it." He winked at her and whispered, "I'll take you up again later in the week when the boss ain't lookin'."

May smiled back. "Thanks. C'mon, I'll help you push the plane back into the hangar."

With the aircraft secured, May pulled the hangar door closed as the noise of another plane overhead caught her attention.

"That's Hoot's last run for the day," she said, glancing at her watch. "It's after seven and I don't think there's anyone else scheduled to jump tonight."

Her gaze traveled to the center of the runway. Two parachutists landed, making a bullseye on the jump target. They gathered their chutes and started towards May and Orrie. Yet another noise distracted her, but this time it was coming from the highway, not the sky.

"Do you hear that?" she asked, turning her head.

"Sounds like a fire truck coming this way," Orrie answered.

The sound grew louder, then faded as it passed the airport entrance and moved on down the road. A moment later, an ancient DC-3 touched down and taxied to the large hangar just beyond May and Orrie. The plane stopped, both engines cut off. Hoot, a white-haired man about the same age as Orrie, stepped from the plane. His weathered hawk-like face bore an expression between a grin and an apology, like a child pleased with himself for breaking a rule and knowing he was about to be reprimanded. He turned quickly as the office door flew open. Hal, a balding, middle-aged man, hurried towards the parked plane.

"Uh oh," May whispered to her companion. "I wonder what he did this time."

The two cautiously approached the scene as Hal's gestures became more animated, his voice rising as he addressed the pilot. The older white-haired man stood scratching his head.

"How the hell do I know how it happened, Hal?"

"Hey, Hoot," May said as she and Orrie approached the plane. She forced a casual tone into her voice. "What's going on?"

Scarlet-faced Hal owned the parachuting company and he cut in before Hoot could answer.

"I'll tell you what's going on. I've got a customer swinging from a parachute fifty feet up in a goddam tree about a mile down the road."

May and Orrie shared a quick glance.

"The fire truck," she whispered.

Hal stood glaring at Hoot.

"Now don't blame me, Hal," he said. "He looked great last time I saw him at ten thousand feet. He said he knew exactly what he was doin', big mouth jackass New Yorker. Braggin' about how great a jumper he was. Serves him right. He didn't hurt the tree, did he?"

Hal, fuming, turned to May and Orrie. "Can you two drive over there and see what's happening? I sure as hell can't send this character."

"Absolutely, boss. No problem at all. We'll check it out and be right back," she promised. The two hurried to Orrie's car.

The long fire engine ladder was already up in the giant pine tree by the time they pulled off the road a mile or so from the airport. They'd been followed by a bright red van that pulled up beside them as they parked. May and Orrie watched as the two jumpers they'd seen touchdown at the airport moments before exited the vehicle and stopped below the towering pine. They looked up. Far above, a chubby young man was swearing and trying to untangle himself from his twisted parachute. A fireman reaching over from the ladder tried to assist him, but the young man slapped his hands.

"Lemme alone, dickhead!" he shrieked. "I'm never coming here again, this place sucks!"

He squirmed, twisting from side to side.

"There's something wrong with this goddam parachute and that plane, what a piece o' crap! That pilot, who taught him to fly—Peter Pan?"

He freed himself and relented long enough to allow the fireman to help him down the ladder. May and Orrie watched as the young man's friends helped him to the waiting van.

"I swear ta God there's something wrong with my chute. And that pilot! Wait 'til I see that goddam pilot!"

"Shuddup, Nickie," one of his friends shouted. "It's always your chute. It's always the pilot. It's your forty-fifth jump, for Christ's sake, and a paraplegic can jump better than you. By now, the least you could do is aim for a short goddam tree."

The men stuffed the parachute and their friend into the van and sped off.

Hoot was working on the DC-3 when May and Orrie returned.

"So where's Captain Bullseye?" Hoot asked. "Did they get him down?"

May relayed the events as he chuckled softly.

"I figured it was something like that."

"I don't know why you take 'em up," started Orrie with a shake of his head. "Back in the war—"

"We gonna have this conversation again?" Hoot groaned. "Yeah, I know, you flew the P51. Why would anybody jump out of a perfectly good airplane if you don't have to… Blah, blah, blah… Horse shit. Listen. We dropped plenty of things out of the B-17s I flew. If people want to jump for fun, I'll take 'em. Are a few of 'em idiots? Sure. It's just like anything else. I had one jump a few years back that didn't know his ass from a hole in the ground. He panicked and didn't open his chute."

Orrie nodded. "Yeah, then his ass was a hole in the ground."

"That's right," Hoot said.

"That's so horrible!" May said, unaware she was falling into a trap. "My God, I wonder what the last thing that went through the poor man's mind was."

"His feet!" the two men roared, slapping each other on the back.

"I don't know why I hang around you guys," May said, rolling her eyes as she headed to the office. "I'll see you later."

*****

"Hey, what do you think of this, Jake?" May asked the man across the table.

"I don't know. What is it?" Jake took the *New York Times* from her hands and looked at the classified ad she'd circled. The bright Saturday morning sunlight made his dark blond hair look lighter and caught the green of his eyes as he scanned the print. "They're looking for flight attendants, but it doesn't say which airline."

"You think one of the big carriers put it in, like TWA?" May said hopefully.

"I wouldn't be too optimistic about that right now, not the way the economy is. It's probably one of those cut-rate upstart companies that are making the big ones go bankrupt."

"You're such a killjoy, Jake," May replied.

A frown crossed her face.

"Sorry," Jake said, "but you know how tough the economy is right now, especially for the airline industry. It's only been deregulated for a year or two, and the companies are all undercutting each other and laying people off. Reagan fired all the air traffic controllers! Some people are still afraid to fly after that bad crash in Chicago."

He stood, sipping his coffee.

"You've been sending out applications to the big airlines for months now, and they're all saying they may hire people in what… 1984? That's three years from now."

Seeing the discouraged look on May's face, Jake softened his voice as he sat beside her.

"I know how much you want to travel. You need to be patient."

May looked into her coffee.

"I know, but there is so much I want to see and I want to get started. I need a job that will let me travel." She couldn't stop the wistful smile that crept across her face. "You know me and airplanes. A flight attendant job would be so perfect. I could travel, get paid, and finally be able to afford to get my pilot's license. My friend, Deb, loves flying for United. She's so lucky that she got hired when she did, right before deregulation hit and sent everything into a tailspin."

Jake put his arm around her and touched her long, auburn hair.

"I know you're frustrated, and I know how much you want your pilot's license."

He stretched his long legs beneath the table.

"At least you've been able to learn something working at that little airport these past months, even if you have to put up with those two crazy, old geezers you hang out with."

May nodded. "You're right. But I'm fond of those two old geezers. They've been great, taking me up sometimes and giving me pointers. I've just have to make enough money to afford to do it right."

Jake looked at the paper again.

"I don't know who placed the ad but I think you need to call and find out. So what if it's some new upstart airline? You could work there for a while and who knows, when the economy gets better, maybe you could apply to a big airline."

"That's true. It's not like there's a lot to choose from now anyway. Pass that paper back."

She read the ad again.

"It says call Monday through Friday between nine and five."

Jake grinned.

"Good. You're off work and I'm off work. That means we've got all weekend to canoe!" A few days later, early Monday morning, May called the number.

"Equity Air," answered a brisk voice on the other end.

May was disappointed. *Not TWA*, she thought, though she did recognize the company name. She knew every airline by heart, even the small ones. She knew every airline logo, where they flew, what every uniform looked like. Equity wasn't an upstart brought about by deregulation. It was a charter airline that had been around since the 1940s. They flew mostly old DC-8 jets and flew all over the world. May recalled Jake's suggestion that she work for a smaller airline until the major ones started to hire again. Suddenly, she was filled with excitement and asked the woman every question she could think of about the airline.

"Yes, we still need people, and if you feel that you meet our requirements, we'd like you to come to New York for a group interview. As a matter of fact, I can set one up for you right this minute."

May was about to accept the offer then stopped.

"What about a language? You fly international flights. Do I need to speak another language?"

"Well, yes. You do."

May's heart sank. She spoke a little Spanish but certainly was not fluent. She was silent. The airline representative eventually broke the silence, speaking in a confidential tone.

"You know, if you meet the other standards, I know for a fact that they're not too strict about the language requirement. I really think you should come for the interview."

May mulled this over. She didn't want to misrepresent herself but the woman on the phone sounded confident and convincing. A small international airline… Low pay… Exotic destinations… Adventure galore… It wasn't TWA, but pickings were damned slim at the moment. What the hell!

"Okay, you've convinced me. I'll do it."

May hung up the phone with directions to the interview in hand.

Oh boy, she thought, *Here we go.*

Early the next morning, May and her younger sister, Lynn, stood in a pile of clothes they'd pulled from May's closet and rejected.

"I don't like any of this stuff! You have to be the most unfashionable person I know!" Lynn chided. "Why don't you ever buy yourself good clothes?"

"I'm not a fashion maven like you are," May answered dryly. "Maybe that's why I want this job. I'll wear a uniform and won't have to worry about wardrobe choices! Here, this one's nice."

She held up a simple beige knit dress. Her sister nodded.

"It's your best one anyway. Shows some curves but not tacky. Wear a little jewelry with it."

"Like what?"

Lynn rolled her eyes and pulled a gold chain from the jewelry box.

"Here, wear this. They didn't exactly give you a lot of time to get ready, did they? One day?"

May smiled. "The sooner the better as far as I'm concerned. Now I need makeup."

Her sister raised an eyebrow. "Oh, no! You're worse at makeup than you are with clothes!

"Well, that's why you're here. Help me out."

Lynn applied mascara to her sister's eyes and added a little color to her cheeks. May looked in the mirror. Her wavy auburn hair hung softly by her shoulders. The makeup Lynn added made her blue eyes pop. At twenty-two, May was slim, average height, and very attractive.

"What do you think? Will this do?"

Her sister looked her up and down. "Not bad. They'll never know what you really look like."

"Good. What time is it?"

"Time for you to go! I hope that old beater of a car of yours makes it." She grabbed May and gave her a hug. "Seriously, good luck! You look great. Tell me all about it when you get back."

May hopped into her ancient Buick Skylark for the three-hour trip from rural Connecticut to New York City. The old vehicle threatened to overheat on the warm June day. She found the hotel where she'd have her interview without much difficulty. She pulled into the hotel lot, parked, and got out, checking her dress. It showed only a trace of a wrinkle after the long drive, and May congratulated herself on choosing the knit. *The only thing more wrinkle-proof would have been polyester,* she thought with a chuckle.

She hurried to the hotel, a place near Kennedy Airport, glancing at her watch as she opened the door. She stepped into the lobby. *Hmmm, about fifteen minutes early,* May thought. The front desk was only a few feet away. She caught the eye of a plump, unhappy-looking female clerk.

"The Equity suite is on the second floor," the clerk said shortly, "and the bathroom is right around the corner over there."

She turned away and didn't say another word.

Wow... we must all look alike, May mused, marveling at the girl's ability to size her up so quickly. She darted into the bathroom to freshen up and then found the elevator.

The elevator doors opened, depositing her on the second floor, where she joined the ranks of a dozen or so well-dressed young people wandering nervously about in the hall. A middle-aged woman, wire bifocals perched on the end of her nose, sat behind a table next to the closed door of the hotel suite. Summoning her courage, May walked to the table to introduce herself. A pair of sharp eyes looked up at her over the glasses.

"One moment," she said as she rummaged through a pile of papers.

May glanced discreetly at the other applicants while she waited, her eyes resting on an attractive brunette sitting in a chair by the door. The girl was impeccable in a navy blue suit and white blouse. There was something about the way she sat: calm, collected, hands folded in her lap. May was suddenly very self-conscious as her eyes moved from the girl's navy suit to her own beige knit dress. Did she look professional enough?

The woman with the glasses found what she was looking for.

"Okay, we have you down here for the three o'clock group interview and it's about to start. You can go into the room now and find a seat."

May stole one more glance at the girl in the navy suit and went in. She chose a seat from the semi-circle of chairs in the center of the room and sat. The rest of the chairs filled quickly as the other candidates poured in from the hall. A bit of perspiration popped out on May's brow. A tiny trickle of sweat moved down the back of her neck.

Oh crap, she thought nervously. *Don't let anybody see that. Please don't let anybody see that. Who wants a sweaty stewardess?*

Everyone snapped to attention as two interviewers entered the room. The first was a very business-like woman of about forty with short reddish hair, and the other a polished, and slightly over-coiffed, dark-haired man of about thirty.

"Hello," said the red-haired woman.

"I'm Joyce, and this is…"

She gestured to the man beside her.

"Roger," he answered, smiling at his partner with perfect white teeth.

May responded with a big smile as did everybody else. They settled into a pair of seats facing the interviewees and politely examined the group. May never let the smile slip from her face. Her cheek muscles started to throb as Joyce told them about the company.

"Now we want to hear about you," the woman said in a brisk, professional manner after she finished her speech. "Why don't we go around the room, and you can each tell us something about yourselves."

When May's turn came, she tried to keep it pleasant and to the point. She was a college graduate with a degree in history, liked to travel, and liked working with people. By the time she finished, Roger was smiling at her but, to her dismay, Joyce didn't acknowledge her at all. May found it impossible to read her.

Maybe if just one of them likes me, it will be enough, she thought anxiously.

From that day forward, the criteria for choosing flight attendants would always baffle May. All of the people in the interview seemed like perfectly good candidates to her. How did they choose? The questions continued until the interviewers stood, indicating they were finished. They handed a slip of paper with a phone number to each of the candidates.

"We want you to call this number in one hour," Roger said. "We will let you know then whether you will be moving on to an individual interview. Thank you so much for coming and best of luck to all of you."

May stood awkwardly in the hall for a moment or two then decided to wait out the hour at the hotel. It seemed like a better idea than leaving and having to find a phone somewhere later. She stepped into the elevator, joining one of the other candidates, a round-faced man of about twenty-five. As they rode to the lobby, they fell into conversation.

"It's gonna be a long hour," the young man said, rubbing his hands together.

"Oh, it will be over before you know it," May answered, not too convincingly. "What's your name?"

"Mike."

"Well Mike, I'm going to wait and call from the hotel lobby."

"That's a great idea! Mind if I wait with you?"

"Not at all."

He's nice, she thought. *I'm sure they want nice. God, he'll be a shoo-in. I wonder if that Roger guy thought I was nice?*

Time crawled and the pair became increasingly uncomfortable. They sat in silence for the last few minutes, having run out of small talk. When the hour finally ended, they looked at each other hesitantly.

"I'll go," May said, rising from her seat.

She reached the lobby phone and plopped a quarter in the machine slot, her hand trembling slightly as she picked up the receiver and dialed the number.

"Yes, we would like to see you tomorrow afternoon at one o'clock," the voice on the line said.

May recognized the voice of the red-haired woman.

Roger must have made the decision, she thought, hanging up the phone. *That lady hardly knew I was in the room.*

Excited to get a second interview, she flashed a thumbs up to Mike. He congratulated her profusely then took the phone from her hand. The tightening muscles in his face and the tone of his voice relayed the answer before he finished the conversation.

May squirmed. He hung up the receiver and shook his head.

"No, I didn't get it."

She murmured some incoherent condolence, not knowing what else to do. The moment was embarrassingly long until the two said an awkward goodbye and parted.

What a tough business, May thought as she headed for her car.

The next day at 12:45 p.m., she jumped out of her car in the parking lot of the same hotel near Kennedy Airport. Once again, she stopped in the ladies' room, checked her appearance, and took the elevator to the second-floor suite.

Right on time, she thought with satisfaction.

Standing ramrod straight, smile nailed to her face, she knocked on the suite door and entered.

Everything was gone. No desk. No papers. No circle of chairs. No receptionist with bifocals, and no Roger. Nothing. Only a maid vacuuming the rug. May scratched her head. Was this the right suite? She looked back at the number on the door.

This is definitely the place, what gives?

She approached the maid who had her back to her. The woman vigorously pushed and pulled the vacuum across the carpet sweating profusely as she worked. She hadn't heard May over the noise of the vacuum. May tapped the woman on the shoulder.

"Excuse me."

The startled maid jumped, dropped her vacuum, and threw her arms into the air.

"*Dios Mío!*" she shrieked.

"Oh! Oh! I'm so sorry to startle you!" May cried. " I'm looking for the Equity Air suite, can you tell me where it is?"

The woman slowly lowered her arms and glared at her.

"*No hablo Ingles,*" she spat in disgust, shaking her head as she returned to her task. She continued to mumble in Spanish, and May was sure she heard the words "*gringa*" and "*muy estúpida*" before the woman switched the vacuum back on.

Jesus, what is going on here? Am I in another universe or something?

In a panic, she hurried down to the front desk. The same clerk from the day before was still there.

May ran to her.

"Excuse me, I was supposed to have an interview here today at one o'clock with the Equity Air people, can you tell me what suite they're in?"

"They left at noon," the clerk yawned, not looking up.

May could feel her stomach sinking down, as if it were going to take up a new home around her ankles. She didn't move.

"Are you May?" the clerk said suddenly.

"YES!" she shouted.

A glimmer of hope! This girl knew her name! There must be a reason.

"I have a note for you," she said with a smirk.

She handed May an envelope. May grabbed it hastily, ripping it open.

"Please come to my office at the Northwest terminal at the airport for your interview," she read aloud. It was signed, "Roger."

"Thank God!"

She reached over the desk, grabbing the clerk's hand and shaking it profusely.

"Thank you, thank you so much! Thank you!"

"Okay, okay, whatever. Gimme my hand back," the clerk answered, annoyed.

May didn't understand what had happened but ran as fast as she could for her car, drove to the Northwest terminal, and found the Equity Air offices and Roger, as polished and perfect as the day before.

"So, you missed our appointment at eleven o'clock, eh?" he said, ushering her into his office.

At least he's smiling, she thought, completely flustered and out of breath.

Somehow, she found her voice.

"Um…It was supposed to be at one," she replied as diplomatically as she could.

She'd written it down so that she wouldn't screw up the time.

"No, no, no," Roger insisted, "it was at eleven."

May swallowed the urge to keep arguing, smiled sheepishly, and he seemed to forget about it.

"Well, no matter, let's get on with your language test, shall we? So you speak Spanish?"

May sat dumb-struck as he rattled off incomprehensible questions at her with a Castilian accent.

Think of something, think of anything! her mind screamed as she tried to hide the overwhelming terror welling inside her. What little Spanish she did remember drained from her consciousness.

"*Es… Es.... Espanol es una lengua muy bonita* and ah.... ah… ah…"

Roger waited expectantly.

"Eh, hem…Well, *Espanol es* ah... ah, huh ah……"

A Spanish phrase suddenly popped into her mind. Thrilled to remember anything, she blurted it out.

"Ah, *mi culo es mucho grande.*" Her voice cracked. It was hopeless. "*Mi Espanol es muy terrible.*"

Roger said nothing for a bit, then moved up in his chair.

"Yes, I will agree with your assessment of your Spanish since you just told me that your rear end is very large."

May's face went absolutely crimson.

"You know, we do require that you be fluent in a foreign language," Roger said.

Trying to recover her dignity, she stammered, "But... but… I was told that the language requirement wasn't that important if I fulfilled the other requirements. I… I made sure I asked before I came to the first interview."

She rattled on in desperation. Roger stood.

"Why don't you take a nice language course and come back and see us in six months?"

With a sympathetic smile, he graciously showed May the door and closed it behind her. She found herself standing alone in the terminal. It had taken all of five minutes. She was crushed, bewildered, humiliated. As she wandered out of the terminal, she tried to make sense of what had just happened. She was angry. Angry because she felt that she'd been misled, but also ashamed of the fact that after three years of high school Spanish and another class in college, the only comment she could come up with was about the size of her rear end.

May got into her old Buick and started the long drive home, the tears of disappointment beginning to flow. How could she go home and face her family members and all of their questions? What would she tell Jake?

She found herself pulling into his lake house. It was dinner time and he'd built a nice fire on the shore near the water. He sat on a log twirling a hotdog on the end of a long stick over the fire, the juices running out of it and sizzling as they hit the flames. He looked up.

"Hey! I wasn't expecting you! How did it go? You want a hot dog?" He gazed into her tear-stained face. "Uh oh, what happened?"

May poured out the story, going over and over the events and generally making both of them miserable.

"Let me get this straight," Jake said. "You told your prospective employer you have a big ass in Spanish?"

He couldn't control himself and burst out laughing. May shot him a baleful look.

"Okay, I'm sorry, but that is really funny and not true by the way. Your ass is just fine. Come on, it's not the end of the world," Jake tried to console her. "Give it time, something else is bound to turn up."

"Like what? I've been looking for so long and this was my only nibble. I'm so tired of hanging around, I just have to get out and see things!"

"Are you tired of hanging around me?" Jake asked quietly.

"No, of course not, that's not what I meant. But you're six years older than I am and you've been around and seen a lot. Your outdoor equipment business takes you everywhere, and with your brother and sister working with you now, your business is only going to grow. Is it wrong for me to want to explore the world, too?"

"No, not at all. I just think you might have to be patient, that's all."

They talked all night, until the sky started getting light and they were both exhausted. Jake doused the last glowing embers of the campfire with water.

"Go home," he told her. "We'll both get some good sleep, and I'm sure things will look better. If plan A doesn't work out, that's when you have to come up with plan B."

May gave him a tired hug.

"I hope you're right. Sorry, I ruined your night."

Jake smiled wearily.

"What's the New York expression? 'Fuggedabout it!' I'll see you later."

May got in her car and drove home. She could smell bacon and eggs cooking as she opened the front door. A chair squeaked as it pushed away from the kitchen table, and her sister raced into the room.

"Where have you been? We called everywhere trying to find you! I finally figured out that you probably went to Jake's house. How can that guy NOT have a phone? I know he's a nature nut, but really!"

"I like him that way," May said wearily. "What's the matter?"

"Some man from Equity called all last evening, and we couldn't reach you. He called again this morning. What happened yesterday? He left this number for you."

May ran to the phone and anxiously dialed the number. As she suspected, Roger answered.

"Hi, May. It's Roger from Equity. I was thinking about you all afternoon and evening after you left and, well, it seems we've had a last-minute cancellation in our next training class. We'd like to have you, if you want to go. We'll hire you on the stipulation that you learn Spanish in the next six months and learn to talk about something other than the size of your butt."

May blushed, unable to believe her luck. Roger came through after all.

"I'll go! I'll go!" she shouted into the phone.

"Okay," he laughed. "You'll come here, to my office, tomorrow morning at nine a.m. to get your ticket to fly to training in Nashville, Tennessee. Bring clothes and money for three weeks. You will not be receiving any type of payment until you actually start working."

"Be in New York tomorrow?" she gulped.

"Yes."

She drew in her breath.

"Okay, tomorrow it is."

"Good. Remember, my office at nine sharp. Your ticket will be waiting for you."

"Thanks, Roger. I appreciate this."

"Welcome to Equity," he answered.

Before she could reply, he hung up.

Years later, when May told the story, she always mentioned that she never took the language course. The airline dropped the requirement a few weeks after she finished training.

CHAPTER 2

May spent the rest of the day frantically packing. She tried to process all of the events in her mind as she hunted through her dresser drawers and closet for suitable clothes for training.

"Business attire and makeup every day," she sighed aloud. "This is going to be tough."

The afternoon was nearly gone when she heard Jake's van pull into the driveway. She quickly dropped her makeup bag, ran down the stairs, out the front door, and leaped into his arms.

"Wow, what's this? A few hours ago, you were acting like life was over. What changed?"

"You won't believe it, Jake! That guy Roger, you know, the interviewer from yesterday?"

"The one you told about your giant butt?"

"Yes! Yes, that's the one! He said someone dropped out of the next training class and they want me! It's a miracle!"

Jake smiled, then planted a kiss on her lips. He dropped her slowly to the ground, keeping his arms around her.

"He probably just realized what a big mistake he'd made not hiring you in the first place. When do you have to leave?"

"I have to pick up my ticket at the airport tomorrow morning at nine."

Jake whistled softly. "Wow, they didn't exactly give you a lot of time, did they?"

"No, they didn't," May gulped, "but it's okay. I'm so grateful that I don't mind a bit."

"Well," Jake said, "can I offer you a ride to the airport?"

May beamed. "I was hoping you'd say that, but I have to leave so early. Are you sure you won't mind?"

Jake pulled her close and kissed her again.

"Not a bit," he whispered.

So early the next morning with the world still dark, May dragged her large suitcase towards Jake's van.

"What have you got in here?" he groaned, lifting it into the back seat.

"Just about everything, I think," she grinned.

She pulled herself into the passenger seat. Jake got in beside her. He turned the key, and the vehicle came to life. The faintest bit of morning light crept into the sky.

"Ready for this?" Jake asked. "Said all of your goodbyes to the family?"

"Yep!" May answered enthusiastically. "Let's get this adventure on the road!"

The van lumbered down the long, dark driveway and onto the open road. May dozed off and on until the sun came up and shone insistently in her eyes. They'd been driving for more than an hour.

"Ready for coffee?" Jake asked with a smile.

"Oh yeah," May answered.

She rubbed her eyes.

"Good, because I'm pulling off at this exit right here."

They found a diner near the highway. As May ate, she mumbled, "There's nothing like hot coffee and a greasy donut to get the day started. And please don't let me spill anything on myself. I'd hate to have to wrestle that suitcase to find a clean set of clothes."

A wry smile crossed Jake's face.

"Oh, don't worry, I'll keep an eye on you. I'm always very cautious around you and food."

May stopped chewing.

"Why, what do you mean?"

Jake glanced at her, a teasing gleam in his eye.

"Oh, nothing really, while you were dozing, I was just thinking about how we met, you know, at that party my cousin brought you to? You can be a little dangerous around food."

May's face reddened.

"I'm sorry about that, my hand sort of slipped. I didn't mean to hit you that hard, but you were cheating at that card game, after all."

Jake answered in mock anger.

"You hit me right between the eyes with a walnut! The whole room went dark, and I was temporarily blind! I was thinking you were nice right up until you almost gave me a concussion!"

May rolled her eyes, then laughed.

"It was just a fun card game, and I kept seeing you cheat. I couldn't take it anymore, and I grabbed the first thing handy and threw it at you. It just happened to be a basket of nuts. It was pretty funny though. The thing I couldn't believe was that you actually asked me out on a date after I did that."

"That's no mystery," Jake laughed, "I figured you must be the girl for me if you did that the first day I laid eyes on you. I mean, who knew what else you'd do? It looked like things could be pretty entertaining."

May touched his arm.

"I'm really going to miss you these next few weeks," she said as they sped on to the airport.

Equity didn't have a scheduled flight to Nashville and instead provided May with a ticket on a Braniff International Airlines flight that flew there daily from New York. She watched the competent cabin crew perform their meal service during the smooth and uneventful flight. She glanced around at the attractive interior of the plane, and when she reflected on it later, she had seen no indication that in a short time this proud company would file for bankruptcy, another victim of airline deregulation.

The flight touched down in Nashville and May made her way to baggage claim to search for her huge, overstuffed suitcase. She was amazed at how much she'd been able to cram into it. The three-week clothing supply turned out to be just about everything she owned. May grinned when her sister brought this to her attention, replying philosophically that "no ne should ever own more than they can fit in the backseat of their Buick."

The black suitcase appeared on the carousel. She grabbed it and started to drag it through the building. Her instructions were to meet the Highway Inn shuttle bus in front of the terminal. She'd barely made it to the terminal door when a tall, lanky young man in his late twenties approached her

"Excuse me, miss," he said with a slight drawl. "I saw you a draggin' that thing across the terminal and I just can't let you carry it any further."

May was instantly suspicious. *Great,* she thought. *I'm going to have my suitcase full of semi-crappy clothes stolen before I even get out of the airport.*

She eyed the young man, looking for signs of the psychotic mind lurking beneath his modest exterior. Her suspicions dissolved as she studied him. He was unassuming, somewhat awkward, and seemed genuinely concerned about her carrying the heavy bag.

May pointed down the curb to a shuttle bus sign, and he deposited the bag under it. She thanked him. He smiled shyly and disappeared.

Wow, how about that! she thought with amusement. *He wasn't a serial killer after all. Chivalry is still alive in Nashville!*

A girl stood beside the bus sign surrounded by suitcases. She was a few inches taller than May with pretty strawberry blond hair, fair skin, and freckles. They both instinctively knew that they were going to the same place.

"Hi," the girl said cheerily, "Are you waiting for the bus to the Highway Inn?"

"Uh huh, are you going to training for Equity?"

"Yes." Her answer was quick and breezy. "Name's Kathleen, it's nice to meet you. What's your name?"

"Hi, I'm May."

The girls shook hands and fell into conversation. In a short time, May felt as if she'd known her for years.

The hotel bus arrived within a few moments, stopping beside the sign. An elderly, rail-thin driver stepped out to load their luggage. He bent and grabbed May's overstuffed bag with his right hand, winced in pain, and grabbed his groin with his left.

Good God, I've given him a hernia with my bag! she thought in dismay.

May gave him an apologetic look. He hurled the huge bag aboard the bus. He settled stoically in the driver's seat and away they went. The two young women chatted amiably as they drove. By the time they reached the hotel, they'd decided to be roommates.

The Highway Inn was an unremarkable two-story hotel just off of the interstate. As it turned out, much of Equity's training would take place right here. It wasn't what May expected at all.

The girls checked in at the front desk and were given accommodations on the second floor. The room was clean but plain, with two double beds and an outdoor balcony that overlooked a courtyard. Every route in and out of the hotel was visible from the entire second floor.

"No one could ever sneak in or out of here," May observed wryly.

Kathleen laughed.

"I'm sure they planned it that way so they can keep an eye on the delinquents, you know… us."

There was ample closet space for their belongings, and as the two unpacked, Kathleen entertained May with stories about her college days as an exchange student in Portugal.

"My room was pretty primitive over there. I used to have to wash my clothes in an old bathtub! I enjoyed the country though, and I did learn to speak Portuguese fluently."

"That's more than I can say for my high school Spanish!"

May laughed describing her Equity interview to the other girl. Kathleen shook her head.

"I'm starting to wonder what kind of outfit we've gotten ourselves mixed up with."

"I know," May nodded. "Me, too."

The girls finished, then freshened up.

"Okay," May said brightly as she and Kathleen stepped into the hall. "Let's go meet the rest of the troops!"

Seventeen more people, mostly women in their twenties, were milling about the hospitality room as May and Kathleen entered for the meeting of flight attendant candidates and instructors. The pair mingled, introducing themselves to their lively, attractive, and excited classmates. Kathleen, working the room like a politician, approached a tall blonde and thrust out her hand for the other girl to shake.

"Hi, I'm Kathleen. What's your name? Where are you from?"

The two stood chatting while May pressed on through the crowd. She noticed an attractive girl standing near a table of refreshments and did a double-take.

It's her! The girl in the blue suit in the hall at my interview! She made towards her.

"Hi," May said, reaching for a soda. "You don't know me, but I saw you the day of my interview. I had a feeling you were going to make it."

"Thanks," the girl answered easily, "I wasn't so sure at the time."

As the two got acquainted, others drifted over to the refreshment table. A dark-haired teddy-bearish man from Boston greeted them.

"How aaah ya? I gotta have a tonic."

He saw the uncertainty in both girls' eyes as he popped open a soft drink.

"I'm Chuck. Tonic is what we call soda in Boston."

Two Black women approached, each grabbing a drink. Both were furloughed Pan Am flight attendants, two more victims of the bad economy and deregulation. They introduced themselves, confiding that they hoped to return to Pan Am and would be with this small airline only for as long as their furlough lasted.

"With the way the economy is," one of them said, "it could be years before we get recalled, if ever."

Tall, clean-cut Evan was another furloughed flight attendant, this time from American Airlines. Louisa, a petite twenty-year-old German girl, had arrived alone in America at age sixteen, and Marta, a Dutch girl raised in Holland and America, spoke English and Dutch without an accent. It was a diverse and friendly group eager to start their adventure, curious about what lay ahead. There were more classmates to meet but, at that moment, a blond woman in her mid-thirties called the room to attention.

"Hello, everyone!" she said, glancing around. "My, what a friendly group you are! My name is Lorna Anderson and I will be your instructor for the first week and a half of training. I'd like to welcome all of you to Equity Air. It seems that I'm the lucky one that gets to tell you about the company, so if you'd like to find a seat and get comfortable, we'll get started."

"Equity," Lorna continued, "started in Tennessee just after World War Two as a family-run charter operation. It was bought recently by a man named J.T. Flint. Our new owner is pouring much-needed money into the operation to expand and to add more scheduled flights. The recent deregulation of the airline industry has made it much easier for carriers to do this. Our company flies predominantly DC-8s and the number of aircraft that we own or lease depends on how good business is. During the slow winter months, we lease some of our planes to other carriers and when business picks up in the spring, we look for additional planes to use."

One of the former Pan Am flight attendants laughed softly. May looked at her curiously

"What's funny?" she whispered to the tall girl, who leaned towards her.

"DC-8s have been around for twenty years. They've got an old fleet and it's going to be like flying in a time machine. Charter operations like this one and upstart carriers are using them a lot because the major airlines are phasing them out. They get snapped up by small companies that can't afford new planes. They're not as fuel efficient as the new planes and they're noisy. Wait until you're sitting on the back jumpseat of one of those old tubs on takeoff, it'll make your teeth rattle."

May slowly sat back in her chair, not knowing what to say.

Lorna went on to explain that the company's business offices were located in New York City, where most of the scheduled flights originated. Aircraft maintenance was done here at an old Air Force base not far from the hotel. They kept the maintenance facilities in Tennessee because it was cheaper.

The Pan Am girl chuckled again, catching May's eye.

"Remind me to tell you the parts of the story that she's leaving out," she whispered.

May was puzzled but turned her attention to Lorna, studying her as she talked. She seemed nice enough and had a healthy, fresh-air look about her.

What wasn't she telling them? May made a mental note to find out.

Lorna's talk had gone on for nearly an hour. As her speech wrapped up, so did the meeting.

"We'll be starting early in the morning," she smiled. "Get a good night's sleep."

May was up, dressed, and at the coffee shop by 7:15 a.m. Class started at eight. May knew that she wouldn't make it through the morning without a strong cup of coffee. Kathleen, opting for an extra few minutes of sleep, moaned and rolled over as May quietly closed the door behind her.

She spied two of her classmates having breakfast and joined them. She'd only met one of the girls the night before, a tall platinum blonde who looked like a high-fashion model. May found herself interrupting an in-depth conversation about cow milking prowess on the family farm in Iowa. May quickly drained her coffee cup, and the three made their way to class.

May learned that most major airlines had their own training facilities for the large classes of flight attendants that they hired. Their facilities contained on-site hotels to house trainees and included classrooms and elaborate aircraft mockups. Equity's facility consisted of a small conference building away from the main hotel. The interior was spartan and resembled a high school classroom. There was a blackboard in the front of the room, rows of desks and chairs, and endless stacks of forms. The large hotel swimming pool was close. Additional training would take place in the pool and at the nearby military airfield whenever an Equity aircraft was available.

The first ten days of training focused on company procedures.

"Get used to paperwork, ladies and gentlemen," Lorna warned. "You'll be doing a lot of it. As flight attendants, you will have to keep track of your expenses while you are away from home."

She explained how to fill out per diem forms for each trip and how to submit them for reimbursement. All flight scheduling was done in Greenwich Mean Time, so they practiced converting from time zone to time zone all over the world.

Lorna handed out long lists of airport identification codes.

"You must memorize all of them."

There were liquor accounting forms, duty-free forms, agricultural forms, and a hundred other forms. It was a series of unending paperwork for every possible situation, normal or otherwise, for anything that could happen on a plane.

"There are so many forms, my God! We're going to kill every tree on the planet," May whispered to Kathleen.

"I know," Kathleen agreed. "If a passenger ever dies on a flight, the paperwork is gonna be a nightmare."

May rolled her eyes.

Lorna moved on to in-flight duties, watching as the class practiced the pre-takeoff safety demonstration with oxygen masks, seatbelts, and life vests.

"I need a model to help us get started with the vests," Lorna smiled, a twinkle in her eye. "Come on up here, Chuck," she said to the chubby young man from Boston. "Show us how to put this on."

Chuck jumped out of his seat, sprinting confidently to the front of the room.

"No problemo!" he said with authority, a big grin on his face.

He grabbed the bright yellow vest, pulling the straps over his arms. A long piece of strap dangled awkwardly in front of his nose— He'd put the vest on backwards!

"I've got this. I've really got this!" he stated, attempting to convince himself. Trying valiantly to pull the whole thing over his head, his grin faded as he proceeded to get himself hopelessly tangled. Now crimson with embarrassment, he surrendered the snarled mess to Lorna.

"You must pre-set the straps before pulling the vest over the top of the head," she instructed. "Imagine what will go through your passengers' minds if they see you getting beaten up by a life vest! Keisha, Margot, you have lots of experience with these from Pan Am, help me out here, ladies."

With just a little direction the group was soon getting in and out of the vests with ease.

There were continuous tests, and all of the candidates were required to earn a 90 percent on each of them or face going home.

A few days later, May rose earlier than usual. She hadn't slept well and finally kicked the covers back and got out of bed at six a.m. Kathleen was sleeping peacefully, snoring in the other bed. Kathleen could sleep through just about anything.

May showered, dressed quickly, and made her way to the coffee shop for an early breakfast. The restaurant was empty except for Keisha from Pan Am. May walked over to Keisha's booth.

"Mind a little company?" she asked.

Keisha nodded. "Sure, have a seat."

They both yawned a little as the waitress filled their turned-up coffee cups.

"How are you liking things so far?" Keisha asked, dropping a spoonful of sugar into her coffee.

"Well, it's work, but it's okay so far," May answered, taking a sip from her cup. "I like everybody."

Keisha smiled, "Me, too."

May looked into Keisha's eyes. May found Keisha's expression intelligent and honest.

"At the first meeting, you said something about them not telling us the whole story about the company. What did you mean by that?"

"Oh, you remember that?"

May nodded.

"Okay, so, before I left my apartment in New York to come down here, I ran into a Pan Am pilot friend. I told him what I was doing, and he told me a few things about the guy that bought this airline. He said that our new owner had another small airline out west ten years or so ago and was forced to give up his certificate because of something illegal."

"What do you mean, 'his certificate'?"

"You have to have a certificate to run an airline. You get it from the Feds. It's never been easy to get one, though maybe it is now since deregulation. Anyway, he couldn't get one for nearly ten years, so when Equity went up for sale, he grabbed the company and the certificate that came with it."

"What did he do that was illegal?"

"My friend said it had something to do with falsifying maintenance records."

May frowned. "That's pretty serious. If he couldn't be in business for ten years, maybe he's learned his lesson."

Keisha laughed. "Yeah, maybe. But my friend said before he had his own company, he was part of Air America in Southeast Asia during the Vietnam War. It was a cover operation for the CIA. He was running guns and who knows what else in and out of countries we weren't supposed to be fighting in."

May stared. "How does your friend know all of this?"

"He has friends. His friends have friends. Word gets around."

"It's word-of-mouth. I mean, we really don't know this for sure, right?"

Keisha laughed again. "I'm not as optimistic as you are. I think it's probably true."

May digested what she heard. "Even if all of that did happen, it's not like it would affect us, right? We'll be flying passengers."

"True. But how do we know what might get put into the belly of a plane? I'll be a little suspicious if we start doing a bunch of charters to, shall we say, the less-than-peaceful areas of the world. Even the regular military charters we'll probably do could be a problem. They're passenger flights. What if someone decides to put something on the plane that shouldn't be there, like missiles or something? Maybe this leopard has changed his spots, but I wouldn't bet my life on it."

The waitress dropped a plate of scrambled eggs in front of each of them. Suddenly, May wasn't so hungry. Keisha reached over and patted her shoulder.

"Come on, eat up! Hell, my friend is probably all wrong. More than likely it's a story that got changed and twisted a million times in the retelling. He could have been flying widows and orphans for all we know."

With a small smile, May shook off her concerns. She dug into her eggs.

The first week sped by. In that short period of time, the class of nineteen morphed into a tightly-knit group. By Friday, they itched to rest and get to know each other outside of grueling classes, but a long drive separated the Highway Inn from any source of entertainment other than its swimming pool and hotel lounge. May and Kathleen returned to their room after dinner and flopped on their beds.

"Everybody's going down to the lounge around nine," Kathleen said, kicking off her shoes. "Wanna go?"

"You don't have to say it twice!"

The lounge wasn't so bad, May decided. It was clean with a nice bar and a dance floor. A popular country song, "Elvira," boomed out of the jukebox and would play at least twenty more times that night. In the center of the room, the trainees pulled a few tables together and ordered some beer. Chuck sat next to a dark-haired, hazel-eyed classmate named Marina. She was fun and wacky, and Chuck was developing a huge crush on her despite their ten-year age gap. Marina had been furloughed from TWA and doubted that she would ever return to work. Eleanor sat next to them. She was tall and very thin with white hair and pale skin. She was brutally honest and had a sense of humor as dry and biting as the winters of her home in New England. May and Kathleen sat in the two vacant seats beside her. The last to join the group was Anne, whom May thought was the most beautiful girl she'd ever seen. The Indiana native was tall and blue-eyed. Her waist-length hair framed a flawless face. She was working in a health club when Equity hired her.

It soon became obvious that word had spread throughout the land to every lonely chicken farmer, trucker, Elvis impersonator, and cattle puncher within two hundred miles of the Highway Inn that a flight attendant class was in progress. May was barely in her seat when the weight of the stare of twenty to thirty men all dressed in their best overalls bored holes through the group with their eyes. It didn't seem to matter that both Chuck and Evan were there. The local boys were on the hunt and ready to use the same skills to find a dance partner that they applied to herding cattle, impersonating The King, corralling horses, or driving an eighteen-wheeler. "Elvira" blared again as three strapping boys approached the trainees' table. The first one zeroed in on pale, blond Eleanor.

"Dance?" the grizzled young man drawled.

The would-be suitor was slightly unsteady on his feet, having consumed several bottles of liquid courage. May doubted he would be able to stay upright long enough to finish a dance, and she was confident that Eleanor, with her New England dignity and reserve, would find a polite way to refuse him.

"No," May heard her say.

It was the only word out of her mouth, and she turned to her drink. All three men stood bewildered for a few moments and then, egos deflated, they walked away.

"Jesus, you're a woman of few words, Eleanor," May said dryly.

"Hey, it worked, didn't it?"

"Yeah, but that guy will be scarred for life."

Her eyes narrowed. "I don't think he'll remember."

Fifteen minutes passed before the next assault was launched. A waitress approached with a note for gorgeous Anne. She read it, giggled, and passed it around the table.

"What does it say?" Chuck asked, resting his head adoringly on Marina's shoulder as the note was handed to her.

"Something about believing in love at first sight across a crowded room," Marina answered, rolling her eyes as she passed it on.

"Who is it from?" Eleanor whispered to the waitress.

"The guy at the very end of the bar. He's in here all the time. Falls in love every Friday."

May stole a glance at him. He was very thin, dressed in white polyester slacks, a white cowboy hat, and boots. A bright, red-and-white flowered shirt opened nearly to his navel exposed a gold chain and a chest sparsely covered with hair.

"He looks like a cowboy mated with a hibiscus plant," May whispered. "I don't think the attraction is going to be mutual."

Eleanor's gaze had drifted behind May.

"Incoming," she said in a low voice, reaching for her drink.

May felt a presence over her left shoulder. She squeezed her eyes closed, hoping that the feeling was her imagination and that it would pass. It didn't. She turned and looked into an acne-pocked face.

"Dance?" he mumbled.

The thick smell of alcohol was overpowering.

God, May winced, *maybe it's the only word they know.*

May wasn't much of a dancer, even with someone she knew and liked. Even then it usually took a drink to get her on the dance floor.

I just don't have Eleanor's way with words, she thought, a little panicked. *What do I say?*

A few seconds passed.

"Uh, no thanks," she replied, "I'm really not ready to dance."

May was pleased. Perfect answer, a polite but to-the-point rejection. "When do you think you'll be ready?"

It was a steady, straightforward return, as if he were asking whether or not it was time to manure the soybean crop. May gritted her teeth as possible responses ran through her mind, including one about the freezing over of a possible afterlife destination.

She settled on "Not tonight."

The light bulb went on over his head and he stumbled away.

A relaxing evening with friends, a chance to get to know one another other away from the pressures of training, time to let off steam… It was just not to happen that evening. It would be a problem any time the trainees went to the lounge, running the gauntlet of the lovelorn. After that night, May kept her lounge visits to a minimum, concentrating on the work at hand. The next free weekend, the entire class went to Opryland.

CHAPTER THREE

Lorna finished with the trainees by the middle of the following week. Equity had no real in-flight service training like the major carriers. They simply couldn't afford to take the time needed to teach new recruits how to serve meals, mix drinks, or open bottles of wine. The small carrier didn't even have first-class service or seating on their planes. Every aircraft was configured for coach only, so there was no need for fancier services anyway. Lorna covered the company's basic serving procedures by demonstrating how to set up meal services and showing them what the equipment looked like, but that was the extent of it. The rest would be on-the-job training with the teaching burden falling on working flight attendants.

The next section of training began. May walked into the conference room, taking a seat next to Keisha and Margot. Keisha was humming an unrecognizable song. She nodded.

"Morning."

May nodded back.

"Morning."

She'd been spending more time with Keisha, finding herself drawn to the girl's dark humor. Keisha had a special way of making some of the potentially difficult work scenarios presented to them seem completely hopeless.

"New instructor today," May said.

As the classroom filled up, a dark-eyed brunette in her mid-thirties entered. She carried herself with a tough, no-nonsense air that was intimidating. She was light years different from Lorna. A feeling of unease crept into the room.

"Hello everyone, my name is Doris Schultz, and I am your emergency instructor. We'll be together for the next ten days. By the time I'm done with you, you'll either be a flight attendant or you won't."

"Okay now," Keisha whispered.

Doris proceeded to outline the program.

"You'll be learning where every piece of emergency equipment is on the DC-8 and on the two DC-10 aircraft that we've just added to our fleet. You'll have to memorize the location and operation of all of it."

May soon discovered that every one of Equity's airplanes was configured differently on the inside, the result of picking them up from other airlines all over the globe. The previous owners had designed the interiors to suit their own specifications and needs. The only changes Equity ever made to the planes when they got them was switching the seat covers and cramming in as many additional seats in as they could. Consequently, none of the plane interiors were standardized and the location of safety equipment was never the same on any two planes.

"Sorry to tell you, but the most junior flight attendant—ah, that will be you for a while—is always assigned to do the safety checklist before each flight. You'll need to keep copies of all of the different checklists with you all of the time."

May heard Keisha stifle a laugh next to her.

"On your final exam, you'll be given a diagram of a DC-8 and a DC-10 interior. It could be any one of them. You'll have to write in the location of all of the equipment correctly. That includes fire extinguishers, first aid kits, all of the walk-around oxygen bottles, and so on. You have to know how to operate every exit on the plane. When we get an airplane in for maintenance over at the field, we'll practice an evacuation. You'll have ninety seconds to do the job. We'll spend a lot of time on first aid initially, and you need to memorize every item in the first aid kit. Then, you'll get CPR certified. Towards the end of our ten days, we'll spend time on over-water equipment and ditching. In case you're wondering what ditching is, that's evacuating an aircraft in the event of a water landing. That is no easy feat, I can assure you. You'll be doing some swimming and doing some practice with a life raft out in the hotel pool. Any questions?"

The atmosphere of the training class had definitely changed.

"I'll tell you right now it's time to learn the most important part of this job. I'm not going to stand for much fooling around. There are FAA standards to be met, or you won't pass."

Doris dove in, discussing every possible safety scenario, forcing the class to suffer drills with oxygen bottles, and teaching them to extinguish aircraft fires. Learning how to use the DC-8's ancient oxygen system turned out to be a complex thing. An oxygen bottle the size of a large man was stored in either the front or rear closet on the plane. Occasionally, it could be found overhead in the rear of the aircraft between two of the lavatories. This first aid system was for those who became ill during flight and needed oxygen. Each aisle seat was equipped with a plug for a first aid mask. When the bottle was turned on, it ran a supply of oxygen to each of these outlets. This system was separate from the one that popped oxygen masks and supplied air for emergencies such as decompressions. A flight attendant would have to check that its gauge read full before every flight.

"If you forget to bleed this system when you finish using it, you could wind up emptying the whole bottle," Doris said as she reviewed each step of the system's operation.

On the third day of emergency training, May, Kathleen, and Eleanor stopped in the coffee shop for a quick lunch break.

"So, how are you guys liking Doris?" Kathleen asked as she took a big bite of her tuna fish sandwich.

"She's tough, but I really like her," May answered, poking at her salad. "She really keeps your attention."

"So did Attila the Hun," Eleanor snorted.

"I like her, too," Kathleen echoed. "She really knows her stuff."

"She could be nicer about delivering the message," Eleanor said.

"She's direct, but she's nice," May said. "What she says could save our lives someday."

Eleanor grunted, glancing at the clock.

"True, true," she said. "Eat up, guys. Lunchtime is about over, and we don't want to keep Attila waiting."

Doris went through every imaginable situation from in-flight fires to hijackers. She drilled them on the procedures for operating aircraft exit doors, and the commands to shout to get passengers out of the plane safely.

And then the day arrived.

A DC-8 was in for maintenance and available for training.

"Casual dress tomorrow, ladies and gentlemen. No business attire. We'll be going to the airport for an evacuation drill in the morning."

After breakfast the next day, Doris and the class boarded an old school bus and headed for the airbase. Equity Operations was located in one of the many World War II-era buildings on the premises.

Doris led the group up one of these buildings' concrete stairs. Graying, middle-aged men filled the equally gray room. One stood to greet the class and provide a short tour. Their guide explained the weather data spitting from one of the computers when May noticed a plywood board leaning against a wall, covered with rows and rows of round tags, each hanging individually from a nail. Some were arranged in groups of ten, others in groups of thirteen. Each tag had a name on it.

"What's that?" she asked, pointing to the board.

"Oh, that's the names of all of our crewmembers, pilots, and flight attendants that are out on trips right now," the man answered.

May and Keisha glanced at each other, then quizzically to the guide.

"Yeah, the smaller groups are on DC-8s and the bigger ones are on DC-10s."

May looked at the board dubiously.

"You can keep track of people this way?"

"Sure, as long as your name tag doesn't fall off the board." He scratched his head. "We lost a young fella once in Spain for six weeks. Name fell off the board and nobody noticed. I heard he had a nice vacation though. I think his mother finally missed him or something. Then, there was the time the whole board got knocked over. Keys everywhere. Talk about havoc! Nobody knew who was where, people lost all over the world... What a son of a bitch that was!"

Doris quickly steered the class toward the door.

"Mmm... Okay, thank you for the tour, gentlemen," she said. "We're heading to the hangar now."

After they left the building, May whispered to Keisha. "Is that the same set up you had at Pan Am?"

Keisha laughed out loud.

The DC-8 parked in the hangar was in for heavy maintenance, but the mechanics disappeared as soon as the class arrived. When the last departed, Doris split the class into two groups. The small group would assume the role of flight attendants and the rest would be passengers. The groups would switch roles frequently. Doris directed those acting as flight attendants. Then, out of earshot from that group, she gave additional instructions to those playing passengers.

"We're going to throw our flight attendants a few curve balls. Kathleen, I want you to pretend that you're blind, and May, you are going to be someone experiencing negative panic. That means you're so scared that you're frozen in your seat and can't move. Margot, you stand in the aisle and scream as loud as you can. Marina, you get really hostile and start a fight at the exit door. Chuck, I want you to shout to everybody to stay in their seats and not move until the flight attendants come for them."

"Really?" he asked, a little confused by the order.

"Yeah, I'll talk about that one later."

May shifted. Doris shouted down the aisle of the plane: "Flight attendants, take your jumpseats! Passengers, get in your seats!"

The simulated crash began. Designated flight attendants yelled commands to passengers.

"Heads down, grab ankles!"

"Unfasten seat belts!"

"Leave belongings!"

"Go to open exits!"

Once passengers reached open exits, they were commanded to "Jump, Jump!"

The cabin was very dark. May sat in her faux numb state watching and listening. She heard a strong male voice yelling for everyone to stay seated, but he was quickly silenced. More commands rang out.

Within a few seconds, a flight attendant, realizing that May wasn't moving from her seat, pulled her up and shoved her toward an open exit. Another flight attendant standing at the door inflated the slide as they'd been trained to do, telling May to jump and slide. She did so, joining the others on the hangar floor. Assuming that all was clear, the class congratulated itself on a job well done.

"Are we good or what?" Chuck smirked, chest puffed out, high-fiving his classmates.

Then, the sound of someone clearing their throat came from above them. The whole class slowly looked to the top of the slide to see Doris and Kathleen standing in the doorway of the DC-8.

"You forgot the blind passenger," Doris chided. "You have to make a final sweep of the cabin and make sure that everyone is out."

The class looked at each other sheepishly. There was no mistaking the disappointment in Doris's voice.

"Okay, gang. We're going to switch groups and do it again. Did all of you hear Chuck telling you to stay seated and wait for flight attendants to come get you?"

They nodded.

"That scenario is based on a real incident. A man on a flight told people to wait for flight attendants to come and save them while the plane was burning to a crisp. He sounded authoritative, so some people actually listened to him. They didn't make it. You have to imagine during these drills that this aircraft is a raging inferno. You have mere seconds to get as many people out as you possibly can."

This time, May served as a flight attendant. As before, Doris assigned others to portray passengers. The second crash test began. Adrenaline pumping, May shouted the evacuation commands. Exiting her jumpseat, she checked that the passenger seats around her were empty. She made her way toward her assigned exit. She flew past a flight attendant pulling on the arm of a passenger hiding in the lavatory.

As she reached her exit, there was tall, athletic, gorgeous Anne pretending to be too afraid to jump out of the plane. Chuck kicked her legs out from under her, sending her sprawling down the slide.

May had rushed to the door, where she was now grabbing people and hurling them down the inflated chute as quickly as she could. When it appeared that the plane was cleared of the last passenger, she and Chuck prepared to jump. Without hesitation, Chuck stepped to the edge, jumped, and slid to the bottom.

Sensing one more body behind her, May didn't turn to identify who it was but grasped the person's arm blindly, preparing to pitch them out of the plane. The arm pulled back hard, and she assumed that she'd grabbed hold of another panicking passenger. She sucked in her breath as she readied a herculean effort to throw whoever it was out the door.

Planting her feet, she turned and looked into the amused face of… Doris. May's face went blank and then reddened with embarrassment. With an apologetic look, she let go of Doris's arm and jumped down the slide.

They were improving dramatically. Doris moved them to their next task.

"You don't know which exits or how many will be usable in an emergency, so you've got to be able to work them all. By the way, that includes knowing how to open up the cockpit windows."

She led them to the center of the DC-8 to its four over-wing window exits.

"There are no slides to inflate at these exits, and you can only use them in an emergency if the pilots in the cockpit have enough time and are able to lower the airplane's flaps. If those flaps aren't down, the height is just too great from the wing to the ground for anyone to get off without sustaining serious injury. Since you people have to know how to do this, the mechanics were nice enough to lower the flaps for us. The first step," Doris told her students, "is to pull out the heavy window exits and roll them onto a seat."

Again, May was dubious. Glancing around the interior of the plane, it was obvious that Equity crammed every possible space with seats to maximize the number of paying passengers. There was barely enough room around the window exits to maneuver. She couldn't imagine keeping these bulky objects inside.

I might have to throw this heavy thing completely out of the plane, she thought.

What had she gotten herself into? She reminded herself of the low odds of a crash but still frowned with anxiety.

"Once you get this open," Doris instructed, "you step on the wing and direct passengers out the opening. You are going to need to convince two brave passengers to slide down that flap and stay there to catch the rest of the passengers."

Kathleen raised her hand. "Shouldn't we go to the bottom?"

"There is only one flight attendant to man these four over-wing exits. You need to direct people to the exits and get them outside. Then, somehow, you've got to get them off the wing. You've got to have help. You should assume that many of the people you ask to help will run away, especially if there is a fire. Keep asking until you get someone with guts enough to stay."

It was a difficult operation even under ideal conditions. After each class member took a turn sliding down the wing, Doris chose some to act as unconscious passengers. Those acting as flight attendants slid motionless bodies off the wing with great difficulty. It was hard to imagine the task with a fire raging.

After hours of work, the drills were finally over. As the class wearily exited the bus at the hotel, everyone mumbled about showers and food. May didn't realize until a day or so later how hard the evacuation experiences had been. She'd smacked her thigh hard against something, probably the flaps of the plane. She had a bruise the size of a football on the back of her leg.

One major training hurdle remained before the emergency procedures final exam. In order to be qualified to fly across the Atlantic or Pacific Ocean, the class needed to learn ditching procedures. Should they ever have the unfortunate luck of entering water in an Equity aircraft, they needed to be able to evacuate all of the passengers safely into life rafts, take care of their first aid needs, and survive until they were rescued.

Ditching on a DC-10 didn't look or sound so bad. The escape slides doubled as life rafts. Once the aircraft door was opened in the water, passengers could walk right out and sit on the raft. Once someone shored up the ends, the staff could detach the whole thing from the door.

If you survived the crash impact and if the aircraft floated, you just might make it.

May shifted uncomfortably as Doris explained the procedure. The old DC-8s were another story entirely. Life rafts were packed into the ceiling of the plane or stored in overhead racks. May couldn't help but wonder how she would pull a hundred-pound life raft out of its compartment amid 250 panicking passengers, then open the door of an airplane that was hopefully still floating, attach the raft to a seat via a metal ring tied to a rope, throw the raft into the ocean, and tell people to swim for it. Only after everyone climbed aboard would a staff member cut the rope with the hope that the survivors would float safely away as the plane sank out of sight.

May liked to think that she was a fairly positive person, but to her, the survival picture the company painted for ditching in a DC-8 was a little too rosy.

Keisha and May discussed it—out of Doris's earshot.

"So, on a DC-8," Keisha said. "The plane goes down. I get my life raft. I attach it to my sinking ass plane. I make everybody swim in ice-cold water. After they all get in, I cut my lanyard, and we float away. Oh, and when the sharks show up, I throw in my shark repellent. I hope it's made out of dynamite. That's the only thing that's gonna kill a big, hungry shark."

"You don't think it'll work, do you?" May said.

"Oh, hell no."

Doris discussed the operation of the ditching equipment. They worked with the life vests again and covered every piece of the survival equipment stored in the raft, including flares, die markers, desalination kits, radio beacon transmitters, and shark repellent.

"Alright, boys and girls, it's time to hit the pool," Doris said. "Meet me over there in five minutes."

May and Kathleen raced to their room and hustled to dress. Kathleen groaned as she struggled into her swimsuit.

"I'm surprised Doris isn't making us jump in wearing our business attire for the sake of realism."

May smiled. "Well, don't go giving her any ideas. Hurry up! We don't want to be late."

All nineteen classmates were milling nervously around the pool as Doris approached. She'd been on the other side of the fence talking to a small group of men, who turned out to be Equity pilots. Word was out that the trainees were doing their ditching exercise, and they'd shown up to watch.

As the men stood gawking outside the fence, May leaned over and whispered to Kathleen, "I think they're here more to check out how we look in our bathing suits than to observe our lifesaving and survival prowess. What do you think?"

"Wonder if they think Chuck and Evan have good legs."

The trainees soon forgot the presence of the pilots, intent on the activities and testing to come. They first had to demonstrate that they could swim to the raft and board it. If they couldn't, they would be sent home.

"Everybody gather 'round," Doris called. "This is a DC-8 life raft. It holds about twenty-five people, but can be overloaded to carry a few more if you have to."

Chuck and Anne threw the heavy raft into the pool. It inflated automatically and popped right side up.

"Alright, everybody, put your life vests on and line up in pairs. You're going to jump in two at a time. Remember, you are not allowed to inflate your vest until AFTER you jump in. Swim to the raft and climb aboard."

The class lined up two-by-two and waited their turn. May partnered with Kathleen and Keisha and Margot stood just ahead of them. As their turn quickly approached, May realized that Margot suddenly seemed very anxious.

May leaned forward. "What's the matter?"

"I can't swim," Margot said.

"WHAT!?"

"Shhhh!" Keisha hissed.

"I don't know how to swim, not a stroke, and I'm deathly afraid of the water," Margot whispered hoarsely.

Kathleen poked her head forward. "I gotta hand it to you, you've got guts. What are you going to do?"

"What did you do at Pan Am?" May asked.

"I... I don't know."

"You don't know? You must have done SOMETHING! You're here. You didn't drown!"

"I really don't know. It's a total blank. I just did it somehow."

Kathleen poked her head forward again.

"How are you going to pull this off? My God, you're going to sink like a rock and drown and Doris will make us all practice CPR on you and…"

"Be quiet!" Keisha snapped. "Let's try to be a little constructive here, shall we?"

She turned to Margot.

"When she says jump, I'm going to be right beside you," Keisha said. "Hold your nose with one hand and the pull tab with the other. Pull it as soon as you go in. You'll bob up to the top and then all you have to do is get on the raft."

She turned to the two girls behind her.

"You two jump in as quick as you can," Keisha directed, "and stay behind us."

"I hope this works," May sighed.

"Me, too," Kathleen said. "My CPR's not all that good. I think my chest compressions are a little too—"

May poked her hard in the ribs. "Shut up!"

"Ow! Okay!"

Eight people splashed into the pool ahead of them, leaving Keisha and Margot next.

"Alright," Doris shouted. "Next pair, go!"

Margot stood frozen.

"Jump," Keisha whispered, waiting for her.

Still, she didn't move. The seconds ticked by, each one lasting a lifetime.

"Jump!" Keisha growled, but Margot didn't budge. Doris was distracted momentarily and hadn't noticed the pause. May and Kathleen were silently pulling for her. Keisha stuck her face in Margot's ear. "Jump, Goddamn it, it's now or never!"

"Go!" Doris yelled.

Margot, one hand holding her nose, the other clutching the life vest pull tab for dear life, jumped into the cold, chlorinated water. Keisha jumped at the same time. Margot's head bobbed to the surface as the vest inflated. Keisha swam beside her as Margot dog paddled to the raft. May and Kathleen jumped behind them, and the foursome reached the raft together. Margot pulled herself onto the raft first, followed by Keisha, May, and Kathleen. They breathed a silent sigh of relief.

"You know," Margot said at last, smiling weakly. "I'm pretty sure that's how I did it at Pan Am."

The others stared at her. She'd done it, and Doris was none-the-wiser. Doris swam to her class of trainees, seated in a circle in the swaying raft. They now had to throw a sea anchor to stabilize it. Then, with instruction from Doris, they would raise a canopy that would offer protection from the elements.

"You could be in the ocean with the hot sun beating on you for quite a while," Doris said.

Next, they removed survival gear from the center compartment and reviewed what they'd learned in the classroom. As they worked, May noticed several small hissing sounds around her. The raft looked somewhat worn and was developing leaks in several places. She brought it to Doris's attention.

"Funny you should notice that," she replied.

Doris pulled a leak repair kit from the center of the raft. She described how it worked, holding a metal patch that could be plugged into a hole.

"Do you want me to do that?" May asked.

"Sure, it will be good practice for you."

May slipped the plug into the closest hole. She patched the spot, but the raft continued to hiss from all directions.

"Ladies and gentlemen, this concludes our ditching class for today. I want you to head to your rooms and change. We will meet in the classroom in half an hour."

When the last trainee was out of the water, a maintenance person from operations retrieved the raft. A major training hurdle was behind them. With quiet satisfaction, the class returned to their rooms.

A number of flight attendant classes completed training that summer, each facing the trials of the ditching exercise in the leaky raft. By the time summer ended, word passed through the flight attendant ranks: the old leaky raft had gotten so bad, that with the very last training class, it sank to the bottom of the pool.

With only a few days of training remaining, May's class received a visit from Chet Ferris, Equity's flight attendant union representative. The flight attendants here were represented by the Teamsters.

"Isn't that a little weird?" May whispered to Keisha. "Don't Teamsters drive horses or something? What were you at Pan Am?"

"Not a Teamster."

The class listened politely. Most of them hadn't been out of college for very long and had little to no experience with unions.

"Hi ya, goils and boys," Chet said in greeting.

He was a short, stocky New Yorker with a thick Bronx accent, just what May imagined a Teamster would be.

"I've been the Equity flight attendants union rep for a lotta years. I'm here to protect your job against any, should we say, inappropriate actions by da company, and I'm here for yous when it's time to negotiate a good contract."

May had to admit, she hadn't given these important issues much thought. She gave him her full attention, even if his accent did make her cringe.

"I'm giving my number to all o' yous, and I want yas to call me if yous ever need me. Ya know, the Teamsters is a great, and I mean great, organization."

A broad smile crossed his face.

"Matter o' fact, Jimmy Hoffa was a good friend o' mine."

An eerie silence fell over the room, but Chet didn't notice. He packed up to leave. Keisha stifled a laugh.

Only one goal remained: passing the final written exam, a cumulative test of everything they'd learned during the last three weeks. The testing would last for several hours. Then, the class would wait while the tests were graded—wait to see who passed and who would be sent home.

They stayed awake long into the night, cramming last minute, sometimes four or five classmates in a room, sitting on beds, quizzing each other about equipment, forms, procedures, and commands.

Then, at 8 a.m. sharp after very few hours of sleep, the trainees filed into the classroom.

Doris' face was expressionless as she passed out the exams.

"Good luck," she said simply.

She took her place at her desk in the front of the room.

The hours of study and practice, plus the excellence of Lorna's and Doris's teaching, made May fairly confident when she handed in her test. Nearly all of the trainees finished at about the same time, then sat on pins and needles waiting for the results. Most felt the way May did—that they'd passed with *at least* the required ninety percent.

"There is always the possibility of making stupid mistakes, I suppose," May said to Keisha. "Something dumb could bring you below a ninety."

"Let's think happy thoughts, okay?" Keisha said.

Still, no one wanted to suffer the disgrace of failure at the last moment and have to go home. Time passed at a snail's pace as the group agonized.

The grading was completed at noon. Word spread quickly among the trainees... Everyone passed!

Theirs was the first group not to lose a single member through the whole ordeal. Whoops of joy rang from the balconies as the classmates rushed from room to room to congratulate each other. The pressure had been colossal, and now it was gone... Gone!

Or so they thought.

A graduation ceremony was scheduled for 2 p.m. Lorna and Doris would be there, of course, and June Knight, the company's chief flight attendant, was flying in from New York for the occasion. She would pin on their wings. Nineteen brand-spanking-new flight attendants looked forward to a wonderful, relaxing afternoon and evening of celebration. There would be cake, punch, and the enjoyment of the camaraderie they'd created during the rigorous program.

A special bond always formed among classmates in every flight attendant training class. They put on their best business attire and strode to the hospitality suite, where they'd met weeks before on their first night in Tennessee.

It seemed a lifetime ago.

The chief flight attendant was already there, talking quietly with Lorna and Doris. Even Rupert Martin, the vice president of inflight services, was on hand for the ceremony.

The modest proceedings got underway. At the major airlines, wing pinning ceremonies were quite elaborate, with graduates allowed to fly out parents or other loved ones to attend. Equity didn't do this, but not having family present to celebrate didn't dampen the group's excitement. Each individual was called to the front of the room to have wings pinned, followed by a handshake by June Knight. May smiled as she touched her shiny, new wings.

When the last pair of wings were awarded, the chief flight attendant congratulated the group as a whole and invited them to dig into their cake and punch.

The new flight attendants beamed with pride, and for the next hour, they dreamed about upcoming adventures and what it would be like to live in New York City.

"Attention please," June said, motioning for silence. "When you signed up for this job, all of you said that you possessed a lot of flexibility, something that you are going to need in your new career. We are going to test just how flexible you are right now. All of you will be flying to New York tonight. You have forty-five minutes to pack your things. I have flight times for some of you for tomorrow."

The group was stunned into silence.

Then, in unison, they exclaimed, "TOMORROW?"

The room dissolved into chaos.

"Tomorrow?" one repeated. "But.. but… we don't even have a place to LIVE!! Where will we SLEEP?!"

"Tomorrow," June said firmly.

There was no room for debate. The party was over. The class scattered to their rooms. They would catch the five-thirty American Airlines flight from Nashville to New York. May and Kathleen sprinted around their room, frantically gathering belongings and throwing them in their bags. They'd accumulated quite a bit in three weeks, in addition to what they originally brought. There were piles of papers from training that they wanted to keep, and there was the enormous inflight manual that they were required to bring on every flight.

"Can you believe this?"

May repeated over and over as she dashed from one corner of the room to the other, occasionally running into Kathleen as she cleaned out drawers and pulled stockings from the shower.

"At least you didn't get a trip for tomorrow, like I did," Kathleen moaned.

May dropped the stockings on the bed.

"Where are we going to stay? They must plan to put us *somewhere*. I mean what do we do—sleep under a bush?"

The girls dragged their luggage to a waiting bus, the old one they'd taken to the airport for evacuation drills. It began to rain heavily. There was so little time, barely enough for a parting glance around the premises. May wanted to memorize all that she could before she climbed aboard the bus, but there just wasn't time.

The bus was quiet as they drove to the Nashville airport. Driving rain splattered the windows, but the flight was still scheduled to leave on time.

May checked her very overstuffed suitcase and headed for the plane.

They took off between showers, and the skillful pilot skirted the large thunderheads along their route. The lightning flashed inside the black clouds, a beautiful sight. May reflected on all that had transpired since her crazy interview roughly a month ago.

Hectic and disorganized as it was and might always be, May was glad that she was here.

PART TWO:

It's Never Dull! (1981)

CHAPTER FOUR

The new Equity flight attendants touched down in New York and released a collective sigh of relief when they learned they had rooms waiting for them at a hotel near Kennedy Airport. Those in the class furloughed from other airlines had been based in New York with their former employers. These lucky ones, including Keisha and Margot, returned to their apartments.

The new hires were assigned four to a hotel room, with May and Kathleen bunking with Louisa and Marta. May hadn't gotten to know either Louisa or Marta during training but packed into the small hotel room, she would get the opportunity now.

Kathleen was the only one of them to get an immediate assignment. She would leave on a flight for Puerto Rico at four p.m. the following day. The girls settled into their room, crawled into bed, and fell into a fitful sleep.

The next afternoon, the foursome gathered in the hotel coffee shop to brainstorm living arrangements.

"We're all getting along pretty well. Why don't we look for a nice big house and live together?" Kathleen suggested.

"That sounds great, but we'll need first and last month's rent to get anything, let alone a big house," May answered. "Good idea, but let's face it, we've got to find a place that's cheap and safe. I think that's going to be hard to come by in this city."

"Keisha and Margot live in the stew zoo in Kew Gardens," Marta said. "That's right near the airport."

Kathleen raised her eyebrows. "What is a stew zoo?"

"A place where lots of flight attendants live. Lots of people live out at the beach, too."

"Well, whoever isn't working is going to have to be looking," Kathleen said pointedly. "We have to solve this problem quick."

"It's going to take a miracle to find a place that will take us without a month's security deposit," May lamented. "Aren't any of you guys rich?"

"No," Kathleen laughed. "I've got to go get ready for work."

Back in the room, Kathleen flew around in a frenzy of preparation. The other three stayed out of her way. None of them had been issued a uniform yet and were required to make their first flights in business attire. They were to wear their wings to make them recognizable as crew members.

Kathleen's trip was a turnaround flight. She would fly on a DC-10 to San Juan, Puerto Rico, drop her passengers off there, load the plane with new passengers, and fly back to New York immediately.

"What time will you be back?" Louisa asked.

"I'm not sure, at least midnight, maybe later."

May learned earlier that afternoon that she would work an identical assignment the following evening. She was anxious to hear about Kathleen's flight. Kathleen finished her makeup, gave a nervous thumbs up to her roommates, and headed for the van to the airport.

The other three girls stood silently in the center of the room for a few moments after she'd gone.

"Well," Marta said, "it's going to be a long wait until she gets back. There's no point holding a wake. Anybody want to go for a walk or something?"

"Yes," Louisa answered. "I'd love to."

"How about you, May? Do you want to go?"

"No, you two go ahead. I want to call Jake."

"Then, we'll get out of here and give you some privacy," Marta replied. "Wait a minute… I thought you said your boyfriend was a great outdoorsman and doesn't have a phone."

"He doesn't," May laughed. "I got hold of my sister earlier today and asked her to bring him to my parents' house late this afternoon. He should be there now."

"God, that sounds complicated. Well, good luck."

"Thanks. See you in a bit."

As soon as they left, May dialed. The phone rang only twice before May's sister picked up.

"Hey! Are you hanging in there? Big day tomorrow, first flight, right? Are you excited?"

"Yes, and nervous. Did Jake make it there?"

"Yup, here he is."

"Congratulations!" Jake greeted her. "I'm proud of you! Tomorrow's the big day. How do you feel?"

"Truthfully? Really excited and really nervous. I don't want to screw up."

"Are you kidding? You'll be fine. I've missed you. I've missed talking to you."

"Yeah, the downside of no phone."

"I know, I know. So, listen, when can we get together?"

"I truly don't know, Jake. This company is just one crazy outfit. I can't wait to tell you all of the nutty stuff that's happened. I might get a day or two off after this first flight. I know they don't want us in this hotel for long, it's too expensive. We've got to find a place to live."

There was a pause on the other end of the line.

"Keep in touch with your sister over the next few days," Jake answered. "Let her know when you're off. If it works out, I'll come see you. I've got some things going on, too, that I want to tell you about."

"Okay, Jake. That sounds just wonderful. I hope it works out."

"Me, too, Sweetie. I miss you. Listen… Good luck tomorrow."

"Thanks. I'll see you soon."

The girls went to bed at eleven, but May could not fall asleep. She tossed and turned, tensing at the occasional footsteps in the hall and then relaxing as they passed. It suddenly occurred to her that the room was too quiet. There were no regular, steady breathing sounds coming from either of the other girls, the kind made when someone is fast asleep.

"Are you guys sleeping?"

Louisa and Marta giggled from across the room.

"No," they both said loudly.

The three laughed and gave up hope of proper sleep. They talked and dozed into the wee hours, speculating about what was happening with Kathleen's flight. Then, at three a.m., the door opened. Kathleen stumbled in, exhausted. It was an extremely difficult flight, she reported.

Equity had advertised a seventy-five-dollar, one-way fare to San Juan. The girls had seen the horrible, tacky commercial advertising it on TV. It starred a fast-talking, middle-aged man in a loud sport coat hawking the low-price fare and pointing to an Equity DC-10, its tail painted with the newly-designed company logo, a rolled up wad of dollar bills.

"I swear that rock bottom fare brought out people who've never heard of air travel, let alone flown on a plane before," Kathleen groaned. "None of the passengers knew anything! The cabin was so full of smoke! I've never seen so many smokers! There was nowhere to get away from it. And babies! Crying babies everywhere, packed in like sardines! The moms wanted to put anything sweet that they could get their hands on into their baby bottles… like soda. Ick! And I swear to God they brought everything they own onto the plane. And the seats are packed in so close there is no place to put anything!"

Listening to Kathleen was anything but reassuring to May. At least she'd found out earlier in the evening that Louisa was assigned to work her flight with her. They'd get through it together.

The next evening arrived too quickly. Now it was May's and Louisa's turn to pin on their wings and tackle their first flight.

The hotel van dropped them in front of the terminal at Equity's New York operations facilities. They wandered through a maze of hallways on the bottom floor of the terminal, far from the upstairs offices where May's interview had taken place weeks before. Eventually, they located the crew scheduler, a harried, heavy-set girl sitting behind a counter.

Mustering as much false confidence as she could, May announced, "We're checking in for our flight."

"Congratulations. You two for San Juan?"

The scheduler's voice was short and curt.

"Yes," both girls replied.

She scratched their names off of a list, then behaved as if they no longer existed. The girls left the room, venturing out into the corridor.

"Nice, wasn't she?" May whispered.

A few pilots stood conversing nearby as more flight attendants arrived. May glanced into the room to her right. A chalkboard hung on the front wall listing the arrival and departure times of the day's flights. They walked farther down the hall and entered the flight attendant lounge, where crew members sat on a scattering of sectional couches, some deep in animated conversations. Everyone in the room seemed to know each other.

Again, May gathered her courage. "Hi," she asked tentatively. "Is anyone here going to San Juan?"

A slim, dark-haired man of about thirty looked up from the clipboard that rested in his lap. He smiled broadly. "You must be my two new guys."

He put a checkmark next to their names on his list.

"I'm Ted, the senior flight attendant on this trip."

He was rather quiet and reserved, but very nice. The rest of the crew shuffled in, each member greeting them warmly as Ted made introductions. May and Louisa discovered that three of their co-workers had been flying for only a few weeks. They seemed like grizzled veterans.

"At least they have uniforms," Louisa whispered.

"We've got everyone, so let's go upstairs and find our plane," Ted said enthusiastically.

May boarded the DC-10 feeling the way most people do on their first day at a new job, like she was all thumbs. Equity spent their training time on company procedures and emergency training, not on service. Both girls realized quickly what an extra burden they would be on their co-workers who would have the responsibility of teaching them in-flight service.

The pilots boarded, giving Ted the flight time, weather conditions en route, and the number of passengers. Armed with this information, Ted held a short briefing with the cabin crew.

"We're full of course, but the captain said it will be a smooth flight, so that will make things easier. Louisa, why don't you work in the back tonight, and May, you can work in the front of the plane. It will be easier for us to show you the ropes that way."

The two girls exchanged a quick glance, and Louisa headed to the rear of the plane. May put her belongings in a storage compartment beneath her jumpseat and stood awkwardly in the front galley.

One of her new co-workers plopped several rolls of toilet paper and tissue boxes in her arms.

"Hi, I'm Tyrone, nice to meet you. I'll show you where these go."

He opened the doors of the two lavatories near the cockpit.

"This is something that the flight attendants just don't get the pleasure of doing at those big, fancy airlines—keeping the passengers' butts in toilet paper. Bet they didn't tell you this part in training, did they?"

"No, no, they left that out."

"Well, that's understandable, they don't want to spoil all of the fun surprises."

May recalled that the most junior person working the flight did the emergency checklist. Louisa was lucky enough to be the most junior on this occasion—in the random assigning of seniority numbers during training, she fell just below May on the list. Oxygen bottle pressure gauges, seals on fire extinguishers, life vests under seats, all needed to be checked visually. The life vest check could be a time-consuming process. May eventually developed her own method of straddling the aisle, grabbing an armrest on each aisle seat, and propelling herself at waist level down the airplane while looking beneath each seat along the way. On the DC-10, she would turn in the back of the plane and come back up the other aisle.

"Make sure you check ALL of the vests," Ted cautioned Louisa. "I don't care how long it takes to count them, don't develop any bad habits!"

A significant feature of the DC-10 was a lower galley located below the passenger level. It had access to the upper galley via elevator. One flight attendant was assigned to the lower galley, or "the pit" as it was known, to stock, count, and cook all of the meals and to send supplies by elevator to the galley upstairs. This person was rarely visible after takeoff and would often change into jeans and sneakers to work more comfortably. A young flight attendant named Charity was working the position. She and two others, Van and Patty, were the three crew members with just a few weeks more experience than May and Louisa.

Marianne, one of the last crew members to arrive in the lounge before going to the plane, reminded May of a flower child from the 1960s. She was friendly, a little flighty, and she liked to wear four-inch stiletto heels during the entire flight. Most flight attendants changed into flat, comfortable shoes after takeoff, but not Marianne.

"Don't your feet hurt in those?" May asked.

"No," Marianne replied, surprised. "Actually, they're very comfortable."

"Oh, I brought some real pancake shoes to wear after we take off," May said hastily. "I'm afraid I'll fall on my face if it gets bumpy."

Marianne laughed as she finished her pre-flight preparations. When boarding time arrived, she walked to the end of the jetway to collect passenger tickets. May stood in the aisle, her best flight attendant smile plastered to her face, trying to look as she imagined an experienced flight attendant should look.

People were coming down the aisle now, an endless stream of tired-looking mothers dragging or carrying screaming children. May never saw so many plastic bags stuffed with belongings in her life. Each woman juggled two or three while still managing to hang on to her offspring. Most of the men boarded far behind their wives and children, hoping they wouldn't be associated with their noisy families.

The crew started stowing bags into every possible location, quickly stuffing the overhead bins beyond capacity. Passengers shoved the bags that wouldn't fit overhead under their seats or into the space between their legs.

"This is a nightmare," May whispered to Tyrone.

She tried to push passenger baggage completely beneath the seats in front of them. FAA regulations called for aisles to be clear of baggage at all times. It had to be done or people would never be able to get out of the plane in an emergency.

"Get used to it, you'll be doing it a lot," Tyrone said. "And it doesn't matter if you're doing it for their own good. They're gonna hate you anyway."

"Thanks. That's great to know."

May was poked, prodded, and asked for help from all directions. Most of the passengers were Spanish speakers, and she thought of Roger's Spanish test during her interview with a sense of grim irony. She winced as she recalled the discussion about her butt. When the last passengers were seated, she and Louisa stepped into the aisle to perform their first safety demonstration. Both managed to avoid getting entangled in the life vests. As they finished, the plane pushed back from the gate. The crew checked each seat to make sure passengers were safely strapped in, and May was surprised to discover that many of her passengers, not being experienced flyers, could not fasten their seatbelts properly. They fumbled with them, connected the wrong ends, and looked up sheepishly to crew members.

The plane taxied onto the runway. May took her jumpseat near the cockpit. Tyrone sat on the seat next to her. They were cleared for takeoff. The power of the engines vibrated through the floor beneath May's feet. The plane hurled down the runway and into the air. She heard the thud of the landing gear as it came up a few seconds later, and the light, grinding sound of the flaps and slats as they retracted.

After that point, there was only the smooth hum of the engines and the unique sound of air rushing past at high speed that is only heard in flight. Other sounds inside the plane took on a muffled and distant quality. As they climbed to their cruising altitude, the "no smoking" sign went off, indicating that passengers could now smoke. It was also safe for the cabin crew to work.

From the front of the airplane, May brought drinks and meals to passengers, learning the service aspect of her job. It was grueling physical work, getting food and beverages to 360 passengers in a flight time of about two-and-a-half hours. The ten flight attendants would handle the considerable needs of the passengers, anything from flight connection problems to sick children.

May and Louisa saw little of each other until the meal service was completed. Scooping up the last of the meal trays, May made a quick trip to the rear of the plane.

"How are things back here?" she asked Louisa.

"Busy, that's for sure, but not too bad. The cigarette smoke is terrible."

Both girls would experience burning throats from inhaling concentrated secondhand smoke. It was something that would be a work hazard for years.

The flight passed quickly. In no time at all, they were making preparations to land. Soon, the aircraft was pulling to the jetway. Passengers collected their belongings as they thanked the crew profusely in English and Spanish for a wonderful flight.

Exhausted, May looked behind her as the last passenger departed.

The plane was a complete disaster.

"Good God, how can a plane get this trashed so quickly?" Louisa commented as she walked up the aisle.

May shook her head in amazement.

"Beats me. I was just wondering the same thing. Hey, our turnaround time is really short, want to look around the terminal?"

"Yes, sure, let's go."

Once they were beyond the jetway, the heat and humidity of Puerto

Rico hit them like a blast furnace. The girls took only a few minutes to wander through the terminal, which had no air conditioning. They walked past the souvenir shops and push carts selling everything from rum to coconuts. As they turned to hurry back to the plane, they spotted the Equity ticket counter. It was mobbed. They were taking another full load back to New York.

"Looks like people are cashing in on that low fare," May said wryly. "I wonder if they're showing that awful TV commercial here."

They hurriedly re-boarded their DC-10, which had made a miraculous recovery to relative cleanliness thanks to some hard-working cleaners. Food supplies were restocked. It was again time to board passengers.

The crew repeated the ritual of stowing the avalanche of baggage, getting passengers strapped into their seats, and performing the inflight safety demo. Once again, it was time for takeoff.

May strapped herself into the jumpseat and looked out the small porthole in the door. Night had fallen. She could see the lights zoom by as they sped down the runway. Then, they were airborne again. The same sensations repeated themselves, the gear coming up, the flaps retracting— sounds that she would become used to, familiar sounds that would indicate that all was well with the plane. The bright lights of San Juan disappeared behind them. The "no smoking" sign went out, and the crew went back to work.

It was well past the dinner hour. May was helping Tyrone prepare the light snack they would serve. A bell rang in the galley, a signal from the cockpit. The pilots wanted to see Ted, the senior flight attendant, immediately.

"They're not wasting any time putting in their coffee order," Ted said as he grinned.

He went forward. May and the others readied the food. Ted returned with a grave look on his face.

"Put everything away now. We've a problem, and we'll be turning around. We're going back to San Juan," Ted directed.

"Did you bring your bathing suit?" Tyrone whispered to May.

"What?" she answered, only half-hearing him, her eyes riveted on Ted.

"You should always bring your bathing suit," Tyrone joked. "You never know where one of these planes is going to break."

May couldn't believe her ears.

"Well, golly, I'll try to remember that in the future, Tyrone," May said, her voice a combination of sarcasm and fear. "Thanks."

Marianne joined the conference in the galley.

"What's the problem, Ted?"

"I don't know, the captain didn't say," Ted answered. "He just told us to stow everything and get ready to land."

"Did he say to prepare the cabin for an emergency landing?" Marianne pressed.

"No, at least not yet. Let's get everything put away and secured, then we'll go from there."

Frightened, May helped secure the carts and returned them to the DC-10's lower galley. A strange sensation grew in her stomach. She asked Ted if there was anything else she could do.

He shook his head and offered her a reassuring look.

With everything safely put away, May thought about going to see Louisa. She was about to leave the forward galley when the bell chimed again. The cockpit was summoning Ted. He returned after a few minutes, looking even more grim.

"Everybody, whatever the problem is, it's bad. The captain said we only have fifteen minutes to get on the ground."

The feeling in May's stomach worked its way to her throat. This couldn't possibly be happening, not on her first flight!

All flight attendants took the job knowing there was a risk of accidents, but the risk was small. Anxious thoughts raced through her head.

DOES IT HAVE TO BE ON MY FIRST FLIGHT? Can't I at least get a little experience before it happens? I can't believe this crap!

Lindsay, a ten-year veteran crew member working the back of the plane, ran forward to talk to Ted. May hadn't had much of an opportunity to get to know her. She was a petite girl with large brown eyes that now flashed with anger.

"Why aren't they telling us what the hell is wrong? Is it a goddamn secret or what?"

"I don't know," Ted answered, frustration obvious. "I don't know if the captain is just a lousy communicator or if he has a reason for not telling us."

Lindsay continued fuming. "Are you sure he doesn't want us to prepare the passengers for an emergency landing?"

"No," Ted said strongly. "He said not to say anything to the passengers, just be ready ourselves."

May glanced from Lindsay to Marianne. Worry glossed every expression.

"It's okay," Marianne said comfortingly. "There's nothing you can do anyway. My philosophy is that if it's going to happen, it's going to happen, so why get upset?"

May said nothing. She wasn't ready for Marianne's philosophy so early in her career.

"I'm gonna die and I haven't been freakin' anywhere," May mumbled.

At last, the captain's voice crackled over the public address system.

"Ah, good evening, folks. This is your captain speaking. We seem to be experiencing a little mechanical difficulty, so we'll be heading back to San Juan."

Click went the intercom.

"He's got to be kidding," Ted whispered. "That's it? Alright, everybody, get out in the aisle and check seatbelts and make sure the passenger aisles are clear. Just try to look confident. Remember, these people will be looking to you."

May walked down the aisle, smiling in a reassuring manner to anyone that caught her eye, but the passengers were strangely quiet. No one said a word or asked a single question about what was wrong with the plane. Time ground to a halt.

The minutes clicked by and with no new information about the emergency, the crew showed signs of strain. Would they need to prepare for a fire on landing? Inflate evacuation slides? Would all of their exits be usable?

Lindsay streaked from the back of the plane to the forward galley.

"You guys, it's got to be really bad! There's all kinds of stuff coming over the wings."

This was their first indication that something was wrong. There were no strange smells. The plane felt and sounded completely normal.

"No," said Ted. "They're dumping fuel. We can take off when we're carrying all that weight, but we can't land with it or the landing gear might collapse. Everybody do a smoking check again. I know the sign is on, but some nervous person might light up."

The crew finished the check just as the lights of San Juan appeared outside of the jet's windows. A chime signal from the captain told the flight attendants to prepare for landing. May made her way to her jumpseat. She was rehashing her emergency procedures in her head as Tyrone sat in the jumpseat next to hers.

"Now, if I die, you know how to open that door, right?" he said.

"What? Yes, of course I do."

Tyrone was grinning.

"Good. How are you liking your first flight here at Equity Air?"

"I'll never forget it. Our fifteen minutes has to be up by now, don't you think?"

Tyrone looked past her, out the window. "Look, runway lights. Just a little bit farther."

The lights were speeding past… then… touchdown. The jet landed smoothly, slowed, and turned off the runway and onto the taxiway. May felt a wave of relief pass through her. The landing couldn't have felt more normal.

She peeked out the portal of the aircraft door. She recognized the terminal in the distance. The aircraft turned away from it and taxied on, farther and farther, to the darkest corner of the airport. There must still be something wrong.

The call bell rang next to Ted's jumpseat. The crew in the rear wanted information and instructions. Ted, having none to give, called the cockpit again. His face reddened with anger and frustration. He whispered into the phone about deploying evacuation slides. After he hung up the receiver, he called the rear of the plane.

"Do not deploy the slides," he whispered hoarsely.

Tyrone leaned towards May.

"If this thing was on fire, we'd be long gone outta here. That's for sure."

The passengers sat quietly, still no questions, and no panic, *yet*. Ted was looking out the window on his side of the plane. May spotted several trucks speeding towards them from the direction of the terminal. Two of the vehicles were carrying mobile stairs that could attach to the side of the aircraft and let the passengers off.

The cockpit door swung open at last. The captain told Ted to get everyone off as soon as the stairs were secured and to do it as quickly as possible. May, now standing next to the cockpit door, locked eyes with the flight engineer. He grabbed her by the arm and pulled her into the cockpit.

"It's a bomb scare," he said. "We get 'em down here every once in a while from a group that wants Puerto Rican independence from the U.S. There probably isn't one on board, but we still had to land quick because the caller gave an exact time that the bomb would go off. They were very specific about the flight and the time."

"Oh," was all she could say.

There wasn't time for anything else.

God, I must have 'it's my first flight' stamped on my forehead, she thought as she hastily exited the cockpit. *Well, at least I know what's going on.*

The mobile stairs were attached to the forward doors now and the flight attendants were assisting passengers from their seats. Marianne immediately went to the bottom of the stairs.

"Go down there and help her," Ted said to May.

The calm the passengers had displayed until this point vanished. A pent-up wave of panic and a sudden urgency to get off the plane took its place. Some passengers stumbled as they hurried down the stairs. Marianne and May did their best to catch them or at least slow them so they wouldn't break their necks. They poured out of two exits now that the stairs in the rear of the plane were connected.

Nearly 360 panicky people, some carrying babies, spilled out onto the taxiway. Several of the flight attendants were outside herding the passengers together and moving them from the plane. A man nervously lit a cigarette.

"Put that out!" shouted Marianne. "You're standing near tons of jet fuel!"

Startled, he dropped it to the ground, quickly stubbing it out.

"Guess he speaks English," she said to May with a grin.

May walked amid the crowd toward the rear of the plane, searching for Louisa. She'd been one of the last to get off. She was visibly upset.

"Are you okay?" May asked.

"Yes, but it was terrible. People were panicking. We opened the doors to hook up the mobile stairs, and before they were latched on, the passengers were shoving, and I almost got pushed out. What a splat that would be down to the concrete! And you won't believe this. We thought everyone was off, and when we made one last check, we found a man going through the stuff people left behind! Evacuating a plane and he's robbing people!"

"Oh my God," May said.

The girls turned, looking in the direction of the terminal. Several buses were coming to pick up the crowd. When the final passenger boarded the last bus, it was evident that there was no room for the crew or the airport officials handling the situation. The buses left for the terminal.

Moments later, a small car appeared and collected the officials. The crew was left standing alone in the dark. Marianne, in her four-inch stilettos, broke the silence.

"Do we have to walk to the terminal? What is it? A mile, mile and a half?"

Far in the distance, a rickety old ambulance came into view, the last vehicle available. Ten flight attendants and three pilots piled in. There was not enough space for all of them, so they squeezed two or three into a seat. May was the last one in, and with no other space available, she sat on Tyrone's lap.

Well, she thought *It's been quite a night. When this day started, who thought it would end with me sitting in a beat up ambulance on a dark runway in Puerto Rico, at one o'clock in the morning on the lap of a man I've just met.*

The crew sat quietly as the captain readjusted himself.

"Okay, everybody!" he exclaimed. "How about a piece of ass and a peanut butter sandwich?"

The flight attendants did not say a word. No one was up for either. The ambulance sped to the terminal.

The crew sat in operations as airport security searched the now-empty plane for explosives. A team of bomb-sniffing dogs would go over every inch before passengers could be allowed on. May was sure that they'd spend the night on the island, and she didn't even have a toothbrush with her.

She was incredulous when long after three a.m. the plane was declared safe. The decision was made to load any passengers still willing to fly to New York. She peeked at the ticket counter. Almost all of the passengers were still there. The intrepid group was ready to get back on the same plane and try again.

Equity didn't bother to taxi the jet to the terminal. They put the people on the same buses, drove them to the dark corner of the airport, loaded them on the plane, and took them to New York.

Two hours and forty-five minutes later, they landed safely at Kennedy. The early morning sun shone brightly as the plane pulled to the gate and released the bleary-eyed passengers. An exhausted crew stood in the aisle bidding them farewell.

The last passenger was gone. As May gathered her things, Louisa came up the aisle. They looked at each other wearily, both desperate to lay their heads on the nearest pillow. They still needed to walk downstairs to operations to sign in on the crew sheet and to see their next assignment.

"Nothing for either of us," Louisa said with relief.

The crew for the morning San Juan run stood in scheduling waiting to turn the plane around.

"Interesting night, huh?" one of them called.

The girls could only nod. May and Louisa left as quickly as possible, intent on catching the next van to the hotel. Midway through the terminal, May stopped.

"Louisa," she said, locking bloodshot eyes with her. "I can't believe it, but I just remembered that I have an appointment this morning to have my airline ID badge made. They need to take my picture for it. They assigned me the time, there's no way out of it. It's at eight o'clock."

It was already seven-thirty.

"I'll wait with you."

"Really? You certainly don't have to."

"I know."

As eight a.m. approached, they trudged to the administrative offices, where the photos were taken. It only took a few minutes. The instant photograph with her company identification number was quickly laminated. The photographer handed the completed ID to May. She held the picture in her hand, her own face staring at her.

It was a mess. Disheveled hair, hollow, bloodshot eyes, exhausted look, her lipstick long since worn off. She managed a ghost of a smile. Somehow, it was fitting. Fitting to have her disaster of a first flight forever captured in the photograph to show to every security agent in every airport all over the world for as long as she flew for Equity.

They reached the front of the terminal. Before they stepped onto the hotel van, May turned to Louisa.

"Do you think every flight will be like this one?"

Louisa looked back to the airport building.

"I don't know," she answered, deadly serious. "I really don't know..."

They returned to the hotel and slept most of the day.

CHAPTER FIVE

"I hope she gets here soon," Kathleen said to May, Louisa, and Marta.

They sipped tea in the hotel coffee shop.

"We only have another two days in the hotel before we get booted out. We've got to eat in a jiffy and start apartment hunting fast!" Kathleen said.

Just as she finished her sentence, their former classmate Eleanor arrived.

"It's so good to see you guys again," she said, hugging each of them.

She pulled up a chair, ordered a cup of coffee, and glanced toward May and Louisa.

"News about your flight is spreading fast," Eleanor said. "I think I've got you beat though. Mine was scarier."

"Oh no," Marta said. "What happened to you?"

"I got back yesterday from a European charter. The whole flight attendant crew was brand new, all from our class, including me, and one veteran flight attendant. We were waiting for a DC-8 coming from Paris. The passengers and crew got off and we got on, the usual routine. We got new passengers and flew them from Paris to London and then on to Belfast in Northern Ireland."

Eleanor pushed her white-blond hair from her tired eyes.

"It was great until Belfast."

She twirled her coffee cup, then stopped, studying its contents.

"So, what happened?" May prodded.

"We were going to ferry the plane home empty to New York. Seven hours, no passengers. It was gonna be great. Relaxing."

"So, what happened?" May repeated.

"They cleaned and serviced the plane, fueled it, and we took off. We were out of Belfast for a while when I went into the bathroom. I looked in the mirror to fix my lipstick, and there was a note pinned to it. It said, 'I'm going to kill you.'"

The girls leaned forward, eyes wide.

"What did you do?" Marta asked.

"I was pretty shaken up," she answered. "I told our senior flight attendant, and she told the cockpit crew. We couldn't figure out when the message got there. It wasn't on the plane in Paris or London. Somebody must have put it there while we were on the ground in Belfast."

She tapped her fingers nervously on the table.

"The pilots contacted the company. They said that no one phoned in any threats. So they decided we might as well continue to New York."

She laughed a little.

"It was actually okay for a while, nothing happened. When we were way out in the middle of nowhere over the Atlantic, that's when the cabin started filling with smoke. Everyone was sure as hell thinking about that note now! All of us new guys were scared to death, but our senior, she was great. She had us check everything you could possibly check on a DC-8 for the smoke source. We didn't find anything indicating that someone tried to set a fire. The cockpit shut down any non-essential electrical equipment and the smoke cleared. Just the same, we decided to strap ourselves into our jumpseats for the rest of the flight."

They waited in silence for Eleanor to finish her story.

"When we got to Kennedy, they sent us out to the middle of nowhere on the field."

"That sounds familiar," May said wryly.

"Shhh, let her finish!" Kathleen said impatiently.

"The FBI showed up! They checked out the plane and asked us a whole bunch of questions, but they didn't find anything. The pilots think the lights probably overheated and made the cabin fill with smoke."

"What about the note?" Marta asked.

"They don't know who wrote it. They probably never will. You know how it's been in Northern Ireland all these years." She laughed. "Talk about your horrible coincidences."

Eleanor looked straight at May and Louisa.

"You know we just got in yesterday afternoon, but the chief flight attendant has heard all about your flight and mine. She's afraid our whole class is going to quit."

No one quit.

Once Eleanor left the coffee shop and the team recollected their nerves after her story, everyone decided to separate to cover more ground in their search for an apartment. Without money for a security deposit, they knew it would be an uphill battle.

In the end, only Kathleen found something: a one-bedroom

apartment in an old building in Jamaica, Queens, not far from Kennedy airport, right on the expressway.

"We have to look at it now," she said. "I know it's one bedroom and we'll have to set up cots or something to fit all of us, but it's the best we can do. It's expensive, but between the four of us, we can do it. It's the only place I've seen that doesn't ask for a month's rent up front."

"Nobody is complaining, Kathleen, at least you found a place," May reassured her. "We'll take my car. Let's go!"

The six-story building was vintage 1940s.

"Who are we looking for again?" Marta asked as they entered.

"Some lady named Dolly, she's the manager. She shows the apartments to prospective renters."

They found the office just off the dimly-lit lobby. A painfully thin, bleached blonde woman opened the door. She wore white slacks and a white blouse covered with silver sequins over darkly-tanned skin that made it difficult to tell how old she was. May guessed her age at about seventy-five.

"Just look at you goils!" the woman exclaimed, lighting a cigarette.

She took a deep breath and pushed a long string of smoke out of her nostrils. After a few hacking coughs, she reached over her desk and grabbed a set of keys from the wall.

"Let me take you right up to the apartment. It's on the top floor. So where are you goils from? I should say women, shouldn't I? We're all women here."

She pointed a skinny, brown finger at Kathleen.

"This one says you're all stewardesses. Oh, that's so exciting! I envy you goils, all that travel."

Dolly talked non-stop until the elevator doors opened into a dingy, grayish-green hall lit by a small, uncovered light bulb. She walked them a short way, then stopped to unlock an apartment door revealing a furnished one-bedroom with a worn, pale green carpet that looked nearly as old as Dolly's skin. There was a spacious living room, one large bedroom, a small kitchen, and a bathroom.

"That sofa, that sofa over there," Dolly said, pointing to the ancient green couch in the living room. "That's a fold-out sofa."

It wasn't a fancy place, and it was old, but it did look reasonably clean. The girls knew that they couldn't be choosy.

"Does it have any kind of a bug problem?" Kathleen asked suddenly. "You know, cockroaches?"

Dolly instantly became indignant.

"Absolutely not!" she declared vehemently. "None! Never!"

The girls talked in whispers a few paces behind Dolly as they followed her downstairs to the office. They decided to sign the lease.

"It's not much, but at least we have someplace to stay," Louisa reasoned.

They left the building, key in hand.

"And we certainly won't be around much," Marta added. "Why did you ask about bugs, Kathleen?"

"I don't know. I remembered that when I was leaving to go to Portugal as an exchange student in college my mom told me to make sure there weren't bugs in my apartment."

"Did you guys notice that funny smell in there?" May asked.

"Yeah, I did," Kathleen said. "What was that? It was kind of sweet, but not quite. Probably some cheap air freshener they use when they show the place to prospective tenants."

May pulled her Buick into the hotel lot. Her heart skipped a beat when she saw Jake's tall, muscular figure leaning against his van. She stopped the car quickly, flung open the door, and ran into his arms.

"Do you think she knows him?" Kathleen dead-panned.

Marta and Louisa smiled. May's friends disappeared quietly into the hotel.

Jake took May to the hotel coffee shop. They had an early dinner. May had so much to tell him and she had to admit, his face made some interesting expressions as she recounted her adventures so far.

"You're right. This is a crazy company that you're working for," Jake said. "Maybe it's a good thing that your first flight was such a baptism of fire. The rest will seem easy now."

"God, I hope so," May answered, taking a sip from her water glass.

"I can't say that the stuff your friend told you about your owner makes me feel too secure," Jake said. "A former gun runner? Lord knows what this guy could be up to. Does he care about anything besides money? You'd better keep your eyes and ears wide open, and for heaven's sake, don't volunteer for anything."

May nodded. "Oh, believe me, I'll watch myself. On the plus side, we did find an apartment today. It's not much, but I have a place to hang my hat."

"Is it safe?"

"I think so. It'll have to do for now."

The two ate, not saying much for a while. Then, Jake put down his fork.

"May, I need to talk to you about something."

"Uh oh," she smiled. "This sounds serious."

"It kind of is."

She stopped eating and looked at him. "What's up?"

"A really great opportunity. A friend of mine is doing some kayaking this summer and he's asked me to come along."

"Why, that sounds great! You'll love it!"

He didn't say anything.

"What's the rest, Jake?"

"It's for the whole summer."

"Well, that's not too bad. Your brother and sister can take up some of the slack at your sporting goods business while you're doing that. That will be great experience for them," May said. "Besides, I'll be really busy, too. We'll just have to fit in our visits when we can."

"It's in Alaska, May."

His news knocked the wind out of her. "Oh."

Jake grabbed her hand across the table. "I know it's a couple of months, but I think we can work it out, I really do."

May held on to his hand for a while. She finally let it go.

"It sounds like you really want to do this, and I think you should. What the heck, you backed me when I went to Tennessee for three weeks. The least I can do is support you."

She leaned across the table and kissed him.

"We'll make up for it when you get back."

After that news, May headed to the apartment. She dropped her bag on the bedroom floor. Marta and Kathleen were working, leaving only May and Louisa.

"I'm so glad this place is furnished," May said. "We'd never find the time or money to go and buy anything."

Louisa nodded. She sat on one of the twin beds. "I'm glad we won the toss for the bedroom. I'd much rather be in here than out in the living room. We'll hardly be here, and I know we'll find something better when we get on our feet."

"You're right," May yawned. "Listen, it's late and I'm pooped. I'm going to brush my teeth and hit the sack."

May headed toward the bathroom. She groped the wall inside the doorway until she found the light switch. She flipped the switch and sent at least half a dozen cockroaches scurrying for cover.

"What the...YUCK!" she shouted.

Louisa came running.

"What is it?" she cried.

May sank against the wall.

"Roaches. Disgusting, creepy...... did I say disgusting? Roaches. I HATE roaches!"

They stood silently.

"We'll get some spray right away," Louisa said finally.

May grimaced. "Hopefully, there's just a few and we can get rid of them. Ugh, I'm going to bed."

A few days later, when all four were reunited in the apartment, May and Louisa warned the other two girls about the roaches. They'd discovered that there weren't just a few, but that the place was overrun. None of them had recognized the sickly-sweet odor of cockroach spray when they initially toured the apartment.

"Every time my eye catches a speck of dust or something on the rug, I jump because I think it's a roach," May sputtered angrily. "I see them in the kitchen, too! I'm having nightmares about them."

"Are you sure it's that bad?" Kathleen asked.

"Yeah, I'm sure."

Late that night, screams from the living room woke May and Louisa. Both women sat bolt upright in bed, dimly making out the silhouettes of Marta and Kathleen in the doorway.

"Wha…? What is it? What?" May asked, rubbing her eyes.

"Co… Cock… Cockroaches," Kathleen shuddered. "I woke up out there in bed, and cockroaches were running across my FACE! I think I'm gonna barf! Can we sleep in here on the floor with you guys?"

"Sure, of course," Louisa answered.

She looked in May's direction, but couldn't see her face very well in the dark. She didn't have to. She knew that May was thinking the same thing that she was.

They'd seen the cockroaches in the bedroom as well.

CHAPTER 6

The next day, Marta and Kathleen set off for Los Angeles on a scheduled flight, and Louisa worked a charter from Des Moines to Toronto. A replacement crew boarded the plane in Toronto and took it the rest of the way to Paris.

May worked the turnaround flight to San Juan—again. She found herself on the flight so often that a coworker took to introducing her to passengers as the newly-crowned "Miss Puerto Rico." May was tired of the flight and becoming jealous of many of her former classmates who were working flights to more exciting locations with long layovers.

In the airline industry, seniority was everything, and the best flights went to the most senior people. Flight attendants bid on flying schedules each month, and the greater a person's seniority, the more likely they were to get their first choice of schedule. People with less seniority got less desirable schedules and flights. The peons at the bottom sat on reserve.

The best these poor souls could do was bid to sit on-call on specific days of the week. On those days, they sat by the phone waiting to fill last-minute assignments. They were often required to get to the airport with as little as one hour's notice. Reserve schedules were supposed to have guaranteed days off, but the company chose to ignore this little inconvenience. They called people to work flights on their days off if they needed them.

May and her former classmates were on reserve and quickly discovered that getting good assignments on reserve was a matter of either sheer luck or buddying up to a crew scheduler. The worst part was that a junior person could be assigned to a good flight on reserve and still get bumped off it by someone with seniority.

The day finally came when May received her first European assignment, a scheduled flight to Brussels, Belgium. The flight left Kennedy Airport in the evening, would fly all night, and arrive in Europe the following morning. May would have a layover of more than twenty-four hours.

She was flying with Evan, her former classmate who'd been furloughed from American Airlines. He'd never been to Europe either and felt just as thrilled for the trip. When flight time arrived, both were greeted by a friendly crew anxious to make the pair's first flight over the Atlantic a good one.

The all-night flight on the DC-8 was full, and it took the seven flight attendants some time to serve dinner and drinks. May and Evan worked together in the back of the plane. When the attendants finished the meal service, the pair dropped side-by-side onto the rear jumpseat to rest. Each downed a quick cup of coffee to rejuvenate as May surveyed their passengers. About half were American, the rest European.

"So," Evan whispered. "How do they stack up? Do you like American passengers better or Europeans?"

May stroked her chin, pretending to be deep in thought.

"Hmm... I don't know. The Europeans smoke more and I could live without that. They do drink healthier beverages, you know, things like juices and tonic water. And they don't like ice in their drinks and that saves time. What do you think?"

"I think the Europeans need to take more baths. I thought I was going to die from the body odor before the air conditioning really kicked in. But the Americans are more obnoxious. I call it a tie."

Little by little, the passengers dimmed their lights. May fought to stay awake in the darkened cabin, as she had little to do until it was time to prepare for the breakfast service. The hours crept by, and it was a very long while before the sky offered hints of dawn. The pilots, aware that two of the crew were crossing the Atlantic for the first time, thoughtfully called to the rear of the plane to see if May or Evan wanted to come to the cockpit to watch the sunrise.

May hardly managed not to run to the front of the plane. She sat in the extra cockpit jumpseat and watched the sky transform into a rosy pink horizon. High clouds changed from black to varying hues of purple. The stars, still visible through them, began to wink out.

May could see the ocean below now, obscured only a few moments earlier by the darkness. The ocean's shades of purple mirrored those of the sky. The thin cloud cover whizzed past the plane, but May could discern no sense of motion from the white-capped North Atlantic below as she watched the world wake up.

A few seconds later, the sun had cleared the horizon and shone too brightly in her eyes. May offered to bring the pilots coffee. They accepted. She made her delivery and returned to work.

The plane touched down in Brussels. The crew breezed through customs at the airport and then boarded the crew van to the hotel. Sleepy as she was, May made an effort to study the scenery as they sped by.

Meanwhile, everyone offered her and Evan lots of advice on coping with jet lag.

"I stay up as long as I can, eat dinner, and go to bed early," someone said.

"No! Don't do that!" someone else chimed in. "You wake up too early the next morning! Sleep a few hours, then get up and go out. Eat dinner and go to bed later."

In the end, May decided that she needed at least a few hours of sleep. She climbed into bed for a nap as soon as they reached the hotel. At two in the afternoon, she awoke refreshed. She ran to the hotel lobby to meet the rest of her crew, who were determined to show the two newcomers a good time.

They hailed two taxis and directed the drivers to the Grand Platz, the ancient square in the center of Brussels. The eight-hundred-year-old buildings bursted with chocolates and lace and more restaurants than May could count. They chose one and devoured an excellent meal of seafood. Then, they walked across the cobblestone square to a favorite drinking haunt of Equity crews.

May entered the packed, ancient bar and stood face-to-face with a full-sized stuffed horse.

Dozens and dozens of inflated objects that she couldn't identify dangled above it.

"Pig bladders," the senior flight attendant informed her.

"Oh," was the only comment she could make.

May followed a co-worker up a winding set of stairs that encircled the gigantic horse, up to the second floor. The crew sat at an old wooden table in a small alcove overlooking the floor below. A tiny window on the opposite side provided a view of the cobblestone square. The flight veterans kept the beer flowing into the wee hours of the morning, determined to break the newcomers in.

"It's a tradition to celebrate your first trip across the pond in style!" the senior flight attendant shouted over the noisy crowd.

She ordered another round.

When May at last crawled into bed, she found herself tossing and turning, the result of jet lag and too much beer.

After she finally fell asleep, her rest was not kind.

May found herself lying motionless on the hard ground. She looked on in horror as a tremendous, enraged elephant placed its front foot on her head. The gargantuan animal gradually shifted its weight, applying more and more pressure to its front foot.

In only a matter of moments, her skull would be smashed to pieces.

An insistent ringing noise could be heard far in the distance. It grew progressively louder, the piercing sound irritating the elephant's large ears and distracting it from its gruesome task.

The ringing produced a similar effect on May. Would she be destroyed by the crush of the elephant's foot or driven mad by the terrible ringing? With a heroic effort, she jerked her body and—

May woke.

Her alarm clock continued to ring. She reached out, fumbling to find the off switch. She silenced it at last. She had a pounding headache, dry mouth, and a general feeling of malaise.

"Oh crap. I really, really overdid it," she groaned, rolling out of bed.

She stood in the warm shower for several minutes, seeking revival.

Maybe if I eat something, she thought, pulling on her uniform.

She crawled to a little hole-in-the-wall restaurant next to the hotel, an establishment frequented by Equity crews. Some of her co-workers were already there, and she squeezed into a seat beside them.

"Have fun last night?" one of them asked, nonchalantly sipping tea.

May moaned, holding her head.

"Not so loud. Does anyone have a couple of aspirin?"

The others laughed, and she ordered a sandwich and a Coke.

"I sure hope this helps," she said wanly when her food arrived.

She forced down the food and drink, but it didn't help at all. As she struggled to keep the food from coming back up, a little old man, white-haired, wearing a long black coat, approached their table.

A small, scruffy, white dog on a leash trailed behind him. He nodded and smiled at the crew, revealing coffee-stained teeth.

"Equity?" he inquired.

The crew looked at one another puzzled, then back at the old man. They nodded.

"Happy landings!" he blurted.

He turned, hobbled to the door with the scruffy little dog, and disappeared out into the street. May gazed after him.

"That was almost as weird as the dream I had last night," she muttered.

He would appear there many more times over the next few years, always with his little dog, always with the same question, always with the same response, like a figure from *The Twilight Zone*.

Sinatra was booming "New York, New York" from the corner jukebox, matching the rhythm of May's throbbing head while she paid for her meal. She returned to the hotel, retrieved her suitcase, and took the elevator to the lobby. As the elevator descended, she wondered how she would ever be able to work.

I've got to muddle through this somehow, she thought, gritting her teeth, *and I will never, NEVER do this to myself again.*

She dropped her key at the front desk and glanced across the lobby at the rest of the crew. An extra flight attendant had appeared from somewhere. May guessed she was in her mid-thirties. She was slim with light brown hair and a friendly yet serious look. The others seemed to know her well.

The woman stood, approaching May with her hand held out in greeting.

"Hello!" she said with a smile. "I'm Penny and I'm a check stew. I'll be giving you and Evan a check ride on the way back to New York."

May's head throbbed mercilessly. She'd known she was to get a "check ride," a verbal test of her emergency knowledge during her six-month probationary period. As she looked at Penny, the color drained from her face. She smiled weakly.

"Great. Okay, Penny …Gee, that's really great."

Evan merely nodded. He was in worse shape than May. As she wheeled her bag toward the bus, she prayed as she had never prayed before.

God, oh please God, if you're listening, I only ask one thing. Please, please don't let me throw up on her.

Somehow, May and Evan worked the flight home, though neither performed at their normal level. May was thankful when service was completed, and it was time to sit down with Penny and go through the hour or so of grilling on safety. The material was fresh in the minds of both new flight attendants. They passed without a problem.

After arrival at Kennedy Airport, May and Evan stood at the end of the crew customs line, the last to pass through.

"Thank God, that's over," Evan said wearily.

"You said it," May replied, retrieving her passport from the customs agent. "How do you feel?"

"Better now, but I barfed twice. I'm glad she quizzed you first. I am pledging here and now to never get that drunk again the evening before a flight."

"I'm taking the same pledge," May said. "This is a sacred vow between us, okay?"

"Okay."

The two spit on their palms, shook hands, and left the terminal.

While the incident may have technically been over, several weeks later, May heard some interesting information through the company grapevine.

In a conversation with some of her friends, Penny had mentioned how she'd given check rides to two brand-new people working their first trans-Atlantic flight. She'd voiced some serious concerns about how the jet lag had made the two new flight attendants terribly sick.

Penny never realized that she'd witnessed the after-effects of two world-class hangovers, and May would never correct her.

CHAPTER SEVEN

May opened the apartment door, dropping her bags inside.

"Anybody else in the roach motel?" she called.

Marta popped her head around the corner from the kitchen.

"Just me."

She was making dinner.

"What's that you're cooking?" May asked, looking in the pan on the stove. "It smells…different."

"It's an Indian dish," Marta answered. "I love Indian food. Do you want to try it when it's done?"

"Sure, I'm always up for a little adventure. Where did you come in from?"

Marta covered the pan and sat with May at the kitchen table.

"I got back a little while ago from a military charter. We took soldiers from Kansas to Bangor, Maine, and another crew took them on to Germany. We flew back to New York on Delta." A wistful look graced her face. "I wonder when I'll get to do the Germany part."

May nodded. "I know what you mean. By the way, I've been hearing all kinds of chatter about this Hadj thing? Do you know what it is?"

"Yeah, some of the more senior people on my trip were telling me about it and it sounds really interesting. Every year the Muslim countries in the world contract with charter airlines from the West to fly pilgrims to Mecca in Saudi Arabia," Marta explained. "They visit all of the holy sites of Islam. Good Muslims are supposed to make it to Mecca some time in their lives if they can. It creates a really big demand for transportation, more than their own countries can handle. They get a company like us during this holy period. It's a month flying them over and another month flying them all back home. It's a pretty big financial boost for the airlines doing it."

May pulled a soda from the refrigerator. A cockroach ran up the door as she closed it.

"Little mother…" she snarled, trying to squash it with a napkin. It was too fast for her. "I hate this place. Go on. So when does this happen?"

"The timing can vary, but it's usually in the summer or fall."

May pondered for a moment.

"There are a lot of Muslim countries. Did you find out where Equity has gone in the past?" she asked.

"My crew was telling me about some of the places. One was Karachi, Pakistan," Marta answered. "They said it was beautiful. Working the flights from there to Saudi Arabia was okay and the shopping was fabulous. The country is pretty westernized."

She suddenly laughed and then continued.

"They also told me about another year when they were flying pilgrims from Nigeria. If you think the roaches are bad here, it sounds like the bugs there are lots bigger, and there's plenty of them. They said everyone slept with one eye open because they were afraid that a giant creepy crawler would get in the sack with them! None of the senior people wanted it, so the junior flight attendants got assigned to it. One of the guys I flew with worked it. He said that the people were nice but not westernized at all. They weren't remotely familiar with even the simplest technology, let alone a jetliner! In their daily lives, they build fires for cooking so flight attendants were going crazy trying to keep them from starting fires in the aisle of the plane! And the bathroom—a flush toilet was an alien concept! He said the language barrier made things just about impossible."

Marta laughed loudly.

"I know I shouldn't laugh, but I couldn't help it when he told me this part," Marta said. "He said that a male passenger went to the lav and couldn't figure out how the doorknob worked. He got inside all right, but he thought that he needed to pull the door in instead of pushing to get out when he was finished. He was in there yelling and screaming, and making all kinds of racket. The door was cracked, and his fingers were sticking out of it. He's pulling the door the wrong way with all his might. Bud— that's the flight attendant telling me all of this— he just couldn't make him understand that all he needed to do was push. The only thing he could think of to get him out was to slam the door on the guys' fingers. When he did, the man screamed bloody murder and pulled his hand out. And that's how Bud got him out of the bathroom."

May laughed.

"Boy, I'd just hate to miss this," she said. "It sounds pretty interesting. Culture shock, but definitely interesting! So is the company going to do it this year?"

"I would think so. With that kind of money involved, I can't imagine that they wouldn't. And you know how our owner is about making money."

"What about the country? Which one would we go to?" May wondered out loud. "Our illustrious owner's supposed past exploits could make for some interesting choices, and not necessarily in a good way. I could see him picking some country that he can run guns to."

"My crew said that we'll just have to wait. It shouldn't be that long until the company decides, though. The pilgrimage isn't very far off. It's in September."

"Well," May yawned, "hopefully, we'll get some good trips in the meantime."

She sniffed the air again.

"Your Indian stuff smells pretty good."

"Thanks," Marta grinned. "It's ready. Grab a bowl and let's dig in!"

A few weeks later, word spread. Yes, Equity would be working the Hadj this year. They would fly pilgrims to Mecca in September and bring them home in October.

"I wish I knew which country we have," May said to Louisa as they walked from the grocery store to their apartment.

Louisa nodded. "Me, too. If it's a good assignment, you know the senior people will take it."

"True," May agreed. "It seems that if all of the senior people take the Hadj, then the good charter lines open up for us. So it could be a good situation anyway."

They entered the apartment building and rode up the elevator.

"I suppose that's true," Louisa answered, "but with our luck Equity will get someplace terrible and we'll have to go."

"I'm thinking positive thoughts," May said resolutely. "You watch, it will be someplace great."

May fumbled with the grocery bags as she put the key in the door. Before she could turn the knob, the door popped open. Marta was standing in the doorway in uniform. She'd just gotten home from her flight.

"Hey guys! Guess what?" she said, as she reached for some of the groceries.

"What?" May and Louisa said in unison.

"Wanna know where we're going on the Hadj?"

"Where is it?" May interrupted. "Is it a great place?"

"Well..." Marta said stalling.

"Oh, God, is it Nigeria?" May asked.

"Pakistan?" Louisa asked hopefully.

"No..."

"WHERE?" the two shouted.

"Libya."

The three stood wordlessly until Louisa broke the silence.

"Libya?"

"Libya," Marta repeated.

May collapsed on the tired couch. A cockroach ran from underneath it.

"Son of a bitch!" she yelled.

May hurled her shoe at the scurrying creature, missing it. She plopped back on the couch.

"Libya, why does it have to be Libya? We don't even have diplomatic relations with Libya!" she whined. "We hate Libya! Moammar Gadhafi is in Libya!"

Marta sat beside her.

"Flight attendants and pilots are in an uproar. Can you just it? Our planes with a big American flag and a roll of giant dollar bills painted on the tail? Who came up with that design anyway?"

"I heard it was the owner's mother," May said. "There's no accounting for taste."

"Well, maybe they would paint over the dollars while we're over there. That would make it a little less offensive," Louisa interjected.

"Are you kidding?" May snorted. "With the stories we've heard? If half the things we've heard about the owner are true, he's not one to care about the safety of his employees, not as long as there is money to be made. This is a legit deal, too, everything above board. No smuggling or hiding anything, just fly the pilgrims where they want to go, collect lots of money, and take your chances that nothing will happen to your workers. If things work out great, if not…"

Despite the pile of potential problems, they were interested in the experience. But what exactly would the risks be? They discussed it from every angle.

"The government will look out for us, won't they?" Louisa asked.

"Sure, they'll send in the Marines if we need them," May remarked. Her smile faded. "I think I'm going to take a wait-and-see attitude."

A key turning in the apartment door stopped the conversation. Kathleen was just getting back.

"You guys heard about the Hadj?" she asked, pulling her suitcase through the door.

"Marta told us," May replied. "We think we might want to do it, but we want to know more."

"Even with what the State Department said?" she asked.

They looked at her blankly.

"State Department?" Marta asked.

"Yeah. It was going around the flight attendant lounge. The State

Department said that if the company takes the job, we'll be on our own, since we don't have diplomatic relations with Libya. If we get into trouble, there will be no help from Uncle Sam."

"Oh, dear," Louisa mumbled. "No Marines."

"Well," May said, standing. "It's a few weeks until we have to bid, so I'm not going to decide until then. Anybody want to go to the diner for strawberry cheesecake?"

The topic didn't die completely. Two weeks later, May was in crew scheduling, signing in for her flight. Two pilots were talking quietly nearby. May had flown with one of them recently and greeted him.

"Hi, Bob, nice to see you again, what's new?" she asked, dropping her bag.

"Have you heard the latest?" he asked.

"About the Hadj, you mean?" she replied. "No. What's up?"

"Not the Hadj exactly, but yeah, the Hadj. An incident," Bob's voice was grim. "I don't know what the circumstances were exactly, but we just shot down two Libyan fighter jets."

As May boarded her plane, she pushed the information she had just heard from her mind and concentrated on the flight she was working. As usual, the flight was full, and soon she and the rest of her crew lost themselves in the demands of working at 35,000 feet.

When she returned, May dashed through her apartment to the bedroom. She froze as she neared the bed, her eye catching a dark spot on the rug.

Just a piece of paper, she thought with relief. *God, I'm imagining that everything is a cockroach. I must be losing my mind.*

She threw enough clothing in her suitcase for her three days off. No new assignment had been waiting for her on the crew list when she'd returned from her flight. She could take a break.

Kathleen arrived, returning from a visit with Eleanor.

"Going somewhere?" she asked.

"Yup," May replied. "Three whole days off and I'm going home to Connecticut. I haven't been back since before training. I know it hasn't been that long, but it feels like a lifetime."

"Don't forget that the flying schedules are coming out in a few days. You don't want to miss bidding for the Hadj."

The sarcasm in Kathleen's voice was obvious. May paused.

"You know I'm still thinking about bidding for it. It's such a once-in-a-lifetime experience."

"As long as you live through it, you mean," Kathleen said.

"That's true. If they'd at least take that damned wad of dollar bills off the tail of the plane!" She glanced at her watch. "I'm out of here. It's late enough that the traffic shouldn't be too bad. See you when I get back!"

It was well past midnight when May pulled into her parent's driveway. The night was very clear, and she stopped to admire the explosion of stars. Her mind wandered to Jake kayaking in Alaska. Several weeks had passed, and she had heard nothing.

I wonder if the sky looks like this in Alaska tonight, she mused. *I wonder if he is thinking about me...*

She drew in a deep breath of the cool, clean night air and stepped into the house. Her family was fast asleep. She didn't see anyone until the next morning, when she puttered to the kitchen to make coffee. Her sister was already there. Lynn reached over and gave May a hug.

"I heard you come in late last night. How's the dream job?"

May laughed. "I don't really know if that's what I'd call it, but it sure ain't dull!"

"Seriously, what are you going to do about that Hadj thing you told me about on the phone?"

"I think I want to do it."

"Are you sure? What are you going to tell Mom and Dad?"

"I don't know, but I guess I'll have to figure it out pretty quick."

"Figure what out?" May's mother asked as she entered the room.

She gave her daughter a big hug.

"Lynn and I were just talking about the Hadj, you know, the pilgrimage I was telling you

about."

Lynn looked at the wall clock above the kitchen cupboards. "Wow, I've gotta run, so I'll see you tonight, okay?"

She gave May a quick kiss on the cheek.

"Don't want to watch, huh?" May whispered in her ear.

"Nope," her sister answered.

May and her mother stood alone in the kitchen.

"I think I want to do it. I want to go to Libya," she said haltingly. "It would be such a great adventure! Really exciting, different—"

"What about your safety?" Her mother interrupted.

May knew she'd been watching the news.

"I know I have to think about that," May admitted. "It's not an ideal situation. If something really did happen to me, say if I became a hostage or something..."

Tears welled in her mother's eyes.

"...If I..."

May's voice trailed off.

"Okay, what if I wait and see how the first phase goes?" May suggested. "And if everything is alright, I'll do the second phase."

Relief flooded her mother's face.

Later that day, May parked her old Buick to walk to the familiar hangar. It was lunch time, and she knew she would find Orrie and Hoot taking a break somewhere. She pushed the door open and found them, cups of coffee in hand, in the middle of an animated conversation. Hoot had his back to her, discussing his latest group of parachutists.

"I just don't know what some of these people are thinkin' that do this, I really don't," he complained. "This young fella thought it would be great to get his ninety-year-old grandma to jump out of a plane for her birthday. It was a tandem jump, but I could see she was scared shitless beyond all reason. She was only doin' it to make the kid happy. When we got to altitude, they all jumped, and she fainted dead away as soon as they cleared the doorway! I saw 'em walkin' across the field just now. She must have barfed as soon as she came to, because I saw the instructor she was tied to, and he had her lunch all over the front of him—"

Orrie spotted May.

"Well!" Orrie exclaimed. "Bust my arms and call me Venus, look who's here!"

May hugged each man warmly.

"Sounds like you're still having all kinds of fun, Hoot," she said with a grin.

"So, young lady, how did things turn out?" Orrie asked.

"I passed the training," she answered, "been working non-stop."

"Which airline are you flying with again?"

May filled both of them in on Equity, including details about their airplanes, and the charter flying. Hoot scratched his head.

"That's a different kind of flying, the non-sched stuff. I did some of it. Unpredictable. Charter companies are usually small," he said. "If the plane breaks somewhere, it can be a long time before you get another one. You can get marooned in some pretty interesting places. Doesn't pay anything."

May nodded. "You got that part right. I work scheduled flying and charters. It's a small company. I know I won't get rich, but I'm hoping to see a lot and I'm having fun."

"Now that's nice. You should do that while you're young."

"Equity," Orrie said. "I know that one."

"It's been around since World War Two," May replied.

"No, I've heard something more recently. Who's the owner of that outfit?"

"A guy named Flint bought it right after deregulation went through."

"That's right, I heard that somewhere," Orrie stroked his chin. "Flint… J.T. Flint. That guy's been around a while and he's been in and out of trouble. I don't know if they still do, but people used to call him 'Skin Flint' because he was so damn cheap."

May looked at Orrie, an uneasy feeling coming over her. She remembered Keisha's comments during training.

"What kind of trouble?"

Orrie and Hoot exchanged glances.

"When the Second World War ended, there were lots of pilots looking for flying jobs. Most of us got on with the mainstream civilian airlines," Orrie caught Hoot's eye. "Some of us sooner than others. The industry really took off. Then there were pilots that wanted to start their own businesses, run their own airlines. A lot of it was cargo, but also charters, especially military charters. Some of those fellows started good companies and did a good job. There was a need and they filled it. Others ran on a wing and a prayer, scraping by financially and cutting corners to do it, especially where safety is concerned."

"How?" May asked.

"Not keeping up with aircraft maintenance, working people to death, going over cargo limits, that sort of thing. Some real fly-by-night operations."

"And what have you heard about Flint?" May pressed.

"He's in tight with the military. Might get preferential treatment when it comes to military charters. That's big money."

"That's not so bad, is it?"

"No, but the scuttlebutt is… He's done some, shall we say, less than above-board work. Gun runner," Orrie said. "Word has it he was flying weapons where we weren't supposed to be. Who knows what else he might have been doing, but I'm sure it wasn't good."

"I heard rumors," May said.

Orrie started to speak, but stopped abruptly. He stroked his chin again.

"What else, Orrie?" May asked. "I should know."

Orrie glanced at Hoot again, then met May's eyes squarely.

"I might as well tell you," he said. "Years back, while ol' Skin Flint put his brother and his brother's wife and kids on a flight to Chicago on one of his company planes. The plane went down over the Rockies and killed everyone on board. The feds investigated the company and found all kinds of safety violations. His company went under right after that."

None of them spoke for several moments.

"He has another airline besides Equity now," May volunteered, if only to break the silence. "It's called Saber Air. It's all charter flying, no scheduled flights, and it's non-union."

"I suppose if he was going to do anything, shall we say, 'unusual,' that's where it would happen," Orrie said. "It would be easier to hide. He could help his old CIA buddies with his own all-charter airline."

He reached over and put an arm around May's shoulder.

"Hell, don't worry about it," he said. "Unless you start flying a bunch of vacationers to every war-torn pit on the planet. Then get out! Just remember guys like that are lookin' to make money—honestly or otherwise—and they're not above gambling with people's lives. They don't mind cutting corners on safety if it saves them a few bucks."

May stifled a sigh.

"Do you two know anything about the Hadj?" she asked.

Hoot grinned.

"I do. That's legit. I did that years ago with a charter outfit, lots of fun if you're flying for a good country," Hoot said. "Are you going to do that? For which country?"

"Libya."

"Might want to skip it this year," Orrie interjected.

"Don't worry," May said. "I already told my mom I wouldn't go on the first phase. I said I'd try to go on the second phase if everything works out."

When the time came for the Hadj, despite the destruction of the Libyan jets, the operation was still a go. The senior flight attendant sat out the first phase. Neither May nor any of her roommates bid on it, and they had just enough seniority to avoid being sent. Junior flight attendants were assigned to the job. The result was the most junior Hadj Equity ever flew.

The company had resorted to shipping new flight attendants straight from training directly to the Middle East.

Four DC-8s and two DC-10s were designated to transport the pilgrims. In the interest of safety, Equity's contract with Libya specified that all crew layovers would be in Saudi Arabia. Much to everyone's surprise, the first phase went off without a hitch. The Libyan government treated the Equity employees well. The pilgrims were well-educated, fairly sophisticated, and a pleasure to fly. Every flight attendant and pilot came home in one piece.

They returned to New York, tanned from sunbathing on the beaches by the Red Sea and sporting new gold necklaces and bracelets that they bought in the open-air markets of Saudi Arabia. Everyone that ducked out of the first phase, including May and her roommates, clamored to work the second phase.

The low-seniority souls drafted to go on phase one didn't have a prayer of going for phase two. Senior flight attendants snapped up the assignment. This time, May, Marta, Louisa, and Kathleen did not have the seniority to go.

Returning the Muslim pilgrims to their homes did not go as smoothly as the first phase. The DC-8s broke down, causing long delays, a situation that did not sit well with officials in Libya or Saudi Arabia. It did, however, leave flight attendants with extra time on their hands.

Crews found Saudi Arabian society very restricted, segregating men and women in most social situations. Western women were allowed a few more freedoms than local women and were vigorously pursued by Arabic men. Some of the pursuers were Saudi Arabians, others were Arabs of different nationalities, including Lebanese, Palestinians, and Egyptians.

Historically, the Hadj was a hotbed of romance among American crewmembers as well. Flight attendants and pilots struck up relationships with each other out of loneliness or boredom. For many, there was little else to do. Alcohol was absolutely forbidden. Crews used their creativity to entertain themselves.

May and her roommates knew of old Hadj legends and unsubstantiated stories passed down through the years about the clashes between Western and Middle Eastern cultures. Like the tale of the German Lufthansa crewmember and his attempt to bypass the Saudi Arabian restriction on pork; he allegedly smuggled a pig into Saudi Arabia disguised as a dog. As the story went, a suspicious customs agent stopped the crew member as he entered the country with the pig on a leash, collar around its neck, proclaiming, "*Mein hund, mein hund!*"

In another story, a pilot employed by an American carrier spotted a beautiful young Saudi woman on the streets of Riyadh. The Saudi woman, obviously from an important and wealthy family, was walking down the street with an entourage, dressed in fabulous robes and covered with jewelry. For the most part, women were locked away and forbidden to have any contact with Western males. According to the legend, the pilot approached her, ogled her longingly and wistfully proclaimed, "I suppose a blow job is out of the question."

Most airline crews stayed in a luxurious downtown hotel owned by a prominent Saudi Arabian family. The family often became friendly with crewmembers and graciously invited them home.

Returning Equity employees described the lavish homes and parties of the privileged class. One wealthy, young Saudi showed off a private disco in his basement, a well-stocked bar, and a solid gold toilet seat in his bathroom. Liquor, supposedly banned from the country, flowed freely for the wealthy who didn't have to worry about harsh penalties.

Even after the necessary repairs of the broken airliners, when the Hadj ended and the last pilgrim was flown home, the Libyan government prevented the departure of the final Equity plane until every monetary problem, real or imagined, was resolved to their satisfaction. Only then was the crew allowed to leave.

The DC-8s and DC-10s were ferried home empty of passengers but full of off-duty flight attendants and pilots. The end of the lengthy, stressful period of hard work, long hours, culture shock, and for most, no alcohol, was a recipe for wild inflight parties. A Hadj Queen was chosen and given a makeshift sash and crown. One returning aircraft made a stop in Antwerp, Belgium, laying over for the night. The plane of crazed flight personnel swooped down on the unsuspecting city, found a local bar, and nearly drove the owner from his own establishment.

May would always regret missing out on this unique experience.

And, as it turned out, it was the last Hadj that the company ever worked.

CHAPTER EIGHT

May, Louisa, and Kathleen sat at the kitchen table quietly chatting when Marta burst into the apartment.

"The bids are out! The bids are out!" she hollered. "I got a charter line! Quick! Call crew scheduling and see what you got!"

The girls took turns phoning crew scheduling. As each hung up, a broad smile lit her face. They had all received excellent flying schedules.

"It's because all of the senior people are on the second phase of the Hadj," Kathleen exclaimed gleefully. "I knew it would happen!"

May scanned her schedule. For most of its existence, Equity was strictly a charter carrier. Charter flying meant long layovers at interesting destinations, which was what most of the company's flight attendants wanted. But, they were also unpredictable. Despite the careful scheduling, you could never be completely sure where you might wind up.

May couldn't go on the Hadj, but this was the next best thing, Europe!

May began her flying month by boarding an evening United flight from New York to Omaha. She and her crew would meet an Equity plane there the following day. Since Equity's scheduled flights were limited, it was not unusual for Equity personnel to fly other carriers both domestically and internationally. It was often necessary to use other carriers to position crews.

May didn't know any of the flight attendants on this Equity crew, but they all bonded quickly. She immediately liked Barb, the senior flight attendant. Barb was a tall brunette about thirty years old. Grace, a soft-spoken blond was flying with her best friend, Dimitra, a dark-haired, dark-eyed, Greek girl. Gail was a feisty, petite redhead from Michigan. LaToya, dark and talkative, hailed from Los Angeles. The only member of the cockpit crew accompanying them on the United flight was Raul, the flight engineer. He was from Puerto Rico and looked to be in his late forties.

"Hello, ladies," he said cheerfully.

"Hello," they echoed.

There was a momentary silence, which Gail broke.

"Where are the pilots?" she asked.

"They're meeting us in Omaha. They both commute."

"From where?" LaToya asked.

"I don't know where the co-pilot is from," Raul said. "He's new. R. J., the captain, is from Minneapolis. You know the company doesn't care how you get to your flight as long as you show up on time and don't cost them any extra money. I believe he usually takes Flying Tigers.

"The cargo company?" May asked.

"Yeah. Lots of people ride their jump seats to commute."

This was something May hadn't heard before. She pressed Raul for details.

"It's easy if you ever want to do it," Raul explained. "Equity has an agreement with them. If you ever want a ride, just get a letter from the company saying that you work here. That's all you need. Then you can go whenever you want. They have flights in and out of the West Coast and through the Midwest. They fly late at night most of the time." Raul chuckled. "You can't be too picky about the accommodations. There's nothing like sitting in the upper deck of a 747 and listening to a herd of cattle bellowing down below."

The team arrived in Omaha and took a shuttle bus to the hotel to await the late-morning arrival of their DC-8. Once they arrived in Europe, the crew would have all afternoon and evening in Paris, then leave midday the following day to ferry an empty plane to Athens, Greece. Once there, they would pick up passengers and take them as far as a crew change point in Prestwick, Scotland.

May and her crew would stay in Prestwick for three days while a fresh crew took the charter to its final destination of Montreal, Canada. At the end of the three-day layover, May's crew would pick up the last, long-leg across the Atlantic of an identical charter and take it to its terminating point in Montreal.

During the night, both pilots had checked into the hotel, so the whole crew was on site. May headed to the restaurant in the morning and discovered the captain eating breakfast with Raul. She pulled up a chair. The captain introduced himself.

"Name's R. J." He extended a large hand and shook hers. "Crew scheduling called me really early. We're delayed until late this afternoon. Pass the word on if you don't mind."

"No problem," May said.

Disappointment crept into her voice. Her very first charter was getting off to a shaky start. Their flight from Omaha to Paris included a stopover for fuel in Bangor, Maine, before heading across the Atlantic. This was common practice for Equity and their aging, fuel-guzzling fleet of jets.

Most fuel stops happened on return trips from Europe. Flights from Europe to the United States often encountered strong headwinds, especially in winter, causing them to burn more fuel. Bangor was a favorite airline fuel stop, along with Boston, Goose Bay, Labrador, and the most frequently chosen place: Gander, Newfoundland.

Charter crews were especially fond of Gander because of a little place at the airport that served out-of-this-world ice cream. May had heard an old story about some Equity charter crew members getting off the plane with the passengers while the plane was being fueled. They made the trek into the terminal for ice cream, not realizing how short the fuel stop would be. The crew members returned to the gate in time to see their plane push back from the jetway and taxi off. Frantically, they ran out of the small terminal onto the tarmac, chasing the plane. When the rest of the crew realized that they were missing, the pilots turned around and returned to the gate for them.

Now, May's airplane was hours late. So there would be no ice cream. Thankfully, the passengers were not overly distraught about the long delay. The crew, however, was dismayed about the loss of most of their layover time in Paris. May was anxious to depart the airport, desperate to salvage what little time remained.

Once the fully loaded DC-8 finally took off from Omaha and the cabin crew served dinner, the all-night flight proved long and tiring. By the time the plane arrived in Paris and the crew got to the hotel, there was minimal layover time left, enough for a good night's sleep, but not enough for sightseeing. May and her co-workers tumbled into bed. They would need their rest for the busy day to follow.

They met their aircraft early the next morning for the next leg of the journey—ferrying the empty plane to Athens and picking up a full load of passengers there. May slept most of the way, waking up about forty-five minutes before landing to freshen up and admire the scenery. The day was brilliant and sunny, and the Acropolis loomed majestically over the city as they approached. The DC-8 landed and taxied some distance away from the terminal. As was often the case with charter flights, there was no gate access for the Equity plane.

A bus brought boarding passengers from the terminal to the aircraft, and May stood at the bottom of mobile stairs to greet them. The travelers approached. Nearly every one of them was carrying a huge metal container.

What the.. she thought.

Olive oil. Container after container of olive oil. Hundreds of them.

The passengers were Greeks who'd moved to Canada and returned to their homeland for a late summer visit. A supply of Greek olive oil was coming to Canada with them. With ALL of them.

May climbed to the plane after she'd taken the last passenger ticket. The captain, senior flight attendant Barb, and the passenger agent argued over what to do with the oil containers.

"They won't fit under the seats and we can't put them in the overhead racks. The racks are not enclosed," Barb said.

"That's right," May agreed. "We can only put hats and coats up there. Not that people don't try to hide baggage up there anyway…"

"And," Barb added, "if we hit rough air and they're not stowed properly, people could get hit by them."

The gate agent, seeing that the chances of the flight making a speedy departure were waning, grew irritated.

"Goddammit," he whispered. "What do they do with all that oily crap anyhow?"

"Put it on grilled vegetables?" Barb suggested.

"I really like it on pizza myself," May contributed.

"Have you ever done any deep frying with it?" R. J. asked. "It's supposed to be really good for you—"

"Okay, okay," The agent growled. "Take 'em away and we'll put 'em in the belly of the plane. Jesus."

He hustled down the stairs and was gone. Despite the surrender of the oil containers by unhappy passengers, the flight was still packed to the rafters with carry-on bags. It took forever to stow them securely. Eventually, when everyone was seated, the plane was cleared to taxi to the runway.

By the time May was able to run for her jumpseat, they'd been cleared into position for takeoff. She scrambled to her seat, near an over-wing exit in the middle of the plane. The crew seat was positioned in a row among the regular passenger seats, but it had a distinctly different shape and a strap with the words "flight attendant only" written across it. They were affectionately known in the company as the "conehead" seats.

May arrived at her destination and spied a 350-pound woman comfortably strapped into it. She froze. The engines revved as they prepared for their takeoff roll. May looked frantically for the woman's correct seat assignment and spotted an empty middle seat several rows away. There was simply no time to move her before the plane left the ground. In a panic, she sprinted to the front of the plane.

"There's a GIGANTIC woman sitting in my seat!" she whispered hoarsely to Barb.

At this point, Barb was strapped into her own seat. The senior flight attendant quickly motioned to the rickety, old jumpseat in the galley. For some reason, the relic had not been removed from the plane.

At one time, most jumpseats were located in aircraft galleys, but these were removed when the FAA finally realized that they were death traps in aircraft accidents. Flight attendants were injured or killed by the modular galley equipment that came loose. Crews lobbied for years to get the seats moved to safer areas. Now May had no choice. There was nothing to do but sit there.

"Damn it!" May swore.

She prayed that nothing would happen on takeoff. She was not at her assigned exit. How would she explain that fact to federal investigators if there was an accident? How would she explain that she was not at her post to perform her aircraft evacuation duties, and that her jumpseat was occupied by a huge Greek woman?

She heard the landing gear come up soon after they were airborne. She got up, ran to her jumpseat, and hustled the woman out. She tried to explain why, but the woman merely gave her a blank look, not understanding a word she was saying. May returned to the front of the plane, shaking her head at Barb and LaToya.

"I guess I'll have to guard my seat with my life," she said ruefully.

Barb laughed.

"Those seats have a magic appeal," she said. "You would think that those big letters that say 'flight attendant only' would discourage people from sitting there. Come on, let's get to work."

The plane landed in Prestwick, Scotland five hours later. As May and her crew exited, a fresh crew boarded to take the flight to Montreal. Her team boarded the hotel van and completed the short drive to their accommodations. May straightened in her seat as they approached the hotel. This was not the typical Equity layover establishment. A stately old stone mansion overlooking acres of well-manicured grounds and gardens had been converted into a lovely hotel. Its location, so close to the Prestwick airport, made it an ideal layover point for visiting airline crews. May glanced around the lobby as she waited for her room key with the rest of the crew.

"How old is this building?" she asked the elderly man working the front desk.

"Parts of the building go back to the 1600s," he replied.

"Wow, if these walls could talk..." she muttered.

"Oh, yes, it has quite a history," the clerk explained. "It was used by the American military during World War II because of its proximity to the airfield."

May took in the country manor décor, Victorian era furniture, walls of rich dark wood, and the large marble fireplace in the parlor beyond.

"Has it changed much since then?"

"Not this part," the man told her. "Of course, they added on a new section of hotel rooms years later, but the main house hasn't changed a bit."

May enjoyed history and had majored in it in college. She let her imagination wander as she looked around the room. She could almost see the military officers, cigars in hand, sipping snifters of brandy and planning airstrikes over Germany. She was quietly, absently humming.

"What's that tune?" LaToya asked.

"'Don't Sit Under the Apple Tree,'" May answered with a smile. "It was a big hit in World War II."

"You need to update your material," she said.

"I really like that old stuff," May said. "My grandfather was a professional musician and played it all the time when I was a kid."

"We also have a couple of ghosts," the clerk told them.

The entire crew gave him a quizzical look.

"Ghosts?" Barb asked.

"Oh, yes," he replied with a grin. "We have a female ghost, a member of the original family that built this mansion."

"She must be pretty damn old and ugly-looking by now," LaToya whispered.

"Many people have seen her," the clerk said, "and even more have smelled her perfume."

May smiled. She didn't believe in ghosts, but thought that if the mansion was truly haunted, it would surely have to be by someone who served in the Second World War. The desk clerk seemed to guess her train of thought.

"Our other ghost is a gentleman, an American officer, to be precise," he said. "He's in his uniform and has been seen looking out the upstairs windows, scanning the skies for pilots that never returned from the missions he sent them on. Must still feel guilty, poor chap."

"Anybody smell him?" LaToya asked.

May stepped hard on her toes.

"Ouch! What'd you do that for?" LaToya asked.

"Thank you so much for telling us such an interesting story, sir," May said hastily, taking her room key from the clerk and grabbing LaToya's arm.

"You're welcome. Hope to see you at dinner."

"What do you think about the ghost thing, guys?" May asked as the crew walked to their rooms.

"I think you shouldn't have stomped on my feet, that's what I think," LaToya complained.

"You were making fun of his story," May said. "What was I supposed to do? What do you think, Barb?"

"It's probably something they tell all of the tourists," she answered. "An old place like this has to have a ghost."

"I don't know, I think there are a lot of things in the world that we just don't understand," R. J. said. "I can believe it."

"What about you, Raul?" May asked.

"I think it's crap," he said quickly. "Who wants a beer before dinner?"

With that, they entered their separate rooms, changed into warmer clothes suitable for the cool, late summer evening, and met in the lobby.

May found the Scottish food to be hearty but a little bland. The exception was a dessert of shortcake, fruit, and cream called trifle. Many of the crew loved it, but it was too much for May. After dinner, R. J. and the co-pilot turned in early while Raul and the girls settled in by a crackling fire in the old parlor room for a nightcap.

"We've got a couple of days here. How are you ladies planning on passing the time?" Raul asked.

The girls glanced at each other. No one had ever been here before, not even Barb. The old desk clerk wandered towards them and they quickly enlisted his help.

"We're not that far from the town of Ayre, and Loch Lomond is fairly close, too."

"Oooo… Like the Loch Lomond from the song?" LaToya asked. "You take the high road and I take the low road and all of that?"

The clerk nodded.

"The very same," he said. "If you'd like to go, I can arrange a van with a driver. I'll pack lunch for you, too."

The girls looked at each other again.

"That sounds wonderful," Barb replied enthusiastically.

"We're in Scotland and I want to see someone wearing a kilt. Where can we do that?" Grace asked.

The clerk thought for a moment.

"We are a little far south for that. They wear them more in the highlands," he said. "You might see someone wearing one in Ayre." He hesitated. "You're not going to be like those Northwest girls, are you?"

They were puzzled.

"You mean from the airline, an airline crew? Flight attendants?" Raul asked.

"Yes, they stay here every now." He grumbled. "You see, a few of their girls wanted to see someone in a kilt, too. They came across a young man wearing one." His face reddened. "They threw him on the ground and pulled his kilt over his head to see what he had on underneath."

May inadvertently sucked some of her beer up her nose as she and the rest of the crew broke out laughing.

"We promise we will absolutely not molest or humiliate any Scotsmen," Barb pledged.

"Now wait, I don't know about that," May said. "How many of you have wondered what they've got on under there? Be honest."

The resulting argument continued until after midnight, when they rose to go to their rooms.

"Raul, you'd better keep an eye out for that female ghost tonight, a good lookin' man like you," Gail said as they reached their doors.

"Yes, Mama," he sniffed. "Good night."

The next day, the girls enjoyed a pleasant time sightseeing, though the cockpit crew remained at the hotel. The flight attendants bought beautiful woolen goods in Ayre, took a boat ride on Loch Lomond, and stopped by the remnants of a castle on a high bluff overlooking a winding river. They climbed the long trail of stone steps to take in the view.

"It's so beautiful," Dimitra said, catching her breath after the strenuous walk.

The girls looked out at the setting sun. The wind was picking up and started to howl through the ancient walls.

"We'd better start back," Barb said.

They began their descent. When they reached the parking lot, they noticed a Mercedes-Benz parked next to their van. An elderly gentleman in a blue and white kilt stood beside it, gazing at the castle. The girls shared a wicked glance. The temptation was enormous, but no one made a move to hurl him to the ground and check out his undergarments.

The entire crew gathered for another Scottish dinner and another evening around the fire. The flight attendants filled in the pilots on their sightseeing.

"You really should have come," Dimitra said. "The lake was beautiful. The town was beautiful. The castle was beautiful."

"Speaking of beautiful, I think I might have encountered the female ghost," R. J. said.

"Really?" May said, raising an eyebrow. "What did you see?"

"Four hundred years worth of ugly, probably," LaToya retorted.

"It's not what I saw, it's what I smelled," R.J. said. "I was in the oldest part of this building, and I know I smelled her perfume."

"What did it smell like?" asked Raul.

The girls turned to him.

"What are you asking for?" LaToya questioned. "I thought you didn't believe in any of that stuff."

"I don't," he replied. "I'm making conversation."

May didn't know whether to believe him or not, but he seemed out of sorts.

"Did you smell something, too, Raul?" she asked.

"Nah, no way," he answered quickly. "What, are you kidding? Come on."

"Okay, sorry, I was just checking," she said. "You don't seem quite yourself, that's all."

Raul grumbled.

"Did you know that they have medieval banquets here?" R. J. said. "They call the basement the dungeon. It's got big, long tables and it's full of mannequins in costumes. There are weapons on the walls, torture devices, and all kinds of neat stuff."

"You saw it?" Barb asked.

"Yup. I scouted around down there while you guys were gone. It would be fun to go to a banquet, but they won't have any while we're here. Too bad. Well, guys and girls…" He yawned and stood up. "It's been fun, but I'm heading to bed."

"Say hi to your ghost," LaToya called as he disappeared around a corner.

The next day, the girls took a long walk around the picturesque countryside, stopping to pet a small group of grazing sheep, taking pictures, and enjoying the peace and quiet. When they returned to the hotel, May wandered through the gardens alone. She imagined the soldiers stationed here long ago.

Some of them probably stood right on this spot, she mused. *Maybe they wandered around just like I'm doing now, only they were probably thinking about who they were going to put in harm's way and whether or not they would get killed.*

She heard a small plane overhead approaching the airport.

"Sending so many pilots into battle and knowing a lot of them wouldn't come back," she whispered to herself. "That would be so hard to do."

That evening, Raul and the girls sat around the fireplace once more. They were the only people in the room, except for a night desk clerk who checked on them now and then to see if they needed anything..

"Any signs of that ghost today, Raul?" Grace teased.

He rolled his eyes, but seemed just a little nervous.

"I told you I don't believe in that stuff."

"I don't believe you, at all," Grace persisted. "Did something happen? You saw something, didn't you?"

"No! Of course not!" he replied. "That R. J.! He was going on about it all day. He really believes in that stuff, and he was driving me nuts."

"You might as well admit it," Grace said insistently. "I can tell that something happened."

"You were rattled yesterday, Raul," May added.

"Alright! Alright, Jesus," Raul said. "I didn't see anything. I just...."

"Just what?" the others said in unison.

"I just....smelled something."

The girls edged closer.

"What did you smell?" Dimitra asked.

"Perfume, okay? I smelled.... perfume," he said. "Right near my room, and nobody was around. Some woman was probably there and walked away, that's all."

"Hmmm... Maybe," Grace said. "You don't know for sure."

"Well, I know it's not some damn ghost."

Barb quietly excused herself. The other crew members teased Raul mercilessly. They were still at it when Barb returned a short while later. Raul stretched and got up.

"There's no such damn thing as ghosts! I'm going to bed," he said. "Goodnight, ladies."

"Okay, go spend a little time with your girlfriend," LaToya added.

Raul glared at her and disappeared. When he was out of sight, Barb jumped up.

"Come on!" she whispered.

"Why? What's happening?" Grace asked.

"I went to the dungeon and grabbed one of the mannequins wearing a medieval dress," Barb explained. "She's in Raul's bed. I sprayed my perfume all over his room."

"Oh, that's so evil!" May said. "How did you get in his room?"

"I got the clerk to give me a key," she said. "Come on! He'll be at his room in a minute."

They giggled uncontrollably as they followed Barb in a single-file line.

"He'll know it's a mannequin as soon as he turns on the lights," Gail whispered.

"I unscrewed all of his light bulbs," Barb answered quietly.

They stopped and waited, crowded together at the corner, and peeked down the hall. Raul stepped inside his room, closing the door. A few seconds passed.

"What's he doing in there?" LaToya whispered impatiently.

"Probably stumbling around in the dark," Barb whispered back.

A split second later a loud, high-pitched shriek pierced the quiet as Raul's door flew open. He tore from his room and raced down the hall, stopping just in time to avoid knocking into the girls.

"Why, where are you off to in such a hurry?" Barb asked him.

Raul sank to the floor, moaning, realizing how badly he'd been had.

"You girls are bad, so bad," he groaned. "How could you do this to a nice guy like me?"

After all those adventures, the three-day layover ended too quickly. It was with regret that May boarded the van for the airport. She'd quickly grown attached to the cozy estate. Gazing at the old building, another song that her grandfather played long ago popped into her mind.

"'Bless them all, bless them all, the long and the short and the tall….'" she hummed.

May froze in her seat.

Was that….a man?

Dressed in a drab uniform, smoking a pipe, gazing from the second-floor window. The man scanned the sky, looking and looking… for something. She rubbed her eyes and looked again.

Nothing.

Good God, I've got some wild imagination, she thought. *There's no way…. Jesus, Raul would never let me hear the end of this!*

The van pulled out of the driveway. May kept her ghost to herself.

A few hours later, the team had assembled on the plane and prepped it for takeoff.

"The agent said this charter of Greeks is bringing just as much olive oil to Montreal as the last group," Grace said.

The jet pulled away from the Prestwick airport gate.

"That's fine, it's all in the belly of the plane now. By the way, the caterers put enough alcohol on this flight to sink a battleship," Barb complained. "There's gin, vodka, bourbon and scotch, all in quart bottles, not miniatures. These people will never drink all of this. Wine or ouzo maybe, but I've never had many Greek people drink this stuff." She rummaged through the customs forms and papers. "There are no liquor seals either. If they don't drink it, I don't have any way to seal it up when we get to customs in Canada."

"Is that a problem?" LaToya asked.

"Most countries are picky about the alcohol that gets transported in and out of their territory."

"What do we do?" LaToya asked.

"Hope they get really thirsty," Barb replied grimly.

By the time they reached Canada, the liquor remained untouched.

"So now what do we do?" May asked.

Barb considered the options.

"We could declare it and spend hours with Canadian customs."

"I don't like that, what else?" LaToya interjected.

"We can pour it all down the toilets."

LaToya was aghast.

"But that's Stolichnaya and Johnny Walker Black!" she moaned. "That's inhuman!"

"I know, and it's all paid for by the charter, too."

"Why don't we give it to the passengers?" Dimitra suggested.

"They'd have to declare it. Customs would ask where they got it. It would be a mess."

In the end, each of the girls packed a few bottles in their luggage and poured a large quantity down the airplane toilets.

"Oh, my breaking heart," LaToya cried as she dumped another bottle of vodka.

The cabin crew stood staring at an entire case of expensive gin in the galley.

"Well, what do we do with it?" Gail asked finally.

"You guys have to deal with this one," LaToya said, walking out of the galley with her hand over her heart. "I can't handle any more pain."

Barb hurriedly pushed the case into one of the bathrooms, covered it with a blanket, and hoped that no one would notice it. When the customs agent boarded, the girls made no mention of alcohol. The crew left the plane without incident. They climbed aboard the hotel van, leaving their baggage for the driver to load. A stocky, middle-aged man grabbed LaToya's bag, throwing it roughly into the back. The glass bottles of alcohol inside clinked together alarmingly.

"Hey! Hey! That's my china! Be careful with my china!" she roared. "That's priceless stuff for my grandma, all the way from Scotland!"

The driver scowled at her and gingerly put the remainder of the crew bags inside.

"That was quick thinking," May whispered approvingly.

To the girls' relief, there was no call in the night from customs. The next day, they sailed through airport security and boarded the DC-8 to ferry it home. Somehow, the case of gin mysteriously disappeared during the night.

They arrived back in New York and found that after spending so many days together, it was difficult to part. This became the thing May cherished about her job—the bonding among crewmembers that took place on the flights in the crazy crucible of events that was Equity Air.

CHAPTER NINE

May awoke the next day to a bright, sunny New York morning and one of those rare occasions when all of her roommates were home. She followed the aroma of coffee to the kitchen and joined the others around the table. May was very tired, but chattered happily about the fun she'd experienced on her Greek-Scottish odyssey.

She finally realized that no one else was saying a word and set down her coffee cup.

"What's the matter with you guys? It's like a wake in here."

"We've been here in this roach hole for a couple of months now and we can't take it anymore," Kathleen answered. "We took a vote and we want to break the lease and move."

"I'm all for that," May replied heartily, "but how do we do it? Is it legal? And where are we going to live?"

"We sort of have a plan," Kathleen's voice dropped a little. "Things will be different though."

"What do you mean?"

"We've had some time to look for other places to live," Kathleen replied. "One of Eleanor's roommates is moving out, and I can move in there. It's pretty cheap and I can afford it. Louisa and Marta found a beach house out on Long Island. They really like it and want you to see it."

May sat silently digesting what she'd just heard. She was happy about the idea of parting with the roaches, but not about losing Kathleen as a roommate.

"We'll all still see each other," Kathleen assured her. "Maybe not as much, but we'll see each other."

"You're right, of course," May answered. "I really want out of this place, too. How does the rest of the plan go?"

"We have a few weeks until the end of the month," Kathleen answered. "I'm going to move my stuff over to Eleanor's place a little bit at a time so nobody notices."

"We can get into the beach house by the end of the month," Marta added. "It's cute and it's furnished. Not having to worry about furniture will make things very easy. I think we should drive out there today so you can see it."

"As soon as we are ready to move out, I'm calling the board of health," Kathleen said in disgust. "This many roaches must be illegal!"

May laughed. "Seriously, you know that Dolly is going to blow her top. What if she sues us?"

"How could she? I asked her about bugs, and she flat out lied and said there weren't any. She took advantage of us because we're… we're… you know… young, innocent, and naive."

"You mean stupid," May answered. "I hope you're right. I want out of this trap so bad, I'll risk it." May turned to Kathleen. "You better stay in touch, and I don't mean when we run into each other in the crew lounge."

Kathleen crossed her heart. "I promise. Have you noticed that there are people that you see all the time and then there are others that you don't run into?"

"I've noticed that," May answered wistfully. "I really miss seeing Keisha and Margot, but I suppose they have their old friends from Pan Am."

Louisa brought the group back to the issue at hand. "Let's get out to the beach and look at that place."

Louisa went to the phone and contacted the real estate agent. May chugged her coffee.

"I'll be ready in five minutes and I'll drive!"

The short trip to Long Beach, just a few miles down the highway, over a little toll bridge and across the bay, landed the girls at a small, well-kept Cape Cod cottage. The street was so quiet that it was hard to believe that the bustling borough of Queens was only a few miles away.

When the agent arrived, she unlocked the front door and ushered them in.

May was instantly taken with the place. It was sunny and cheerful, and each room was clean and nicely furnished. After the tour, the agent walked outside, giving them time and space to discuss the matter.

"The great thing about this deal is that the owner told the agent to give it to us without a month's rent up front," Louisa said eagerly. She winked. "I think she told the owner how respectable we look!"

The girls walked outside.

"We'll take it," Marta told the agent.

They signed the lease. In the car, May couldn't stop thinking about the price of the cottage.

"You know that it's too expensive for us, right?"

"Right," Louisa and Marta answered.

"We need another roommate then, right?" May said.

"Right," they answered again.

"We have to find somebody, and fast," May concluded.

"Right," the three of them said together.

As they discussed, Kathleen relocated her belongings little by little to Eleanor's apartment. An extra bag here and there as she walked through the lobby did not arouse suspicion. After all, they usually walked around with suitcases. Meanwhile, May, Marta, and Louisa sought another flight attendant to move into the cottage at the beach, but no one they knew wanted to move. They were getting concerned.

"We have got to get someone! We're running out of time!" May moaned. "Not only that, I've been gone so much I haven't been able to pack a thing."

"I think I might have something," Marta said.

May looked at her with hope-filled eyes.

"Who?"

"You know that new crew scheduler, the girl from Boston?"

"Yeahhh..." May said dubiously.

"She's looking for a place."

"A crew scheduler?" May was incredulous. "How can we live with a crew scheduler?"

Crew schedulers and flight attendants were mortal enemies, always at odds over trip assignments. Crew scheduling was a thankless job, and May didn't envy anyone that did it. They got heat from the flight attendants about being assigned to bad trips on short notice, often violating contract work rules. On the other side, they were constantly pressured by management to get flights out on time with full crews. May experienced a crew scheduler's wrath more than once when the pressure was on. This solution was by no means ideal, but they were out of options.

"I guess we don't have much choice," May said, the resignation evident in her voice. "We might as well try it. The worst thing that can happen is that she's a real jerk, and we have to kill her in her sleep. Louisa's coming in tonight, so we can see if she'll go along with it."

"I'm going to call Jessie right now and tell her," Marta said, reaching for the phone.

"Is that her name?" May asked, pulling off a shoe.

She threw it as hard as she could at the scurrying cockroach climbing the opposite wall. The shoe fell, leaving the bug flattened in place. A second later, the roach dropped onto the rug, leaving a brown smudge behind.

May picked up a pad from the table next to her and made a hash mark.

"That's… that's twenty-three so far this week," she announced.

Marta cringed. "That's disgusting. I can't believe you do that."

A few days later, May, Louisa, and Marta met their prospective roommate at the beach house. Jessie was slim and brunette, a streetwise city girl from the north end of Boston with a thick accent. The girls found her outgoing and friendly, at least when she was away from the crew scheduling desk. May started to feel more hopeful about the possible living arrangement. Jessie toured the cottage.

"This is nice, I like it," Jessie said. "With four of us, I can afford it."

"Us, too," Louisa agreed with a smile.

"There is one thing we need to talk about," Marta said.

Jessie's eyes opened wide.

"What's that?" she asked.

"You know the whole flight attendant crew scheduler thing. How do you feel about that?"

"I can handle it if you can," Jessie remarked.

"We just want to be up front with everything," said May reassuringly. "We felt that we should ask."

"Actually," Jessie said, a change coming over her tone. "I applied as a flight attendant, but the company was done hiring for the year. I wanted to get in somehow, so I took this job. I really would rather fly and when they hire flight attendants again, I'm gonna go for it."

The four glanced at each other.

"That settles it," Marta said with a smile. "It looks like we have a deal."

With four roommates, the girls were ready to move into their new home as quickly as possible. Kathleen departed first.

"I called the board of health," she told May. "The shit should hit the fan any time now. "

"Louisa and Marta are pretty well-packed," May replied. "I've been doing San Juan turn-arounds all week and I've barely started! And I've got to do another one tomorrow! I'll never get out of here at this rate."

"I know, I feel really bad about your schedule. I'm leaving today. I think Louisa and Marta are out tomorrow sometime." Her face tightened. "I should tell you that I wrote everything in a letter to the manager and put it on her desk in the office when she was out. I left my new number. If she wants to do anything about it, she can call me."

"Guess that makes me the last one out," May said. "What the hell, somebody has to lock up and turn out the light. Maybe I'll get lucky and I won't run into her."

A few nights later, May trudged up the street, pulling her bag behind her. The San Juan flight was exhausting as always, with hoards of passengers, screaming children, the works. She was not looking forward to the hours of packing that lay ahead of her. She slowed her pace as she approached the apartment building.

Please don't let *me run into Dolly right away*, she thought.

Dolly, with her bleached blonde hair and skin that had seen way too many seasons in Miami Beach, cornered her in the lobby and steered her into her office. She stood beside her desk, ranting about the broken lease and the call to the board of health. May stood silently. She decided to let the woman blow herself out.

"After everything I've done for you goils!"

The words dripped melodramatically from her lips and hung in the air. She was in such a state that May feared she might have a heart attack. There was a momentary lull in her tirade as she looked May squarely in the face.

"As a woman, you can understand everything I've said, can't you?"

May took this statement as an invitation to reply.

"We asked you point blank if there were bugs in the building the first time we set foot in it. You lied to us," May said. "That's why we felt we had the right to break the lease. You've got every roach in New York City crammed in this building, and it's not healthy living."

The phone rang. May turned and walked out of the room. Flustered, Dolly stood sputtering, watching her go. She reached for the receiver. As the door closed, May heard her shouting into the phone to one of the maintenance men.

"And I don't want to see any of you helping her move anything!" Dolly yelled.

May shook her head and got on the elevator.

Long after midnight, she loaded the last of her things into her Buick. Now she only had to turn in her key and leave. The office was dark and empty, so she stooped to slide the key under the door. As May rose, she caught sight of a large cockroach sitting on the door knob. It stared at her, taunting her in triumph.

"It's all yours, buddy," she said. "It's all yours."

The beach house proved to be a happy change and its four bedrooms offered privacy for all. The neighborhood was filled with flight attendants, firefighters, New York City police officers, and no cockroaches.

"I can finally look around and not jump when I see something on the floor!" May exclaimed.

Louisa smiled in agreement. "It's such a relief, but I wonder why we don't see any at all here when there were so many in Queens."

"Who knows," May said. "Maybe they can't swim across the bay!"

May got into the habit of running or taking long walks on the beach whenever she was home. September ended, taking the summer sun worshippers with it. The change in seasons left the beach uncrowded and cozy.

She also discovered that the supersonic Concorde arrived at Kennedy Airport from Europe late each afternoon. On her days off, May found herself sitting on the beach, listening for its unmistakable roar. She would then watch the sleek machine with its swept-back wings approach over the ocean.

The girls also found Wiley's, the local beach bar and restaurant and second home to off-duty flight attendants, firefighters, and police, a fun, friendly place. The girls frequented it when they were in town.

May was delighted with her new home, more comfortable in her job, and getting to know her new Boston roommate. Jessie had a passion for flying that equaled May's own.

"I've loved airplanes since I was a little kid," Jessie said. "My friends at home used to tell me that my neck would lock up from looking into the sky at planes. As soon as I get some money, I'm going for my license."

"I've been working on mine off and on for ages," May admitted. "I've never been able to get enough money. We should do it together! We could go to ground school together and help each other study. I'd love to take lessons back home—but it's so far away. There's got to be some place close. Let's start as soon as we can, deal?"

"Deal!" Jessie agreed heartily.

Unexpectedly, Jessie changed the topic.

"When do I get to meet this mystery boyfriend of yours?" she asked. "You know, the one with no phone that hangs around in the woods? Does he wear clothes?"

A shadow crossed May's face.

"I haven't seen or heard from him in quite a while," she said quietly. "My sister saw him when he got back from Alaska. I tried to reach him, but he was off with some new friends. With my schedule, I might not have time to get out there until next month."

"Hard to keep a relationship going that way," Jessie said.

"Tell me about it."

May walked to the window and pulled back the curtain.

"It's a nice day for a stroll on the beach," May said.

She turned to face Jessie. Jessie said nothing.

"I care about Jake, I really do," May said, "but... It's been so long since I've seen him."

"And?"

"And? Well… I think I kind of don't want to see him," May said.

"What does that mean?"

"I don't know," Jessie said. "Have you met somebody else?"

"No, not at all," May said. "I feel like I need to be free, free to see the world, no ties and no worries."

"If you really feel that way, you have to tell him," Jessie said.

"I know and I dread it," May said.

"You can't string him along," Jessie said.

May sighed heavily.

"You're right, you're right," she told Jessie. "I'll get in touch with him as soon as I can. You know, there is something else about this that's bugging me."

"What's that?"

"It doesn't feel like he's trying very hard to see me, either," she admitted.

There was a long silence.

"I think I'll go for that walk on the beach. I'll see you later, Jessie."

May ambled along the water's edge, the waves breaking over her bare feet every now and then as the tide came in. The cries of the gulls normally soothed her, but today they added to her anxiety. She couldn't escape the desire to be free, but how could she tell Jake?

I still care about him, she thought. *Do I really want to do this?*

She'd walked nearly a mile before she stopped, her mind made up.

I just have to tell him, and I have to do it right away.

She turned and started back to the cottage. The beach was empty except for a tall figure approaching from a distance. Walking was a little more difficult now, the incoming tide forcing her to step in the soft sand higher on the beach.

She looked ahead. The figure drew much closer. There was a familiarity to it, the way it moved.

Jake.

Lightheadedness flooded over her, and her knees went weak.

Oh God, what do I do? What do I say?

He was here now, and she had to deal with it. She forced a smile.

"Hey, stranger! It's been a while! How did you find me?"

Jake gave her a peck on the cheek.

"Your roommate told me you went for a walk on the beach," he said. "I thought I might get lucky and find you."

For the first time ever, May felt uncomfortable around Jake.

"I know we've been having a hard time getting together," he said, "but

I really needed to see you, so I took a chance and came down."

"I'm glad," she answered. "I've really wanted to talk to you, too."

Jake hesitated, and May realized that he was as uncomfortable as she was. The late September air suddenly felt chilly. He'd come to tell her something.

"May," he said, "I don't know how to say this, so I'm just going to say it. I'm moving to Alaska."

A million thoughts ran through her mind but only one stuck: *He beat me to it.*

That's how she and Jake said their goodbyes. When May pulled the front door closed behind her, she didn't wave to Jake as he drove away in his van.

Jessie put down her newspaper. "Want to talk about it?"

May flopped into a chair.

"Not a lot to say, really," she replied. "Turns out we both wanted space. How about that? I want to fly around the world, and he wants to live in Alaska. We always were on the same page."

"So how do you feel about it?" Jessie asked.

"I don't know. I know I care about him. He's a great person," she said. "I know I'm going to miss him, but I'm relieved at the same time. I'm confused."

She couldn't help the tears. For better or worse, May was free.

CHAPTER 10

May and Marta threw their bags in May's Buick and started for the airport. They had the same flying schedule for October.

"The charter flying has really dropped off this month," Marta remarked. "I've heard rumblings that the last of our late season vacation charters got moved to Saber Air."

May frowned. "I don't think I like that much."

"Me either, I hope it's just a one-time thing and that there's a good reason for it," Marta agreed.

A broad grin broke out on her face. They were working an evening flight to the West Coast.

"I guess there are worse things than having to fly a scheduled route to Los Angeles," Marta said.

Their plane would make a stop in Chicago, then continue to Los Angeles. They had a 24-hour layover. Rock bottom ticket prices meant a full flight, and the first leg from New York to Chicago would be especially hard.

The DC-8 included a drink and snack service for its 252 passengers. Depending on the weather, they only had about an hour and a half to serve it. Service on the old aircraft was primitive. A rickety, three-level beverage cart had to be set up by hand. That alone was time-consuming. Most planes used modern carts pre-loaded with drinks in easy-to-reach drawers, but not the DC-8. Meals and snacks were loaded in bulk and needed to be separated and organized in the galley.

When the attendants completed service, they picked up the refuse and emptied the trays into large trash bags. These were smashed to fit into the small modules that the supplies originally came in. The only way to make the bags fit back in the modules was to do what the flight attendants called the "stewardess stomp." They stood on the bags and crushed them, then taped the modules shut to ensure that they wouldn't open. Some flight attendants used so much tape that they were accused by co-workers of "gift-wrapping the garbage."

The glamorous part of the job, May thought.

May, Marta, and the rest of the crew loaded passengers for the first leg and worked at a furious pace to serve them before they landed in Chicago. Most of the passengers disembarked in the Windy City. The plane was quickly cleaned and resupplied as the crew prepared to take a second full load to LA.

Once the aircraft cleaners left the plane, May made her way to the jetway door to take tickets. The October night was unusually warm for Chicago, making the terminal stuffy and uncomfortable. May was in position for only a few moments when a middle-aged man approached her. He was visibly upset.

"Excuse me, m…m…miss," he stammered, his voice low. "There's an unusual passenger waiting for this flight, and I hope you will not allow them on the airplane."

May frowned.

"Why, what do you mean? What's wrong?" she asked.

"You'll see," he replied cryptically.

He moved toward the plane. May didn't know what to think. Seconds later, a distraught, elderly woman hurried to her.

"Stewardess! Oh, stewardess!" the woman called. "You can't possibly let that man on this airplane, you can't possibly!"

The woman, wringing her hands, stood very close to May.

"What man? What's the matter?" May asked.

She wondered who or what could possibly have these people so terrorized.

"There's a man, he's VERY BIG. I believe he's drunk, and he's been bothering everyone in the boarding area." The woman gazed imploringly into May's eyes. "You're not going to let him get on the plane, are you dear?"

May didn't reply. She turned and made a beeline for the gate agent, a young and very frazzled dark-haired girl.

"Hi," May said.

The agent glanced up from her computer, barely acknowledging her.

"I've been getting some complaints about a passenger, a man. What's it all about?"

The agent's reply was curt.

"Don't worry about it."

The gate agent picked up the public address system and made the first boarding announcement. May had to resume her position by the jetway door. Families with small children and a few elderly passengers handed her their tickets. She noticed no one suspicious. Boarding continued by row number. May, head bowed, checked each ticket handed to her.

A huge pair of cowboy boots appeared in her line of sight first, followed by faded denim jeans. Her gaze continued upward. A denim jacket covering the rest of a long, lean body. The man stood at least 6' 7". His long, dirty brown hair reached his shoulders. He zigzagged slightly as he loudly addressed May.

"Hey, man… I wanna get on, n… n… now."

His breath reeked of alcohol. May didn't move a muscle as she glanced at the wrinkled ticket in his outstretched hand. She steeled herself. She dug deep to summon her most professional voice.

"We haven't called your seat number yet, sir."

He leaned towards her, his face millimeters from hers, his breath so putrid it was paralyzing. He spoke louder.

"I SAID… I wanna get on… NOW."

He staggered erratically, unsure of his footing, and stumbled to a nearby pillar. He leaned on it, recovered his balance, and harassed a few nearby passengers. May would need every bit of her experience to handle this situation. She stopped the boarding process and walked over to the ticket agent behind the counter.

"I can't let this guy on the plane," she tersely told the agent.

"Just get him on, he'll be okay," she snapped.

The agent was swamped with passenger seat assignments. It wasn't too difficult to see that the agent wanted this literally-huge troublemaker out of her hair and out of the terminal any way possible. Confronting him and removing him would be tremendously difficult, but May was determined.

"I can't let him on," she repeated. "He's big. He's drunk. He's obnoxious. He's scaring the customers to death."

Her words fell on deaf ears. The agent glared at her and resumed her boarding announcements. Once more, May took her place by the jetway door. The tall disorderly man returned, the passenger straight from Airline Hell. He loomed over her like a yeti.

"I'm sorry, sir," May said. "You'll have to wait for a few more minutes."

It was the only thing she could think of to do: stall. She hoped that some more permanent solution would present itself.

"Hey man, what is your PROBLEM?" the man exploded. "I wanna get on and I wanna get on NOW!"

Oh God, oh God, she thought in fear and panic. *I'm gonna die. Pull yourself together, pull yourself together. He can probably smell fear.*

She cleared her throat and said with a voice that was so deadly calm she didn't recognize it as her own—

"Sir, you'll just have to wait."

Her demeanor momentarily confused him and the drunken yeti stumbled away once more. By this time, boarding passengers were relaying what was happening in the terminal to the flight attendants on board who, in turn, notified the cockpit.

Caroline, the senior flight attendant, stood in the front of the aircraft with her close friend, Cole. Caroline sent Cole on a scouting mission to the end of the jetway.

"Is that him?" Cole whispered, motioning to the denim-clad giant.

"That's him," May answered quietly. "I still have him off the plane, but the agent wants him on board so she can get rid of him."

"She needs to call a cop," Cole said.

"She doesn't want the hassle. She knows it will take a SWAT team."

"Well, screw her," Cole said. "She doesn't have to put up with the psycho six miles up in the air."

Cole strode quickly up the jetway to speak with Caroline and the captain of the aircraft, Woody. Woody was a plump, gray-haired bachelor of about fifty. He always looked a little rumpled, especially in his uniform, with his tie and hat slightly askew. He was friendly, liked to socialize, and accompanied flight attendants on most layover outings, intending to join them on a trip to Disneyland that the crew was planning.

As the captain of the aircraft, his was the last word on who boarded the plane and who did not.

Twenty-five minutes passed. With nearly everyone on board, May turned to gather tickets from the last remaining passengers. The belligerent customer was talking with another man dressed in identical clothing.

Great, just great, she thought. *He's brought reinforcements.*

Both men turned their backs to May at precisely the same moment, allowing her to see an insignia and the words "Hell's Angels" emblazoned across their jackets. Her heart sank.

"Could things get any worse?" she groaned.

They did get worse. Woody gave the word to allow the man on-board. May couldn't believe her ears. Both men handed her their tickets, the taller man leaning on his sober traveling companion. They proceeded up the jetway.

"This really pisses me off," Caroline fumed to the others. "So Woody thinks that the psycho is going to fall asleep. Well, that's great if he does, but what if he doesn't? He's up there behind a closed door in the cockpit. We're the ones that have to deal with him."

There was nothing to do but make the best of it.

The crew dealt with the usual overflow of carry-on luggage, stuffing it in closets and under seats. The surly gate agent even managed to take a loose motorcycle chain away from the drunken biker as he staggered in the aisle, explaining to him that it needed to be placed in the belly of the plane with the other luggage. She walked down the jetway with it, a baggage claim check dangling from one end. It looked ridiculous.

It quickly became apparent that the tall, inebriated Hell's Angel was too drunk to find his assigned seat. He shuffled from one row to the next, each empty seat that he fell into conveniently located next to a single female passenger.

Each horrified woman immediately became alarmed and asked that he be removed. Rejected at every turn in his quest to find a seat beside a woman, he finally, in utter drunken frustration, stood in the center of the airplane aisle, all six feet, seven inches of him, in a plane packed with passengers, and yelled at the top of his lungs.

"WHAT'S THE MATTER, LADIES? I DON'T HAVE CRABS!"

Somehow, Caroline herded him into the correct seat and quieted him. The plane was behind its departure time now, and the crew worked furiously stowing the remaining passenger bags. As they were finishing, the companion of the drunken man approached Nan, another crew member working in the rear of the plane.

"Excuse me," he said to her with extreme politeness.

Nan gave him her complete attention.

"I'm sitting over there," the man said.

He pointed to a row of seats. A middle-aged woman sat in the window seat. The center seat was empty. An older black gentleman occupied the aisle seat.

"Look, miss," the polite man said. "I'm a Hell's Angel, and I'm also a member of the Ku Klux Klan. I'm gonna kill that guy over there."

He pointed to the black passenger. There was no anger in his voice. His voice was quiet, almost deadly in itself, and very matter-of-fact.

"Right," Nan answered.

She had no idea how else to respond to this new bombshell. She thought fast. Brushing past the freshly, self-identified Klansman, she approached the black passenger in question.

"Excuse me, sir," she said gently.

He looked up. "Yes?"

"We have a problem with your bags. Could I talk to you for a moment?"

"Okay…"

"Over here?" Nan led the man to the galley. "I didn't want to say anything back there…"

Nan carefully repeated the man's threats.

"I understand, miss. Thank you," he responded.

Nan was impressed. The information didn't appear to rattle him. She escorted him to a new seat and then walked to the front of the airplane to inform Caroline.

"Jesus H. Christ, what else tonight?" Caroline said.

"I know, it's pretty bad, isn't it?" Nan said. "It's probably a good thing that I didn't tell that Klan guy I'm Jewish."

To the relief of all concerned, both the drunk and his friend fell asleep for the duration of the flight, just as Woody predicted. Never was a crew so happy to touch down at its destination. They arrived much later than usual at the hotel, checked in, raced to their rooms, changed, and set a speed record getting to the hotel lounge. A waitress approached Caroline to take her order.

"I'll take three scotches, just line 'em up."

The waitress stood staring at Caroline as the group howled. Everyone else ordered doubles. It was just that kind of night.

CHAPTER ELEVEN

May slammed the front door shut and walked into the living room, where Jessie and Marta were watching television. Her face was beet red and her hair wind-blown.

"That's it," she exclaimed. "I can't walk out on the beach anymore until spring. The wind is blowing sideways and my face feels like it's been sandblasted."

"Like what you've done with your hair," Jessie said. "Did you see anybody else out there?"

"No, not a soul, not for the last month or so."

"That's because you're the only one crazy enough to walk on that beach in December."

"You're right," May said. "November wasn't so bad, but I guess I have to admit to myself that winter's here now."

She flopped on the couch next to Jessie.

"You know I'm so glad that we got hired when we did," Marta said, lowering the volume of the TV. "I heard today that we've furloughed more flight attendants and pilots because the flying has dropped. One of the pilots told me that it happens every year at this time. At least there are still some people junior to us who will be laid off first if it gets worse. We'll probably wind up on reserve or with some pretty bad flying schedules."

"I don't care that I got some bad trips this month," May replied. "I got Christmas Day off! If my flight works out, I'll be back early on Christmas Eve and I can get home to Connecticut in plenty of time. It's the one holiday I don't want to miss with my family."

"Yeah, and hopefully your plane doesn't break on your trip," Jessie said. "Where are you going?"

"It's a military charter to Frankfurt. Louisa and I have been working together all month without any glitches, so let's hope our luck holds through Christmas."

May liked military charters. They were a pleasure to work because the passengers were polite and courteous. The next afternoon, she and Louisa stood with the rest of the crew at the Delta Airlines gate, waiting to board a flight to Charleston, South Carolina. The flight would put them in position to meet their own DC-8 and work the Equity charter to Frankfurt, Germany.

"Hey, Bert," a voice said from the back of the line.

May and Louisa spun around. A tall, lanky man in his early thirties with tousled blond hair, a blond mustache, and wire-framed glasses smiled at them. The girls looked at him quizzically as he introduced himself. His name was Benny. He was the flight engineer and would be flying with them for the whole month. Benny was friendly, liked to talk, had a good sense of humor, and as the girls quickly found out, he called everyone, male or female, "Bert."

The Equity flight departed from Charleston early the next day, the military passengers a pleasure to transport as always. After a short fuel stop in Bangor, Maine, they continued across the Atlantic without a hitch and landed in Frankfurt.

"Are you going to visit home?" May asked Louisa as the van drove to the hotel.

Louisa had grown up in the Black Forest area of Germany, some distance from Frankfurt.

"No, I wish I could, but my family lives hours from here and there isn't time. I'll give them a call, but you're stuck with me."

May was sorry that Louisa was unable to go home, but glad to have her friend there, not just for company, but as an interpreter while they explored the city and bought Christmas gifts. It was cold in Germany, and with only a few days left before Christmas, Frankfurt was packed with shoppers. May, Louisa, and Benny shopped for several hours before they stepped into a small restaurant for something to eat and drink. Bratwurst and beer were ordered all around. While they waited for it to arrive, May got up to find the restroom.

"What do they call the ladies' room here?" she asked. "The little fraulein's room?"

Louisa raised her eyebrows. "Very funny."

Louisa gave May instructions. She managed to find the bathroom. She opened the door and stepped in. Many things in Europe were different than they were in the United States, but a urinal was a urinal anywhere. May turned quickly and fled, bumping into Louisa, giggling.

"Thanks, thanks a lot!" May said.

The next day, their return charter bound from Frankfurt to Delaware was boarded and ready to go when Benny informed the captain that he'd discovered a mechanical problem on the DC-8. The cockpit crew talked quietly with the gate agent, who made an announcement to the passengers. There would be a delay, and it could last for many hours. Disappointed military personnel anxious to make it home for Christmas trudged to the terminal. May and Louisa cornered Benny.

"What's the story, Benny?" May asked anxiously. "How long is this going to take?"

"I don't know," he answered. "I really don't. This is gonna be one of those things."

May groaned.

"This is all Jessie's fault," she said. "I'm going to kill her when we get back."

Louisa looked at her, surprised. "Why, what has she got to do with anything?"

"She put the whammy on this whole trip," May said. "I was talking about how I was going to make it home for Christmas, and she said, 'Yeah, if the plane doesn't break.'"

Louisa smiled. "We might as well sit down. It could be a long wait."

The crew sat on the cold airplane all day as Benny and the mechanics worked on the problem. May found these creeping delays to be one of the most difficult parts of flying. Because the plane might be fixed and ready to go at any time, they couldn't leave and go back to the hotel. And while pilots enjoyed certain FAA limits as to the number of hours they could work, flight attendants were bound only by the hour limitations of their company contract. Needless to say, these were often of much longer duration than the restrictions governing pilots.

The delay dragged on and on.

Late in the afternoon, Benny stopped in the front galley, poured himself a cup of coffee, and flopped in a seat next to May and Louisa.

"How are things going?" May asked.

"I don't know," he said. "We're getting somewhere, I think."

He was agitated. The girls attributed it to the ever-lengthening delay and too much coffee.

"How many cups of that stuff have you had today?" Louisa asked.

"The coffee's not the problem," Benny said. "The delay is bad enough, but we just had an argument with some military guys that wanted to put a bunch of crates in the belly of our plane. Seems they couldn't fit all of them on a Saber Air military charter that's out there on the tarmac. The captain said no, we're just within our weight limits now. We'd be too heavy if we took more cargo. They were not happy and started cursing us out. The captain stuck to his guns though, told 'em to go piss up a rope. They stopped to talk to this skinny, white-haired older guy. I've never met Flint, but I've seen his picture and I swear it looked like him."

He gulped the rest of his coffee and got up.

"I don't know, maybe I'm seeing things," he added. "Gotta get back, I'll see ya later, Bert."

May glanced out the windows of the plane.

"Sure, see you later," she muttered.

By the time the plane was finally ready to go, the pilots and flight attendants were over their duty time limits. The tired crew had been sitting in a frigid airplane for more than sixteen hours when the captain came to speak with them.

"Look, I know these creeping delays suck and I'm sorry we couldn't go back to the hotel," he said. "You guys know we could leave in five minutes or fifteen hours."

He looked at each crew member.

"I don't want to pressure anyone. I know how tired we all are. I just want to say that all of our passengers are tired, too. They haven't been on board with us, but they've been waiting in the terminal. Some of these folks are trying to get home for the first time in over a year. Some of them are at the end of their tours of duty and are trying to get home for good," the captain said. "If we don't take them, it will take a long time to get another crew with enough duty time here to work this flight. And it's almost Christmas. So what do you people want to do?"

May and Louisa conversed in low voices amongst themselves. They were within their rights to request some time away from the plane before flying— but did they want to stay in Germany any longer than they had to?

"I'm so tired, but the only chance I have of getting home for Christmas is if we work this," May said. "Even then, it's going to be very late Christmas Eve before we get back."

"I know, I want to get back, too," Louisa replied quietly.

The crew took a vote. It was unanimous. They would get the soldiers home. Benny, after making one last walk around check of the airplane to confirm the state of the repairs, ran up the mobile stairs. He made one final quick stop in the galley for more coffee.

"What's wrong?" May asked as she handed him a cup.

"You know those sons of bitches with those crates?" he whispered. "They were trying to sneak that shit on. I told them I was coming up here to get the captain. There must be some kinda Christmas presents in those crates if they want to get them out of Germany this bad. I gotta get to the cockpit. I'll talk to you later, Bert."

A cold shiver went through May, but she was too tired to do anything but nod at Benny as he walked away.

The crew finished their final cabin preparations and the airplane took off. May, Louisa, and the others served drinks and a hot meal. The passengers fell asleep soon after. Crew members were never supposed to sleep under any circumstances, but after being on duty for more than twenty hours, they decided to ignore the rule and spot each other taking short naps.

The headwinds going west were relentless. Two-thirds of the way into the flight, the captain came over the intercom.

"Ladies and gentlemen, I know this isn't what you want to hear, but with the headwinds being what they are, we've been using a great deal of fuel," he said. "Sorry, but we're going to have to make a fuel stop in Bangor, Maine."

A groan went through the cabin as the endless flight dragged on. Hours later, after a fuel stop and another leg, the exhausted passengers and crew touched down in Delaware. The passengers were able to escape at last, but the day was not yet over for the crew.

The airplane was needed in New York immediately. As the flight attendants flopped into the cabin seats, the pilots prepared for the short ferry flight to Kennedy Airport. May scrambled to take the extra jumpseat in the cockpit. She loved watching take-off and landing up front, but also wanted to assure herself that the pilots were awake. The plane arrived in New York. After passing through customs in the International Arrivals building, the crew headed to their own terminal to check in. A congratulatory telegram from the company bigwigs in Tennessee awaited them. The co-pilot held up the paper.

"Anybody want a copy of their attaboy?"

"Atta what?" May asked.

"Your attaboy, you know, when they pat you on the back and say 'attaboy' and that's all you get."

The company was thanking them for working despite surpassing their duty time and dealing with the difficult circumstances.

They weren't stupid. If the crew didn't work the flight, the company would have lost huge sums of money due to the delays and the expense of flying in a replacement crew. They'd been up for thirty-two straight hours at this point.

"Sure," May said. "I'll take a copy of my attaboy."

She and Louisa dragged themselves through the nearly deserted terminal. As they neared the exit doors, May readjusted her baggage. A short, stout man approached her mumbling something that she could not understand. Perhaps he was Indian or maybe Pakistani, she thought. She was exhausted, but made an effort to be polite. He mumbled to her again. It was only when she leaned in close to the man that she realized what he was saying.

"You rub me, miss?" he repeated.

May stared at him blankly for a moment as the meaning of his obscene comment registered in her over-tired mind.

"Jesus," she said.

She rolled her eyes and resumed walking to the exit.

"What did that guy want?" Louisa asked when May caught up to her.

"Nothing. He just wanted to welcome me home to New York."

A potent storm had dropped several inches of snow while they were out of the country, and the girls struggled to find Louisa's car. Airport plows had passed through the parking lot several times and completely buried it.

"Great, just what we need," May said in disgust.

Somehow, they unearthed the car and got in. Louisa's Volvo was nearly as old as May's Buick. She turned the key, the engine grinding away over and over, but it would not catch. May snapped and turned to Louisa.

"I can't believe this hunk of junk won't start! Damn it! I knew we should have brought my car!"

"Your car?" Louisa fumed. "YOUR CAR? Didn't the skirt guard fall off of it onto the freeway on your last trip to Connecticut? Didn't it roll up in a little ball and land on the side of the road? AND YOU WENT BACK TO GET IT!"

There was dead silence in the car. A minute passed. May started to laugh. Quietly first… then the two girls laughed until tears streamed down their cheeks.

"I'm so sorry, Louisa. I'm just so tired."

"I know, me too," she answered. "Maybe we shouldn't fly together. This is our second disaster."

"Oh, it's really not so bad," May said. "Besides, it's still Christmas Eve. I can get my car and make it to Connecticut by daylight."

"You're such an optimist," Louisa said.

The engine finally caught and they headed to the house on the beach.

CHAPTER TWELVE

"What is the Rose Bowl again?" Louisa asked.

She and May threw clothes into their respective bags in preparation for their trip. May, preoccupied with her own thoughts, didn't hear her.

"Hello, anybody home over there?" Louisa asked, raising her voice.

"Huh? What did you say?" May responded absently.

"What's the matter with you? You haven't been yourself the last day or so since you got back from Christmas," Louisa said. "What's going on?"

May dropped an extra uniform shirt on the bed and shrugged.

"I don't know, it just felt a little weird at home, that's all. It seemed strange... you know... without Jake around."

Louisa raised an eyebrow. "Are you having second thoughts about him now?"

"No. I don't know. It was just, you know... strange. Anyway, I'm hardly ever at home now. A relationship would never survive that. What's done is done," May said. "I made my decision and I'm good with it. Look at us, we're taking off on a trip. Come on! We'd better hustle."

As the two piled into May's old Buick, Louisa repeated her question.

"Like I was asking, what is the Rose Bowl?"

"It's a college football playoff game," May replied as she backed out of the driveway. "Iowa is playing USC. We're taking a plane full of fans from Des Moines to see the game in Pasadena."

"I've heard of the Rose Parade. Are they connected?"

"Sort of," May explained. "They're both on New Year's Day. We should try to go to the parade. It's so gorgeous on TV. It must be fabulous in person."

That evening, they took a United flight to Iowa to meet their own aircraft. On the following bright, sunny winter morning, 252 Iowa football fans decked out in school colors of black and bright yellow, wearing yellow hats and carrying yellow pom poms streamed aboard the Equity DC-8. The bright sunlight pouring through the airplane windows accentuated the yellow accessories, making the interior of the plane look like a sunburst. Iowa was playing the USC Trojans and hoping for a shot at the national title.

"You think any of them have extra tickets?" one of May's coworkers whispered.

"Are you kidding?" May said. "Not a chance."

The flight landed in Long Beach, California, not too far from Los Angeles. As the last passenger gathered his bundle of yellow gear and departed, the crew realized that New Year's Eve was upon them and not one of them had any plans.

"What do you think, Louisa?" May asked. "How about the Rose Parade tomorrow?"

"Are you two going to the Rose Parade?" an excited female voice asked from behind them.

The voice belonged to Leslie, another member of the crew.

"Yeah, we really want to go," May replied. "Do you want to come along?"

"Oh yeah," Leslie said. "I've always wanted to see it and who knows when I'll be here again on New Year's Day!"

"Hey, Bert," Benny said, emerging from the cockpit. "Did I hear Rose Parade? Mind if I come along?"

The foursome made plans to reserve a car and drive to Pasadena early the next morning.

Two regularly scheduled Equity flights and two Equity Rose Bowl charters were laying over at the hotel on New Year's Eve. The evening was young as May took the elevator to the hotel lobby.

She poked her head into the lounge to see who might be hanging around. She spotted Caroline from the Hell's Angels flight sitting at a table with her crew. Leslie and Louisa were also there. May quickly joined them. Leslie was chatting with a group of young men at the table beside her, roadies working for a band playing next door at the Los Angeles Coliseum. As concert time drew closer, the young men bid them farewell.

"Hey, everybody," Leslie said, turning her attention to her friends. "There's a New Year's Eve country music concert tonight next door. I have a bunch of free tickets and backstage passes! Who wants to go?"

"I do," Caroline said. "Who am I to turn down a free concert ticket?"

"Me, too, I'll go," May echoed enthusiastically.

May, Louisa, Leslie, and Caroline paid their tabs and headed toward their rooms to change. On the way out, they ran into Benny on his way to the lounge for a beer and hors d'oeuvres. The aroma of food drifting out of the lounge to the lobby was irresistible.

"Hey, Bert," he said, nodding to the girls.

He sniffed the air and smiled.

"Mmmmm… I smell fish."

Caroline looked up, down, turned in every direction, then stuck her head toward her crotch and sniffed.

"Nope, not me," she said firmly. "See you ladies back here in a few minutes."

She sauntered to the elevator.

"What… What the hell was that?" Benny said, stunned.

"That's Caroline, we flew together a few months ago," May said. "You should hear her on the PA system! Gotta run, I'll see you later!"

At the concert, the girls sang and danced and thoroughly enjoyed the music, but they decided to skip the trip backstage.

"It's turned out to be a pretty good New Year's Eve so far," Leslie observed as they returned to the hotel. "Does anybody want to go up to the top floor?"

As a perk for flight crews, the hotel set aside a large suite on the top floor to be used as a private lounge. It was spacious, comfortable, and available 24 hours a day. The suite was also open to the Korean Air crews that stayed at the hotel, but they never showed in the evening, probably because the Equity people were so noisy.

"Sure, okay," May replied. "It's only eleven, maybe a few people from the other Equity crews will be around."

They heard the racket as soon as they stepped out of the elevator. May cracked open the door to the suite and found every flight attendant and pilot from every Equity crew staying at the hotel.

"Hey, Raul!" she yelled over the din, seeing her engineer friend from her Scotland trip.

He nodded and waved. To her delight and Louisa's, Marta was also there.

"I wonder what Jessie is doing tonight," May said as the three gathered together.

"I know she had plans to do something," Marta answered. "She's not sitting home alone."

May walked Louisa and Marta over to meet Raul.

"So, did your roommate tell you what she and her buddies did to me in Scotland?" Raul asked.

Louisa and Marta nodded and giggled.

Raul winked.

"She was bad, but I have seen a lot worse in my time."

"Like what?" the girls asked.

He thought for a few seconds.

"There were these two pilot friends of mine that got drunk in a hotel in Limerick, Ireland," Raul began. "They grabbed a lawnmower, brought it inside the hotel, and mowed the carpet in the lobby. We haven't been allowed back for the last five years."

"I can see why," Louisa said. "I thought I was being terrible when someone asked me if we were going to show a movie and I told them to look out the window and watch *Gone with the Wind*."

"I heard something about a guy on a DC-10 a month or so ago," May said. "How did that go—"

"Oh yeah!" Louisa said with a grin. "An engineer, Gary something, I heard about him, too."

"I haven't," Marta said. "What did he do?"

"He left the cockpit to check out some minor mechanical problem and slipped into the downstairs galley while most of the passengers were sleeping," May explained. "Then, he crawled through the emergency hatch from below, you know, the one that comes out of the floor in the middle of the passenger cabin. He messed up his hair and uniform and pretended to be out of breath. Then, really loud and right in the middle of the cabin, he says, 'Geez, this plane is really moving. I didn't think I was ever going to catch up to you guys!' Then, he went to the cockpit and closed the door. I guess people were freaking out for a few minutes."

"Then there's Toni Blake," Marta said. "She likes to leave fake poo on the seat in the lav for people to find."

"She did that to me!" May chuckled. "I didn't fall for it though, I'd been forewarned. Did you hear what she did when she found out that the president of inflight services was going to be on her flight? I don't know how she did it, but when she was serving him breakfast, she was apologizing all over the place saying how sorry she was that she overcooked his eggs. That girl managed to get little baby chicks, and they were scurrying around on his plate!" May stopped.

"There is something else that she did and I can't believe she didn't get in trouble for it."

"What? What?" asked Marta.

"I don't know how I feel about this one," she answered slowly.

"Well, tell us anyway," Louisa prodded.

"She was working on a DC-10 to LA out of New York and she wanted to play a trick on a friend of hers working in the lower galley. There was an orthodox rabbi on board, a really sweet old guy, and he asked her if there was any place on the airplane where he could stand and pray privately. So, she says, 'Yes sir, as a matter of fact, we have a special room provided by the airline to accommodate people of all religions who need a quiet place to pray.' She puts him in the elevator. He's happy, nodding and bending in prayer, and she pushes the button and sends him down to scare the crap out of her friend working in the lower galley."

"How does she get away with it?" Louisa marveled.

"I think it's that angelic face of hers. And she's so deadpan, you don't know you've been had until it's all over."

Marta pointed to the largest of three burly characters stocking cases of beer into a refrigerator.

"Speaking of characters, have any of you flown with Wes yet?" she asked.

"I haven't," May said. "But I've heard of him."

"Ol' Wes and I go way back," Raul interjected. "He's a fun guy, nice. Gets a little wild sometimes. He's a reserve pilot in the Marines, too."

"Who are the other two guys?" Marta asked.

"Wes said he met them in the lobby, a couple of Flying Tiger pilots."

Raul leaned in closer to the girls.

"You've gotta watch those Flying Tigers," he said, "they can really get nuts."

The party went on for hours, becoming progressively louder as the time passed. Fortunately, there were no other guests on the entire floor to be disturbed by the ever-increasing level of noise. May gazed at Wes. He was on all fours on the floor now, barking like a dog. He jumped over a nearby couch, crawled to the refrigerator, grabbed a beer, bit a huge hole in the side of the aluminum can with his teeth, and proceeded to drink the contents.

"Holy cow," she whispered to Raul. "That could be the greatest thing I've ever seen."

Just beyond him, the two Flying Tiger pilots were carrying a door that they'd just removed from its hinges. A middle-aged Equity pilot lay passed out on a couch near the lounge's floor-length windows. The Flying Tiger pilots set the door down beside him, lifted his motionless body, laid it out on the door, and threw a sheet over it. One of them began to tug at the windows.

May stared, mystified. "What the hell are they doing?"

"I don't know," Raul replied with concern. "But I'm gonna find out. Come on."

She and Raul quickly made their way over to the two men and their unconscious victim. May stepped beside the pilot splayed on the door and looked out the window, down to the ground several stories below. The window was perfectly situated over the swimming pool. It was supposed to slide open only halfway as a safety precaution. Somehow, the two burly characters managed to pull it all the way open. Both men snapped to attention, faced each other, saluted each other and tipped the door to the window.

Raul grabbed the top of the door just as the body started to slide. May shoved the window shut.

"Just what the hell are you two guys trying to do?" Raul asked.

Both men stood weaving.

"Why, we're having a burial at sea for this fine officer, of course."

"Holy Christ, are you kidding? Do you know how many floors up we are? Go do something else and leave the 'fine officer' alone!"

Raul and May pushed a large couch in front of the window. Hopefully, no one would open it again. The two drunken, disappointed pilots staggered away.

Another hour passed. Music blared. Beer flowed. The noise grew even louder, if that was possible. The party showed no signs of letting up. May looked at her watch. She yawned. It was almost 3 a.m.

"I'm tired," she said to Louisa.

"You know we have to get up at six to get our rental car, right?" she said. "If we're going to the parade, we've got to get at least a little bit of sleep. Let's see who else is still interested."

"I'd love to," Marta said, "but I'll be long gone before you get back from Pasadena."

"I'm still coming," Leslie said through a yawn. "Somebody better check with Benny."

Benny was nowhere to be seen in the suite, so May poked her head out into the hall. Benny, along with a crowd of crewmembers, had gathered around the same unconscious pilot she'd helped rescue an hour before. The pilot's crew stripped him to his underwear, put him on a large room service cart, and covered him completely, head and all, with a sheet. A homemade paper tag was tied to his big toe, the only body part protruding from beneath the sheet.

"Let us all bow our heads," a voice in the crowd said.

A short makeshift funeral followed, then the crew pushed him into the elevator and sent the body to the lobby. May, covering her mouth in disbelief, returned to her friends.

"Let's go," she said, tugging at Leslie's arm.

"Is Benny coming?" Leslie asked.

"We'll see in the morning. Do you guys mind taking the stairs? It's only two floors."

"Why?" Louisa questioned.

"Don't ask," May said.

The girls reached their floor, separated, and headed toward their separate rooms.

"Happy New Year, you guys," May called as she closed her door.

Three hours later, her phone rang. She groped around the nightstand next to the bed in earnest, trying to silence the noise. She mumbled into the receiver.

"This is your recorded wake up call," the machine answered. "It is six a.m. This is your recorded wake up…"

May dropped the receiver and looked at the clock. She turned toward the window. It was still dark and it was pouring rain. She called Louisa's room. She sounded a bit more awake than May, but not by much.

"Do we still want to do this?" May asked.

May desired nothing more than to roll over and go back to sleep.

"The parade starts at nine," Louisa answered. "Maybe it will clear up."

She's right, May thought. *Who knows when I'll ever be here on New Year's Day again?*

"I'll call Benny, if you'll call Leslie," May replied. "Let's try to get to the lobby as quickly as we can."

The bleary-eyed group met downstairs a half an hour later, hung over, tired from lack of sleep, and determined to see the parade.

"It'll be over by mid-day," Leslie said as she yawned. "We don't work until tonight. We'll still have time to get back and nap for a few hours before the flight."

They took the hotel van to a local rental car establishment, picked up their vehicle, and drove to Pasadena.

The weather did clear. The foursome sat on a curb on the parade route. They admired float after colorful float as they cruised past the noisy crowd.

"The flowers are so incredibly beautiful," Louisa marveled. "I'm so glad we came."

May nodded emphatically as a fabulous, rose-covered float passed by.

"They look amazing on TV, but the screen just can't capture the workmanship that goes into this. I can't get over the flowers! Gorgeous!"

The four couldn't stop talking about the parade as they drove back to the hotel.

"That rose queen wasn't so bad either," Benny said with a twinkle in his eye. "Good call, guys! It was worth it."

Back in her hotel room, May climbed into bed for a good, long nap.

On the flight that night, they would take a high school marching band from the Rose Parade home to Kansas City. They would drop off their passengers, ferry the empty plane back to Los Angeles, and spend another night in the hotel. May, Louisa, and Leslie decided to leave their luggage behind in their rooms.

"We're coming back late tonight anyway, so why pack up and bring it all with us?" Leslie reasoned as the hotel van drove them to the airport.

Daisy, their senior flight attendant, shook her head in disapproval. She was petite, very nice, and a ten-year veteran. The girls liked her very much.

"I don't know if that's such a good idea, ladies," she chided them. "I usually bring mine along anyway no matter what. You never know what might happen or where you might wind up."

The three girls glanced at each other nervously.

"You know she's right," Benny chimed in. "The plane could break anywhere and there's a bad snowstorm in Kansas City tonight."

His words made the girls squirm.

"Jesus, how could we be that stupid?" Leslie sputtered.

"It's too late now," May groaned.

Benny was right. It was snowing heavily when the aircraft touched down at their destination.

As was often the case, there was no available jetway for the charter. The passengers departed down the mobile stairs into the storm. May, Louisa, and Leslie paced and wrung their hands as they waited for the pilots to file a flight plan back to Los Angeles. The captain did a great job getting them into Kansas City. Now, they hoped he'd work more wonders and get them back in the air.

Benny went out into the storm to do the preflight walk-around check of the airplane. He was an excellent engineer. May felt confident having him on board, especially on a snowy night. He stopped by the landing gear to check the hydraulic fluid in the lines. Without it, most of the controls on the airplane wouldn't work.

May and Louisa were chatting in the galley when they heard him run up the mobile stairs yelling.

"Water! I need water now!"

The girls stared at him.

"I need water now!" he shouted again. "I have hydraulic fluid in my eyes!"

Both girls scrambled for cups so they could get water from the sink in the lavatory. The airplane water tanks were empty.

"Milk! Milk!" he shouted.

A few small cartons remained from the incoming flight. May and Louisa tore them open and handed them to Benny. He stood in the galley, pouring them into his eyes.

After a few minutes, he seemed all right again.

"Whew! That happened to me once before. That shit really burns."

He tossed the cartons in the trash as the girls cleaned the milk from the floor.

"Milk is a pretty good eyewash if you need it," he grinned.

"I think you're pretty lucky it wasn't worse," Louisa said, shaking her head.

Benny went out into the swirling snow again to finish his pre-flight check. The plane barely managed to make its escape from Kansas City. The aircraft thundered down the runway through the blinding snow, and the airport closed immediately after they took off. The plane climbed and climbed to get above the storm, up to forty-two thousand feet, as high as the old DC-8 was supposed to fly. The plane's fuel would last longer at the higher altitude. There were no airports open anywhere, not until the West Coast.

They reached cruising altitude. May looked down upon a solid carpet of clouds. A huge system of storms covered the entire western part of the country. Far above the storm, a bright, nearly-full moon rode along beside them. May felt an uncomfortable heaviness in her chest and pressure building in her ears. The old aircraft didn't pressurize as well as it did in its younger days, and she found herself continuously trying to clear her ears. May stepped into the rear galley for a drink of water. Most of the lights in the airplane cabin were off. She switched on a small light that dimly illuminated the galley and a few nearby seats. Then, she left to join the rest of the crew sitting near the cockpit.

Perhaps it was the quiet darkness of the cabin or the bright moon that followed as they sped west, but the crew fell into a strange mood. They started to tell each other ghost stories. One gruesome tale of the supernatural followed another until the darkness of the cabin began to feel ominous.

"I've seen movies about crazy killers on airplanes," Leslie said. "What if someone sneaked aboard and is hiding somewhere on this plane right now?"

"Oh, stop," Daisy laughed nervously.

The others persisted. The dim light from the rear galley silhouetted objects in the back of the plane. The crew's imaginations ran away with them.

"I know it's just the magazine rack back there," Louisa observed with a whisper, "but doesn't it look like a person?"

The little galley light in the rear chose that moment to go out. They all jumped, startled.

"W…What do you think happened?" Daisy said.

No one moved. May, plucking up her courage, grabbed her flashlight.

"I'm sure the bulb just burned out or something," she said, feigning nonchalance. "I'll check it out."

She hesitated as she stepped into the aisle. It was too late to back out. She made her way down the pitch-black aisle to the rear galley. Finding the switch with her flashlight, she flipped it on and off a few times. The light came back on.

"Probably just a loose wire," she mused, then smiled to herself. "Wow! We really let our imaginations get the better of us this time."

She walked up the aisle, and when she reached the over-wing area, she switched her flashlight off to look out the window.

"It is such a beautiful moon…"

A steel grip grabbed her ankle and yanked hard. She let out a piercing howl. May tugged and tugged, desperate to free herself, but the hand was like a vise, refusing to release, yanking, pulling her off balance. She looked for any place to escape whatever held her. If it were possible to jump out the window, she would have.

A giggle gave way to hysterical laughter as Leslie stood from between two rows of seats.

"You suck, you know that?" May said weakly. Her heart was pounding. "You scared the living shit out of me."

The others laughed as the two made it to their seats in the front of the plane. Twenty minutes later, with May nearly recovered, Louisa noticed a strange rumbling. It sounded as if it were coming from the lavatory closest to the cockpit. Louisa got up, looked inside, listened, and finding nothing, returned to her seat.

A few minutes later, the sound returned. All of them heard it this time.

They checked the lavatories and the forward galley area, finding nothing.

"We should tell them in the cockpit," Louisa said.

"I agree," May answered.

She and Louisa made toward the cockpit.

"Benny," May said, "we've got a strange noise somewhere back here and we can't find it."

Benny swiveled in his seat, his face grave.

"I didn't say anything back in Kansas City, but it looks like we've developed a mechanical problem, and it's getting worse. I don't think we're going to make it to LA. We're going to have to find somewhere else to land, if we can find an airport that's open."

Leslie joined them in the cockpit. The three girls were beside themselves.

"But what about all of our stuff back at the hotel?" Leslie wailed.

"I wonder what they'll do with it," May moaned. "I didn't even pack anything up. It's still all over the room."

"They're gonna love going in there," Benny laughed.

"Dirty underwear all over the room," she muttered.

"They'll probably throw it against the wall to see if it sticks," Benny snickered. "Maybe they'll sell all of your stuff."

The three left the cockpit, kicking themselves for not bringing their suitcases. They flopped into the front row of seats.

"We're on the road for how many more days?" Louisa grumbled. "Who knows what city we'll wind up in. No clean clothes, no blow dryer!"

The rumbling started again, louder this time and more persistent. The three jumped from their seats and scrambled for the cockpit.

"You guys, that sound is really bad back here now," Leslie said anxiously.

May was suddenly struck by the fact that the captain and co-pilot remained strangely silent through the crisis. She glanced from the pilots to Benny. His face contorted. He couldn't hold back any longer and exploded in laughter.

"That's a compressor you've been hearing back there," he said, wiping a tear from his eye. "I can hit a switch right here and it makes that noise."

"So no mechanical problems?" Louisa said tersely.

"Nope," Benny said. "No, ma'am. No problems at all. Should be in LA in an hour or so."

Benny was still hooting as the girls retreated. Fuming, May wanted to strangle him with her bare hands. Everyone sat together without saying much for the rest of the flight. Unbeknownst to each other, they'd all come to the same silent conclusion—revenge was an absolute necessity.

Later, when the van pulled up to the hotel, May ran to her room. Everything was exactly as she left it. She and the others learned a valuable lesson. No matter how short the flight, she never left her bag behind again.

May, Louisa, and Leslie sat in the hotel coffee shop the next morning, brainstorming ways to seek their revenge on Benny.

"We've got to get into his room," Leslie said. "It's the only way we can really do anything. We have to get a key."

"Do you think the front desk will give it to us?" Louisa asked dubiously.

"I think so. I know one of the clerks pretty well. He works in the afternoon. I'll come up with some excuse to get Benny's room key."

A few hours later, the three met in the lobby. Leslie discretely pulled a key from her pocket.

"Piece of cake, let's go."

They took the elevator to the third floor. The girls' rooms sat at one end of the hall and Benny's room at the other. He was out for the afternoon. None of them knew where. Leslie put the key into the lock and pushed the door open.

"We'd better be quick," she said, "We don't want to be here when he gets back."

They tiptoed into the room. The open curtains allowed the bright sunlight to flood in.

"You sure about doing the underwear thing?" Leslie said to May.

"Oh yeah," she answered, pulling a roll of tape from her pocket. "He was going on about the hotel staff throwing mine against the wall to see if it sticks. I think it's only fair to stick his."

The girls rifled through Benny's suitcase searching for his underwear, clean or dirty, and after several minutes found one pair.

"One pair? That's all he has, one pair? This is a six-day trip!"

May shook her head in disbelief.

"We're definitely going to have a discussion about this."

The girls taped their lone discovery to the large mirror next to the TV.

"What's that other thing he says all the time?" Leslie asked.

"Yahoo," May and Louisa said in unison.

In big red lipstick letters, Leslie wrote the word next to the hanging underwear. Job completed, the three girls poked their heads one by one out the door and peered into the hall. Looking both ways and seeing the hall empty, they dashed to their rooms and ducked inside. May sat smugly on the bed, congratulating herself. She turned on the TV and stretched back, her arms behind her head. There was a tap at her door. She sat up with a start.

"Who is it?" she asked cautiously.

A young male voice answered.

"Room service."

She scrambled to the door.

"I didn't order any room service," she said.

The voice mumbled something. She looked out of the peephole in the door. A young man stood dressed in a red jacket, holding a silver tray.

"Just a minute," May answered, perplexed.

She dashed to the phone and called Leslie's room.

"Leslie," she whispered, "there's a guy from room service at my door."

"So? What does he want?"

"I don't know, but I don't want to let him in."

"Go ahead," Leslie said reassuringly. "I'll step out in the hall and I'll watch him."

"Okay, that will work."

By the time May got back to the door, the room service boy was gone. The silver-covered plate was on the floor next to her door. Leslie's head poked out from her room. As she did so, the attendant reappeared, bearing another silver tray for her.

Louisa opened her door and stepped into the hall. The three girls stood staring at the silver plates.

"I don't think I want to know what's under there," May said finally.

"Me, either," said Leslie.

Gingerly, they reached down and removed the covers. There on matching dinner plates were two pairs of soiled, white men's briefs, BVDs to be exact. A roar of laughter drifted down the hall. Benny stood near the elevator.

At this point, the girls conceded defeat, realizing that they were way out of their league. Benny was a master practical joker, and there was no way to out-do him. Enjoying having a joke played on him as much as playing them on others, Benny told the underwear story to anyone that would listen.

"Benny," May said as they boarded the plane the next morning. "There's just one thing we want to know. Why did we only find one pair of underwear in your bag?"

He mumbled something hastily about doing his wash at the hotel, and the girls never did get a straight answer to their question. May and Louisa told Jessie and Marta all about their trip and all about Benny. Not long after that, Marta met up with the master of practical jokes. They dated for many months.

CHAPTER THIRTEEN

May stomped the late January snow off her boots as she entered the house.

"Hey, Jessie, are you here?" she called.

Jessie popped her head around the corner from the kitchen.

"Yeah, what's up?"

"Not much, just getting back from L.A. What are you cooking? It smells pretty good."

"Just baking a chicken with budaydas."

May frowned.

"What the hell are budaydas?"

"Oh, excuse me, I meant to say po—tay—toes."

"That's much better. I don't speak fluent Boston."

"You want some?" Jessie asked, returning her attention to the stove.

May noticed a bottle of wine open beside Jessie.

"No thanks, I ate on the plane. I'll take a little of that wine, though."

May sat at the kitchen table, sipping from her glass of pinot grigio as Jessie ate.

"It's supposed to snow more tonight," May said. "Our plane was freezing on the way back from LA. We kept calling the cockpit to warm it up, but it didn't help."

Jessie took another bite of her chicken.

"The systems on those old planes just don't work that well anymore," she answered. "I heard a couple of pilots in operations talking about how the mechanics are supposed to drain water lines on the planes that might freeze up in the winter. They don't do a very good job."

May took another sip of wine. She and Jessie had become close friends over the past few months.

"Knowing our owner, he probably doesn't want to pay the money to have it done right. Louisa and Marta got on the plane when I got off, they're working the trip back to LA. Maybe it will be warmer for them."

May looked at her wine glass.

"What is this?" she asked.

"You like it? It's Italian. I got it at the store down the street." Jessie reached back into the refrigerator and pulled the bottle from the door. "Here."

May looked at the label.

"I thought I recognized it! It's one of my favorites. Jake liked it, too."

"You still think about him, don't you?"

May looked out the window.

"Yeah, I do sometimes, but…"

Her voice trailed off.

"What about you?" she said. "I haven't seen you stick with anyone for more than a few dates. I've never even heard you talk about anybody except your brother the boxer. And he's the only one you visit. Where's the rest of your family?"

Jessie was very quiet, her eyes fixed on the floor. May suddenly wished she could take her comment back.

"My brother is the only one that I want to see," Jessie said with a strange expression on her face, something May couldn't read. "My dad is dead, thank God."

May didn't know what to say to that.

"My dad… He tried to molest me when I was little, but I managed to stay away from him. My little sister wasn't so lucky. She's a stripper now in Boston. My older brother almost killed a guy, so he's wanted by the police. Last I heard he's hiding in Florida. So, yeah. You know about my brother the boxer, but he drinks too much."

May froze.

"Your mother?" she finally managed to croak out.

"Mental hospital," Jessie said.

"Holy crap," May burst out. "How did you turn out so well?"

"I looked at the shit going on around me and I promised myself that was not going to be my life," Jessie said, just as matter-of-factly as she had stated that she was making chicken and potatoes. "I did well in school, stayed out of trouble, and… And May, I have a dream," Jessie said. "I'm going to fly."

May stood and hugged her friend tightly.

"You know we all love you, right?" May said. "Me, Marta, Louisa. Don't ever forget that."

Jessie said nothing. She picked up her fork and poked at her potatoes.

"Damn things are cold already."

May did her best to shake the heavy feelings.

"I'm going to take a shower," she said. "Anything good on TV tonight? It's a good night to drink wine and watch a comedy."

"I don't know," Jessie said. "It's already pretty late, but I'll take a look at the *TV Guide*."

Once showered and dressed in her pajamas, May emerged to find Jessie giggling. The mood had completely changed.

"Look! It's a Three Stooges marathon!" she shouted gleefully. "I love these guys!"

Moe was twisting Curly's nose with his hand.

"Me, too," May said. "Move over."

The two sat on the couch drinking wine and laughing into the wee hours of the morning. That's why, when the phone rang at 6 a.m., May didn't hear it at first. The ringing persisted. She stumbled out of her room as Jessie reached for the receiver.

"I hate it when the phone rings early," Jessie groaned. "It's never good news.

"Hello!" she said into the phone.

The muscles of Jessie's face shifted into a grim expression.

"Are you guys alright?" she asked.

May stood next to her.

"What time are you getting back to New York?" Jessie asked.

May tried to reign in her imagination.

"Okay, we'll see you later," Jessie said.

"What was that?" May asked.

Jessie had barely replaced the receiver on the cradle.

"What's going on?" May asked.

"Marta," Jessie said. "They had a gradual decompression on their flight."

"Are they okay?" May exclaimed. "What happened?"

"They're fine," Jessie said. "Marta didn't have time to talk. They never made it to L.A. They're in Denver. Once the plane is fixed, they'll ferry it back."

Even with their friends on their minds, Jessie had no choice but to drive to the airport to work. At home, May busied herself with errands. Louisa and Marta returned late that evening. The four roommates sat together in the living room sipping hot chocolate.

"We were pretty close to Denver. Service was done. I went to the cockpit to see if the pilots wanted to eat," Marta began.

"And I was sitting on my jumpseat with my dinner," Louisa interrupted. "I just started to eat when the plane went into a steep dive. My food fell off of my tray onto the floor. I looked up and saw all of the oxygen masks in the cabin fall out of their compartments and into the passenger's faces. They looked pretty surprised! I did just what they told us in training. I went for some oxygen for myself so I could help passengers. My mask fell out right in front of my face, but when I grabbed it, it pulled right out of the ceiling!"

"Did you pull a little harder than you should have? " May asked gently.

"No! I didn't! The thing came off right in my hand! I sat there staring at it," she replied. "It seemed like a long time, but it was probably just a second or two. Then the people started yelling like crazy. We were running around like idiots."

"I was in the cockpit," Marta said. "The engineer couldn't maintain cabin pressure. As soon as we reached 14,000 feet, there wasn't enough air, so the captain had to drop to a lower altitude fast. It was a steep dive, but we got to 10,000 feet. Then there was enough air whether the plane was pressurized correctly or not."

"The masks popped out automatically at fourteen thousand feet," Louisa added. "You should have seen it. Of course, NOBODY ever watches the safety demo, so no one knew to activate it. Passengers were screaming."

"It turns out that we didn't need them anyway," Marta said. "We still had breathable air and got down to a safe altitude so fast that we were okay. It's not like a hole blew open in the plane and all the air got sucked out. It was a small leak somewhere. There was this young guy. He was wearing headphones, listening to music with his eyes closed. He missed the whole thing!"

"So what then?" Jessie asked.

"The captain said we were making an emergency landing in Denver. When we got on the ground and the passengers felt safe, they just exploded, screaming, yelling, crying. Of course we don't have scheduled flights to Denver, so there wasn't anybody from the company to help them except us. We didn't know what to say. We're not ground personnel. It was an absolute nightmare."

"How did things end up?" Jessie asked.

"Honestly, I don't really know," Marta replied. "I think the company got another airline to help the passengers. I really felt sorry for them. We eventually got out of there and went to a hotel. I was never so glad to get away from an airport in my life."

"Which DC-8 was it?" May asked.

"115," Louisa answered.

"That's the one we got from the French. I thought it was one of our better planes," May said.

"Guys, I am so tired," Louisa said, taking her cocoa mug to the sink. "I'm going to turn in."

"Me, too," Marta said. "I'm sure we'll hear more about this."

A few days later, May sat at the kitchen table, drinking coffee and reading the *New York Times*. A small article on the third page caught her eye.

"Hey, look at this!" she yelled to Jessie.

Jessie walked into the kitchen and looked over her shoulder, reading the words aloud.

"An Equity Air DC-10 had an uncontrolled loss of altitude over Denver…"

When she finished reading the article, she made a gesture to May.

"The only thing they got right was the location," she said.

"And this is a good newspaper," May answered in disbelief.

Some weeks later, Marta ran into the captain from the flight that had the decompression incident.

"You know what he told me?" she said to her roommates later. "A chunk of ice clogged a water line to one of the lavs near the tail of the plane. It choked off some valve, and that's what caused the plane to gradually lose cabin pressure. Can you imagine? A frozen toilet!"

"Everyone was okay, that's what matters," May answered.

"True," Marta said. "Just the same, I'm glad that spring isn't all that far away. Winter flying has some strange hazards!"

CHAPTER FOURTEEN

By early March, the days grew longer. Spring waited around the corner. The number of flights increased and the possibility of furlough faded.

May, Louisa, and their former roommate Kathleen sat on reserve for the month of March when they received an assignment to work a long charter to Europe. IT began with a DC-8 full of tourists headed to Zurich, Switzerland, just in time for the carnival. The layover would allow them to attend an elaborate holiday parade during the day and observe the wildly-costumed people reveling in the streets and bars at night.

After a day and a half, they moved on to the U.S military base in Rota, Spain. They would work a series of short charters transporting military personnel from Spain to the American bases in Italy. Equity put the crew up at a small coastal resort near the town of Santa Maria, not too far from the base in Rota. Summer vacation season was months away, but resort owners realized the money they could make by opening for airline personnel.

"It's so quiet and peaceful," Kathleen sighed.

She took a deep breath of sea air as she exited the hotel van.

"That's because we're the only people in the place," May answered, grabbing her bag.

"Not quite," the captain declared. "A Saber crew is staying here, too. I ran into their pilots at the airport. They are doing the same military charter loop through Italy, so we could bump into each other."

"I don't know if I like that," Kathleen grumbled. "Are they trying to take our flying away from us? I just don't understand. What's the point of having two airlines anyway? I don't get it. Well, at least the beach looks nice. Anyone want to go for a walk after we unpack? We have a few hours."

The whole crew took a relaxing walk on the beach, ate a quick meal in the hotel restaurant, and headed to the base to await their plane. The flights were short and easy, and, as expected, the military personnel were well-disciplined and polite.

"I just love these flights," Kathleen said.

"I know, me too," May answered. "The only time I don't like them is when we have to take a whole plane full of them home for the last time. You know, when their duty is up. Have you ever done that?"

Kathleen shook her head.

"I hope you don't have to. It's a drunken party for them and a nightmare for us. I had one trip where they drank the plane completely dry. We were going from Germany to the States. Guys kept coming to the galley to buy drinks for themselves. I didn't know who was drinking what. After a few hours, everyone was barfing up a storm."

"Ick," Kathleen said.

"You said it. We couldn't keep track of how much they drank, so we couldn't cut them off. They probably would have killed us if we tried. Thank goodness we ran out of alcohol."

This voyage flew to Sicily, took troops from there to Naples, then took other military personnel from Naples back to Spain. The crew repeated this series of flights several times and were rewarded with a 36-hour layover at the Spanish seaside resort. They rested and explored the town of Santa Maria. May even tried to revive her limited Spanish.

"If Roger could only hear me now," she said with a grin.

She, Louisa, and Kathleen stopped in front of an outdoor café. They stared at the menu.

"I really think my Spanish is getting better. I can understand some of this."

"Okay, then," Kathleen challenged. "What's this?"

She pointed to one of the menu items.

"Oh, that's a salad," May said. "See that word there? It means salad."

"Good, perfect, that's just what I want," Kathleen replied.

The girls sat at a table in a sunny courtyard surrounded by flowering shrubs.

"Sometimes, I just love my job," Louisa said.

She smiled while drinking in the atmosphere. A waiter sauntered over to them, handing each of the girls a menu. He helped May and Louisa each choose a fish soup, then turned to Kathleen. She pointed at the salad they'd seen on the posted menu.

The waiter nodded, scribbled on his pad, and disappeared. The fish dishes appeared swiftly, but several minutes passed before Kathleen's salad arrived. The waiter delivered it at last. He stooped, placed a large bowl of greens in front of her, smiled graciously, and walked away.

Three pairs of eyes were riveted on the salad. On top of the greens, a pile of suction-cupped tentacles moved lazily in different directions. Kathleen stabbed one with her fork.

"Maaay," she said slowly, "just what the hell did you make me order?"

"It said salad. It must have been a seafood salad."

"Why, yes, May," Kathleen said, "and it's so extremely fresh. Did the menu say it was going to be raw and try to shake my hand?"

"I don't know. I don't know the word for raw," May said. "Are you going to eat it?"

Kathleen shrugged and took a small bite.

"You're braver than I am," Louisa said.

Kathleen chewed, not saying anything for several moments.

"Well?" May asked.

"Mmmmmm…" Kathleen grinned. "Tastes like chicken!"

Louisa didn't look convinced, and May tried to keep her face neutral.

"No, really, it's very good. Just the same… Let's ask the waiter what the Spanish word for 'raw' is for future reference!"

After lunch, the girls wandered around the town, inspecting shops and observing the locals. They spied a large arena in the center of town.

"Bullfighting ring," Kathleen said.

May frowned.

"You'd never get me in there," she said. "I'd smuggle the bull out!"

The threesome completed their day by joining the rest of the crew for dinner at a local restaurant in an ancient Moorish building.

"Right out of the *Arabian Nights!*" Louisa said, enchanted.

"Or *Casablanca*," Kathleen said.

When she returned to the hotel, May was dragging her feet, exhausted from a long and enjoyable day.

A good night's sleep is definitely in order, she thought.

She climbed the steps from the lobby to the second floor. She slowed when she spied a young woman of nineteen or twenty descending the staircase from above. May had seen her before, recognizing her as one of the Saber crew staying at the hotel. As they passed on the stairs, both stopped.

"Hi," May said in greeting. "How are your flights going?"

"Great!" the young woman answered. "We're working one more loop through Italy tomorrow, then as soon as we land, we're picking up a military group and taking them to Germany. We get a six-hour break before another charter to Delaware."

May whistled. "Wow! That's a lot of flying in a short time! How are you doing it with so little sleep?"

The Saber flight attendant laughed.

"It's tough," she admitted, "but what the heck, I can sleep when I'm dead, right?"

"That's true," May said politely.

She wished the girl good night.

Once she reached her room, May lit the candle on the table next to the bed and opened the large wooden doors leading to the balcony. A light breeze stirred the night air as she looked over the ocean. Waves crashed continuously up and down the coastline. The twinkling lights of the villages dotted the shore. The view directly ahead was total blackness. She thought about the name of the town.

Hmmm... Santa Maria. Like one of Columbus' ships. May stared out into the nothingness of the dark ocean. *How could three little ships just go out there, into that, with absolutely no idea what they'd find or if they'd ever come back?*

She had crossed this ocean time and again, many times a month, in the relative safety of an aircraft.

Brave souls, brave, brave souls.

She closed the balcony doors and prepared for bed. The next day, the crew drove to Seville and caught an Iberian Airlines flight to Madrid and then on to Brussels. They were working a regularly-scheduled Equity flight from Brussels to New York.

After completing meal service, May and Louisa paused in the rear galley. They spoke briefly as Doug, a fellow crew member, picked up the last of the trash from passengers. Doug was sweating and moving slowly through the aisle.

"He doesn't look well at all," May whispered.

"I know," Louisa answered with concern. "He said he started to feel ill last night. I've been keeping my eye on him."

As the hours passed, Doug's left eye began to swell. By the time they started the descent into New York, he couldn't see out of it at all.

"We only have about thirty minutes left," May reassured him. "You can make it."

Doug gave her a tired smile. He rose from the jumpseat.

"It's time to pass out the sour balls," he said.

Flight attendants on Equity flights distributed sour balls before landing to help the passengers' ears adjust to the change in altitude. It was a nice touch, especially on the international flights.

"Don't be silly," May said. "Stay where you are. I'll do it."

Doug shook his head. "I'll do it, it'll make the time go faster."

May shrugged and dumped a bag of the round, sour candies into a basket. She handed them to Doug.

Here you go, Igor," she said.

"Igor?"

"Yeah, you know, Igor. Dr. Frankenstein's assistant with the hump and the funny eyes?"

"Wait a minute," Doug said, grabbing a pillow from the overhead rack.

"I think I know where you're going with this," Kathleen said from her nearby vantage point.

Kathleen walked over and stuffed the pillow inside his shirt to create a hump. May handed him the basket and sent him into the aisle. Despite everything, Doug was a wonderful actor, stooping over and dragging one arm, his horribly swollen eye completing his costume.

"Would you like a sss…sss…ssour ball?" he said to each passenger.

He dragged himself up and down the aisle. Some of the startled passengers looked puzzled, others smiled, and some laughed. After they landed in New York, the departing passengers thanked their crew heartily for an entertaining flight.

Doug nursed his cold and eye infection for a week before he was able to get back to work.

New York had warmed during the time May was gone. The next day, she took her first walk on the beach in a very long time.

PART THREE:
It's Always a Nice Day Up Here, Spring 1982

CHAPTER FIFTEEN

May pulled up in front of the beach cottage and opened the door of her Buick. She turned her face to the warm, late-April afternoon sun and took a deep breath of sea air. She was returning from a long and difficult flight to the Caribbean Island of Trinidad.

Jessie was watching TV and eating a bowl of cereal in the living room when May unlocked the front door.

"Hi," Jessie mumbled, her mouth full of cornflakes. "How was your day?"

"Rough," May groaned, dropping her bag. "The passengers were friendly enough, but there were a zillion kids on the plane. They were everywhere. I swear none of them was older than six. And they needed everything! I was bringing all kinds of extra drinks, blankets, pillows. You name it. You'll love this. I was walking a bunch of drinks to the front of the plane and right across the aisle from me a woman flopped out an enormous boob and started feeding her baby."

Jessie laughed as May threw up her hands.

"Hey, I'm not squeamish about breastfeeding and natural motherhood and all that stuff, but most women are pretty discreet about it. They use a towel or something to cover up. This giant breast was just out there."

"What did the other passengers do?"

"That's the funny thing. Nobody else seemed to notice or care. Maybe I'm not worldly enough yet for some of these things."

Jessie put down her cereal bowl.

"Speaking of worldly, I found out that the company is hiring more flight attendants."

"Are you going to apply?" May asked.

"I did, a month ago."

"Have you heard anything yet?"

"I got in," Jessie said. "I start training in two weeks."

May reached over, grabbed Jessie, and hugged her.

"Why didn't you say anything?"

Jessie cocked her head, embarrassed.

"I don't know. I didn't want to say much of anything in case I didn't get in," she said, "but wow! I'm really going! I can't wait!"

May's face was a mask of mock gravity.

"Are you sure you want to do this?" May asked. "Go out there, flying with wild breastfeeding passengers?"

Jessie threw a pillow at her.

"I'll pack my sense of humor on every flight," Jessie replied.

Jessie had joined the flight crew just in time. Flying exploded during the month of May. Regularly scheduled flights were added, and there were charters galore. May and Marta were flying together once again while Jessie completed her training.

"Do you realize that we've been doing this for almost a year?" Marta said.

May and Marta walked into operations.

"I know," May answered, shaking her head in disbelief. "I can't believe it. It's like one adventure blends into the next and all of a sudden, a year is gone."

Their month together was a mix of scheduled flights and charters, including the one from Minneapolis to Oslo, Norway. May was excited to visit the land of the midnight sun and looked forward to the two-day layover. The crew ferried an empty DC-8 to Minneapolis to position it for the trip to Oslo.

The day dawned clear and sunny as 250 excited passengers walked up the outdoor mobile stairs to board their winged chariot to Norway. The flight attendants stowed baggage and settled people into their seats as departure time drew near. Outside the aircraft, the flight engineer was completing his walk-around inspection of the jet when something peculiar caught his eye.

He ran up the mobile stairs just as the gate agent prepared to give a departure speech.

"You can forget making any speeches," he told the crew. "We're not going anywhere."

Marta was working in the front of the airplane with the senior flight attendant and overheard the remark. She drew near the engineer and the agent.

"Somebody punched a nice big hole right through the fuselage," the engineer said.

The agent gasped. "How? How did it happen?"

"It looks like someone drove the mobile stairs into the side of the plane at some point, maybe last night. They probably got scared when they saw the hole and didn't say anything."

The agent sputtered in frustration. "What does this mean? I guess we can't go like this."

"No," the engineer answered, "we can't go like this. When we pressurize the plane, the hole might get bigger. We could have a nasty decompression in flight."

The agent clenched his fists. "How long will it take to get it fixed?"

"It's going to be a while. We're going to have to find a seal somewhere to plug the hole, and then we're going to have to test the pressure of the airplane while it's on the ground."

Marta drifted to the back of the plane to talk to May.

"We're going to be here awhile," she whispered to the remaining crew members in the galley. "Somebody knocked a hole in the plane."

"A hole?" May asked in disbelief.

"Yep, a hole."

May shook her head. "Well, that's a new one."

The agent reluctantly announced the delay. Passengers groaned, gathered their belongings, and headed back to the terminal. Hours passed. Equity couldn't get a proper seal from another carrier to fix the hole and had to have one flown from Tennessee to Minneapolis.

Once it was installed, extensive tests were performed to make sure that the seal worked. Twelve hours later, the plane was declared airworthy.

"So much for that two-day layover," Marta grumbled to May as they prepared for takeoff.

Fortunately, once they'd arrived at their destination, enough of the layover remained to see some of Oslo.

"What do you want to do first?" Marta asked.

May pointed to a large excursion boat loading at the waterfront dock.

"How about that boat tour over there? That looks like a good place to start."

The girls were the last two to board and both shivered as they pulled away from the shore. It was mid-May, but there was still a chill in the air this far north.

"It's an attractive city, don't you think?" Marta commented.

"Beautiful," May agreed.

They cruised along past evergreen trees and a rugged coastline.

"Lots of nature so close to a big city," May said. "Look at the people sitting on the rocks along the shore sunbathing, that's so nice."

May did a double-take. The people on the rocks looked awfully exposed and beige.

"Is it my imagination," May said, "or are a whole bunch of those people naked?"

Marta sat up and studied the scene.

"They're naked all right. Maybe they don't see the sun that much way up here and they want to get all they can."

"Maybe. Another one of those cultural differences, right?" May said with a laugh.

"I guess so," Marta said. "Those people are tough, too. It's too damn cold to be naked!"

When the boat returned to the harbor and docked, the girls wandered around the city before returning to the hotel. Marta pointed to a stone figure several yards away.

"What's that statue?"

They walked over to view the seated figure carved in stone, and May recognized it as they got closer.

"Look, it's Franklin Roosevelt. It's nice that they have a statue of him. It must be from World War II."

She noticed an unpleasant smell in the air.

"Is that what I think it is?"

Marta grimaced. "They're peeing on President Roosevelt."

"Oh, that's too bad," May said. "I always kind of liked him."

"Come on," Marta said. "We're going to be late for our dinner reservations."

May and Marta's last flight of the month was a scheduled DC-10 flight from New York to Los Angeles. Rain fell steadily as the plane sped down the runway and continued as it climbed through thick clouds. In a matter of minutes, the jet shot through the storm and into the clear blue sky, leaving the bad weather far below.

May hummed as she and Marta prepared the drink cart for the beverage service.

"This is one of the things I like best about the job," she said as the sun's rays poured through the aircraft windows. "No matter what's happening down on Earth, it's always a nice day up here."

Marta emptied ice into a bucket.

"I never really thought about it that way, but you're right."

When they'd completed the meal service, the girls opened the back galley to accommodate any passenger desiring a beverage. People often got up to stretch their legs during long flights, and many would stop for a drink and hang around the galley. Most crewmembers were happy to converse with passengers when their duties allowed it.

May and Marta were manning the galley when an older gentleman approached and asked for a soda. May handed it to him and smiled.

"Taking a little vacation time in California?" she asked.

"No," he replied, taking a sip of his drink, "visiting my daughter and grandkids. I do this a couple of times a year."

They talked quietly so as not to disturb the other passengers. A short while later, a man in his early thirties approached and asked for a drink. The two passengers and two flight attendants spoke casually for a while.

Eventually, the conversation turned to both men's military experiences. As they reminisced, May and Marta faded out of the conversation and just listened.

"I was in the Army Air Corps in the Pacific. Bombardier. World War II," the older man explained. "The Japanese shot us down, and we ditched in the ocean. We spent a lot of time in the water, but everyone made it out. We were damn lucky."

May looked at the older man with new interest. He seemed so average: slim build, grandfatherly, an air of quiet confidence about him. She was itching to ask him about the hours he spent in the ocean. Was he injured? Were there sharks? She wondered if he was willing to talk about it or perhaps he would rather forget. Though she was tempted, she kept her questions to herself.

"You got the good war," the younger man said. "Everything was clear for you. You knew your enemy. You knew right and wrong. I sure couldn't say that about Vietnam. I didn't know a damned thing, you know? Not a goddamn thing about what I was doing there. I did a lot of recon work, intelligence gathering. Went on a lot of patrols at night."

There was no emotion in his voice.

"We needed each other to survive, my buddies and me. Needed to have each other's back. Every bush could potentially have the enemy behind it. One of my guys was getting heavy into drugs. Got to the point where he wouldn't shut up, kept tripping, making noise. Stupid son of a bitch gave our position away more than once."

There was still no emotion in his voice.

"It got bad, really bad. We had to kill him."

May and Marta's eyes met in a flash. They said nothing, and after a few more exchanges between the two men, the conversation ended. The passengers returned to their seats.

"Did I hear him right?" Marta asked in a low voice.

"I think so. They call it fragging, I think, killing one of your own. Never thought I'd hear it for real."

The conversation disturbed the girls, who busied themselves in the galley to get their minds off of it. Diandra, their senior flight attendant and a fifteen-year flight veteran, appeared in the galley. She was an American citizen, but had spent most of her years growing up in Europe with her Irish parents. She stood outside the galley as the two girls worked silently.

"What's the matter with you two?" she asked.

"Oh, nothing really," May answered. "We were listening to a couple of war vets talking back here. One was a Vietnam vet. He was telling the other guy a gruesome story about the war."

"Yeah, war is disturbing," Diandra agreed. "I flew plenty of charter flights in and out of Vietnam during that war."

"Equity flew charters there?" Marta asked.

"Yes, lots of carriers did, not just Equity. Those military contracts were big money for airlines."

"So, Equity was doing the military stuff before Flint came along?" May asked.

"Yes, that was way before his time here."

"What was it like working those wartime military charters?" May asked.

Diandra laughed softly. "First thing the company did was ask us about our politics. They didn't want anti-war protesters on the flights. I was just out of school in Europe and had just come back to this country, so I really didn't know that much about American politics. There was a temporary West Coast base in San Francisco and one in Hawaii. Lots of the flights came from bases across the U.S. and then refueled on the West Coast, Hawaii, or in Alaska. They went from there to Tokyo."

"That's a lot of flying," Marta commented.

"Yeah. Some crews would fly the troops from the West Coast to Tokyo. Other crews got temporary duty assignments and were based there. Those crews would fly the troops to Saigon, drop them off, and bring another flight full of military personnel back to Tokyo."

"What were the trips like?" May asked. "Were they scary?"

"There were some scary moments," Diandra said. "There were times when we landed in Saigon without lights at night so we didn't get attacked. One day, we landed and unloaded troops and we were waiting for the plane to be serviced so we could take people back to Tokyo. The crew was hanging around on the plane when they started shelling the airport. I got on the P.A. and told everybody to hit the deck." She laughed ruefully. "Being on the floor wouldn't have made much difference if we got hit by a shell, but it might have helped in dodging bullets."

Another long-time Equity flight attendant working in the front of the plane stopped in the rear galley. Ursula, a gruff Swedish girl and one of May's favorite co-workers, dropped a bag of trash into a container.

"Remember our Vietnam charter days, Ursula?" Diandra asked.

"Hmpf," she grumbled. "How could I forget?"

"Remember the flight we worked when they bombed the Saigon airport?"

Ursula's eyes rolled. "They always bombed that damned airport."

"What about the time where you went into the terminal and got caught in there?"

Ursula looked at the two younger women.

"The rockets were flying, and I crawled under some rows of seats in the terminal. It was the only shelter," she said. "I crawled beside this young G.I. He looked like he was twelve years old. I leaned over to him and asked him if this happened often. You know what he said?"

"What?" May asked.

"He said, 'I don't know, I just flew in here with you.'"

"Those boys were so young," Diandra said. "Planes filled with boys that were so young and so afraid. They didn't know what was coming or if they would ever make it home."

"You know the worst?" Ursula added. "The worst was looking out the window at the cargo coming home. The caskets. The rows and rows of caskets."

"When did the charters end?" Marta asked.

"Early 70s," Diandra answered. "That was when Equity had its only fatal crash. In Alaska. Right, Ursula?"

A strange expression crossed Ursula's face.

"She was on it," Diandra said quietly.

The younger women stared.

"It was a miserable rainy day," Ursula said. "I was working with Ingrid, my roommate. We knew each other from Sweden. The flight was full as usual, and on the takeoff roll the plane just didn't feel right. It was sluggish. I thought for sure the captain would abort the takeoff, but he didn't. The front end of the plane barely got airborne when it crashed down on the runway. The plane burst into flames. Thank God it was a military flight. That's why so many people got out alive. Out of 250 passengers, 200 survived. So many of the flight attendants were injured, buried under debris. Soldiers dug them out and carried them away. All of the crew made it, except for Ingrid."

May and Marta murmured condolences.

"It was so strange, the way Ingrid was," Ursula said. "When she died, they found $1,000 in her pocket. It was all the money she had in the world. Like she knew she was going to die or something. They flew her body back to Sweden to be buried."

"How were you ever able to come back to work again?" May asked.

"I don't know," Ursula said. "Some of the others tried to fly again, but they eventually quit. For me, after a while, it just seemed like the same old airplanes, my same old galley, and I was okay. Maybe it was because I didn't get injured."

A call button chimed in the aisle. Diandra looked at her watch.

"Wow, where did the time go? Looks like the natives are getting restless. We'd better be thinking about our second beverage service."

Ursula jumped.

"The captain asked me for a cup of coffee a while ago, and I told him I'd bring him one."

She reached for a paper coffee cup. Before she filled it, she grabbed a pencil and started to write something in the bottom of the cup.

May was curious. "What are you doing?"

"I can't stand that captain, he's such an asshole. He knows I can't stand him, too. Whenever I have to get him coffee I write 'Fuck You' in the bottom of the cup so he'll see it when he finishes."

May howled with laughter.

"That's why I love you, Ursula."

CHAPTER SIXTEEN

The hectic summer months sped by. Brand new flight attendant Jessie toughed out her time on reserve.

"I feel so bad now about giving you guys those San Juan turn-arounds," she groaned as she dropped her bags and fell onto the couch. "God, they're hard!"

May, running from one room to the next in preparation for her flight, was only half paying attention.

"Uh-huh," she said absently as she grabbed a shampoo bottle from the bathroom.

"Where are you off to?" Jessie asked.

"Rome. I've got a three-day layover there."

"September in Rome. Leave now before I kill you," Jessie said. "I'm so jealous."

May laughed.

"Oh no, I paid my dues," she said. "You know that better than anybody. It might take a while, but you'll get good trips, too."

"Who are you flying with this month?"

"It's the first trip of the month, and the only one I know of so far is Carly Miller. I saw her in the crew lounge a few days ago. We noticed that we have the same schedule."

"Flying with the crazy Australian, that should be fun."

"Yeah. Did you know that her father is an undertaker?"

Jessie grinned. "Does that make him a down-under undertaker?"

May winced. "Clever, very clever. I don't know, but any undertaker's kids I've ever met have all been a little nuts and lots of fun. They have a great attitude about life."

"And death," Jessie added.

"I guess so. Listen, I've got to get going," May said. "Maybe you'll get a nice trip while I'm gone."

"Nope," Jessie said. "I'm doing San Juan again tomorrow."

May pulled her suitcase toward the door.

"Chin up!" she called. "See you in a few days."

May arrived in the crew lounge as Diandra walked in. Their eyes met.

"Rome?" May asked hopefully.

"Yup," Diandra answered. "I'm the senior."

"That's so great, you can tell me more stories about the good, old days."

Two more flight attendants entered. May recognized Starla, a southern girl from Alabama, and her companion, Patrick. They'd gone through training together a few classes after May's and were close friends. The pair shared an apartment in Queens with two of their former classmates. This was the first time May would be working with either one. Once Carly and the rest of the DC-8 flight attendants arrived, they walked together to the airplane, where their cockpit crew already waited. The flight engineer was young, tall, and weighed about 275 pounds.

"My friends call me 'Ox,'" he said cheerfully.

Diandra nodded. "Makes sense."

May couldn't take her eyes off the first officer—a dark, handsome man in his mid-thirties.

Carly leaned over and whispered in her ear in her thick Australian accent, "He's married, mate."

"Well, that figures," May mumbled.

The captain—rather Nordic-looking, lanky, and also in his mid-thirties—introduced himself as Derrick. The name jogged a memory. May's old friend, Benny, from the Rose Bowl trip, had mentioned him.

"That guy can be a real dick to work with, a real hard ass, always right about everything," Benny had said. "I call him E.T."

"Why?" May had asked. "Does he remind you of an extra-terrestrial?"

"No, he reminds me of an extra testicle."

May snapped back to the present. She wondered if she would have to spend a three-day layover with him. Suddenly, the trip lost some of its allure.

"I want to tell all of you this right now," Derrick said to the crew. "I won't be with you for the Rome layover of the trip. Since we're working the first leg to Zurich and then deadheading to Rome for three days, I'm going to spend the layover in Zurich with my girlfriend. I'll meet you in Rome."

"Gee, Derrick," Diandra said blandly, "we'll miss you, but have a good time."

They worked the long, busy flight to Zurich, left the DC-8 there for the next crew, and boarded a Swissair jet to Rome. With the exception of Diandra and Lara, a Finnish girl with many years of seniority, it was everyone's first trip to The Eternal City.

May's interest in history piqued as she eagerly peered out the hotel van window at the passing remnants of the Roman Empire. To her delight, the hotel was only a block from the Coliseum. Their lodgings were simple but nice. The rooms, though not fancy with their iron twin beds and plain furnishings, were very clean.

She walked to a window and opened it, letting in a warm September breeze. Buildings glimmered in the afternoon sun. Rows of clothing hung on lines strung between the rooftops. She heard a woman calling in the distance. The city was just as she imagined it would be, the residents of Rome living casually, surrounded by the remains of thousands of years of history. Were they conscious of it? Did they think about the miracle of touching a stone crafted by a builder two thousand years before, or was it just that she was from a place where everything was new and ancient structures were nearly non-existent? Roman builders turned to dust long ago, but their handiwork survived in the buildings, aqueducts, and roads that remained. The whole crew met in the lobby for an afternoon of sightseeing.

"Where do we go first?" little Carly asked eagerly.

All eyes turned to Diandra and Lara.

"We could start at the Vatican," Diandra suggested. "But I warn you, we could spend the whole three-day layover there and not see it all. I suggest that we stay a few hours and let it go at that if you plan on seeing anything else."

The crew piled into two small taxis. The cabs took off from the hotel, driving at breakneck speed through the city.

"What the hell are they doing?" Ox shouted.

They careened around corners and darted in and out of traffic. One particularly sharp turn tossed Ox to the left, so he smashed into Carly and nearly squashed her. In a flash, they pulled up to a curb near the Vatican. Ox paid the drivers as the others escaped the vehicles.

"Thank you, I think," he said.

Both cabs sped away.

"Look at this place," May marveled.

They walked through rows of columns and exquisite sculptures.

"I see what you mean about this, Diandra," May said. "I could spend hours and hours here."

From the Vatican, they moved on to the Spanish steps and visited the Trevi Fountain.

"Take my picture!" Carly shouted.

She turned to throw a coin over her shoulder into the fountain.

"They say that if you do that," she explained, "you'll come back to Rome someday!"

"Let me at that fountain, then!" May grinned, moving forward.

The whole crew dug in their pockets for change. The group strolled past shops selling jewelry, clothing, and leather goods. May found herself picking out a new wallet. Later, tired from hours of walking, they returned to the hotel.

"Who wants to go to dinner?" Lara asked.

"Everybody, I think," Ox answered.

"Let's meet here in the lobby in, say, half an hour," she said. "I know a really good restaurant that's within walking distance." The restaurant proved to be a warm and cozy family affair only a few blocks from the hotel. Its cheerful, portly owner continuously filled their glasses with wine as they stuffed themselves with pasta. It was late when they paid the bill and prepared to leave.

"Oh, I ate way too much," Carly groaned. "I think I'm gonna explode."

A block or so from the restaurant, May stopped, groping frantically through her pockets.

"Guys, I think I left all of my money on the table back at the restaurant," she said. "Either that or I dropped it." May was in a panic. "What do I do? If I left it there, somebody probably took it by now."

"Either that or the waiter thinks you're a world class tipper," Diandra said dryly.

May turned and ran full speed to the restaurant. She reached the cash register and suddenly had no idea what to say to the friendly, generous owner standing behind it. Her face flushed with embarrassment, May explained what she'd done. She'd only gotten a few words out when he smiled.

"Bellissima!" He exclaimed, slapping her on the shoulder.

He handed her wad of lira. It wasn't a fortune, but it was all she had. She thanked him profusely as the large man suddenly grabbed her by the shoulders and planted a kiss on each of her cheeks. He waved as she stepped back into the street. The rest of the crew had followed her to the restaurant, and they were standing on the curb.

"Well?" Diandra asked.

"You know, these Romans are all right," May answered with a sigh of relief. "I'm going to be able to eat for the rest of this trip."

Back at the hotel, the crew eyed a few guests having a drink, sitting in the lobby in comfortable chairs. May was so excited about getting her money that she agreed to join the others for a nightcap. They plopped onto cozy couches surrounding a central coffee table and settled in as the bartender delivered their drinks.

"I brought my Uno deck," Carly announced. "Does anyone want to play?"

"What's Uno?" May queried.

"It's a card game and it's lots of fun. Let me get my deck, I'll be right back."

The card game was easy and entertaining. After a few rounds of alcohol, it deteriorated. Carly stood.

"You know what we need, don't you?" she said, wavering. "We need to get a tattoo."

May and Starla nodded vigorously in agreement. Suddenly, Starla stopped.

"Oh my," she said unsteadily in her southern accent. "It's three in the morning. We'll never find a tattoo parlor open at this hour."

The three sat forlornly.

"I know!" Carly screeched.

She reached into her purse and pulled out her ballpoint pen. May and Starla gleefully followed suit. Each completed a ballpoint pen tattoo masterpiece on their legs. They looked at them admiringly, then turned to Cliff, the handsome co-pilot.

"What will it be?" Carly shouted.

"I know! I know!" May shouted. "An anchor across his chest!"

"With 'Mother' in big letters under it!" Starla shrieked.

Try as they might, the girls couldn't pin Cliff down to tattoo his chest, and so they settled for drawing the Equity Air wad of dollar bills insignia on his leg. The foursome then made a solemn pact not to wash off their tattoos, a pact none lived up to except for Cliff. He proudly displayed the drawing on his leg when the crew met for another round of sightseeing the following day.

May, Cliff, Carly, and Starla walked the short distance from the hotel to the Coliseum. May gasped in amazement as they approached.

"I can't believe so much of this is intact," she said.

They walked through the arena's ancient stone passageways.

"This part used to be underground," Cliff said. "This is where they kept the animals and where the gladiators waited until it was their turn to fight."

"I think there must have been cat fights, too," May commented. "Have you noticed all the cats running around?"

They walked from the Coliseum to the ruins of the Roman Forum, the column and stone remnants of the center of the old city.

"The cats are all over here, too," Starla exclaimed. "Every time I look around a corner or in a hole, a cat jumps out!"

"Some of them are sick, too," May added. "Some of those cute kittens have runny eyes. I wonder if this place has always been full of cats."

Cliff was walking behind them.

"Haven't you heard the story of how they got here?" he asked.

Both girls turned, waiting for the answer.

"It was a *cat*-astrophe," he said quietly.

The girls groaned.

"It's almost dinner time," May said.

They returned to the hotel to join the others. Once the crew gathered, they headed to a bustling restaurant, one recommended by the concierge. A charming outdoor patio filled to capacity opened into the crowded interior of the establishment.

"It must be pretty good, judging from the size of the crowd."

After a short wait, they were seated. The cuisine was tasty as promised, and the crew consumed mounds of wonderful food and bottle after bottle of wine. The evening flew by. Ox was the first to realize that they were the only people left in the restaurant.

"I think we should help these guys clean up," he declared, motioning to the two waiters clearing tables.

The entire crew stood up and without a word started hauling in chairs from the patio. The restaurant owner stood dumbfounded and perplexed at the sight of his customers pitching in, but the waiters seemed pleased to have the help. Starla stood in a corner, conversing with one of them.

"Say," she drawled with her Alabama accent, "I know it's Sunday, and all but do you fellas know of some place where we can go and dance?"

"Most places are closed," the waiter informed her, "but I do know of one."

Starla ran to the others.

"Hey y'all! The waiters are gonna take us out dancing! Isn't that just the best?"

The others looked from Starla to the waiters.

"Okay with me, I guess," Carly said.

"Sure, why not?" Ox seconded.

The waiters proceeded to hail two taxis and whisked their new friends to an obscure nightclub several blocks away. The establishment was located in the basement of a large, old building, and music boomed from a doorway at the bottom of a long flight of concrete stairs. Two young men stood in the doorway collecting a cover charge. May did a quick dollar-to-lira conversion in her head as she relinquished her money.

"This is a pretty steep cover charge to go dancing," she whispered to Carly.

"It is Sunday and there isn't anything open. Maybe that's why they can charge so much," Carly whispered back. "We're here, let's make the best of it."

The disco was nothing out of the ordinary. There was a bar and a large dance floor surrounded by bleachers for seating. The newcomers quickly ordered drinks and joined the crowd. Ox picked up Carly, twirling her in circles. Cliff and Lara danced up a storm, and Starla worked herself into a frenzy with one of the waiters.

"Great way to work off that big dinner!" Diandra shouted.

She and Patrick drifted by. The frantic dancing continued for several hours. May took a turn on the dance floor with one of the waiters. As she moved to the blasting music, a young blonde woman crossed her path and disappeared.

A minute later, the blond returned, pushing past May and her dance partner. May's partner motioned as if he wanted to tell her something. She leaned forward, and the waiter mumbled something that she couldn't hear over the roar of the music.

"What's that?" she yelled without breaking her pace.

"*Prostituta!*" he shouted.

May was not sure she'd heard what she thought she'd heard.

"Beg pardon?" she asked again.

"*Prostituta!*"

He nodded emphatically, motioning to the blonde girl. She didn't need a translation for "*prostituta*," and had no idea how to respond.

May could only stutter, "Oh! ...where do they go?"

He pointed to a few doors barely visible in the shadows just off the dance floor. Rooms for customers.

The song stopped, and they walked to the bar. It was getting late. Patrick sat with his elbows propped under his chin, a slightly irritated look on his face. May followed his gaze to the other side of the dance floor, where Starla was peering beneath the bleachers.

"She lost one of her shoes," Patrick said wearily.

"She lost a shoe?" May repeated.

"Yeah."

Patrick was obviously tired and wanted to go back to the hotel. The rest were ready to call it a night as well. May glanced at the dance floor. Starla had recruited several people to help her search for her missing shoe. Men were crawling on the floor, looking under every bleacher, to no avail. Starla ran over to the bar breathless.

"Oh y'all, I can't find it anywhere," she said. "Did Diandra come back with that flashlight yet?"

May looked towards the bleachers. Starla's helpers were fed up and deserting.

"What am I going to do now?" she wailed.

Starla hurried to the bleachers.

Diandra returned. She'd taken Carly with her on the flashlight search. The two were perplexed.

"I don't know what it is," Diandra said, "but there is something really weird about this place. I was looking for anyone who might have a flashlight, and I tried those doors over there."

She motioned across the dance floor.

"I tried to see if someone back there had one, and every room I went to, a weird guy came to the door and told me to get out!"

May's mind instantly flew to the waiter's comments.

"Diandra, I think prostitutes take their customers to those little rooms over there where you were poking around."

"What?" she exclaimed.

"This place is a cat house, Diandra."

The stunned silence gave way to roars of laughter.

"OMIGOD! OMIGOD! And I'm over there looking for a *flashlight?*"

Starla ran to the group, shoe in hand.

"Found it! Found it!" she squealed in delight.

Patrick rolled his eyes. "Does that mean we can go home now?"

The next day, it was nearly three in the afternoon before May was able to crawl to the little sidewalk café near the hotel. Cliff, Lara, Ox, Carly, Diandra, and Patrick were already there. They looked no better than she did. Starla was nowhere to be seen.

"She went shopping," Carly volunteered. "Can you believe her last night? She was driving me nuts with that shoe. And asking us to find her a flashlight and Diandra and I wind up with a bunch of hookers! You know we have to do something about this."

May was sipping on a Coke and nibbling on a plain roll with butter.

"What do you have in mind?"

"I think I can get the key to her room," Carly answered, a mischievous look on her face. "I'll decide what to do when I get there."

"Want any help?" Diandra offered.

"No, I've got this."

Carly set off on her mission. Twenty minutes later, the rest of the group returned to the hotel to find her in the lobby by the elevator with a smug look on her face. May stepped towards her.

"We're going to try to see the Sistine Chapel if it's not too late, wanna go?"

"Sure," Carly answered.

The elevator bell dinged behind them. The doors opened, and Starla stepped into the lobby. She'd returned from her shopping trip, gone to her room, and hurried downstairs. She nearly tripped over May and Carly, shrieking.

"Oh, y'all are just too much! I can't believe it! Y'all are just too much!"

"What are you talking about, Starla?" Carly dead panned.

Starla turned to her.

"Oh, did you do that? I can't believe you did that! That's great!"

"Goodness, Carly!" Ox said. "Whatever did you do to Starla?"

"It was just so great!" Starla gushed. "I went to change my shoes and I could only find one. I looked for my other pair and there was only one of them, too. And only one of my sneakers. And even only one of my slippers! Y'all are just too funny!"

A smile appeared on everyone's face as Diandra broke in.

"We better hurry if we're going to make it to the chapel."

The late afternoon walk to the Sistine Chapel was pleasant, but all were disappointed to find out that they'd arrived too late and the chapel was closed.

"Guess we just took too long to get here," May said in resignation.

Starla, who'd been chatting constantly during the entire walk, fell silent. They'd turned to go back to the hotel when her face brightened.

"I know! It's too bad that this place is closed, but after dinner tonight, we can all get together again and go dancing! It'll be great! Maybe we can even go find those waiters again," her voice trailed off as she absorbed the grim looks of the others.

Finally, after a long pause, she asked softly, "Hey, Carly, do you think I could have the rest of my shoes back?"

"Our last night in Rome," May said wistfully.

The crew decided to eat at a small nearby restaurant and hang around the hotel. Lara went to bed early, and the rest took their positions around the table in the lobby, engrossed in another game of Uno. All except Starla, who did her best to coax the others into another dancing excursion.

"For the last time, nobody wants to go!" Diandra said irritably. "Why don't you join the game?"

Starla sat sulking as Ox glanced across the lobby to the front desk.

"Look," he whispered, "It's our evil counterparts. A Saber Air crew is checking in."

"I swear, sometimes I feel like I'm being stalked," Diandra complained. "They show up where we are more and more, like an annoying little sister."

One of the male flight attendants, an attractive young man in his mid-twenties, walked across the lobby and introduced himself.

"Hi, folks! You can probably tell by the uniforms that we're a flight crew.

"We're an Equity crew," Ox countered.

"Do any of you know where there might be a good restaurant close by?" The young man asked. "You been here long?"

"This is our third night, we're taking a charter out tomorrow."

"That sounds like a nice trip. You guys get much better layovers than we do."

"I don't know how you work some of the hours you do," Ox said. "I heard that you do Europe turnarounds!"

The young man nodded. "Yeah, on occasion."

Diandra interrupted, "Are you ever going to get a union?"

"We're trying, but I doubt it will happen. You know how the boss is. Although there are rumors about us starting some scheduled flights soon," he said. "Maybe that would change things."

A shadow crossed the faces of the Equity crew as they digested this bit of information, but no one said anything.

"So, do you guys at Saber think the stories about him are true?" May asked abruptly. "Is he really a gun runner?"

The young man considered the question carefully.

"We've heard all the stories, too. He was with the CIA in Vietnam, was a gun runner, all that," the young man said. "Personally, I haven't seen anything obvious. We've started flying some military charters through the Middle East lately, soldiers on training missions or something. We've also been going to Central America a little more."

"That's an interesting choice of places to fly, what with the Sandinistas, the Contras, and all that political upheaval," Ox said. "Who exactly do you take to Central America?"

"I don't know, families mostly. At least that's what they look like." He grew uncomfortable. "We're here until tomorrow. Have you been seeing the sights?"

"We've had a great time, especially when we've gone dancing," Starla said loudly. "I LOVE to dance."

The others rolled their eyes. Starla glared at them.

"She wants to go dancing tonight, but the rest of us are too tired," Carly explained.

The Saber Air flight attendant looked at Starla intently. "I'll take you."

Starla squealed in delight. "Would you? Would you really? That would be so great! Oh, wait a minute, I have to check something." She fumbled through her purse looking for her wallet. "Oh my, I don't have a dime left, and there'll be a cover charge for sure no matter where we go. Oh, y'all, I wanted to go so bad!"

With lightning speed, Diandra, May, Carly, Ox, Patrick, and Cliff all jumped up, reaching into their purses, wallets, and pockets. Seconds later, they were shoving a wadded-up ball of lira into Starla's hands.

"Here, take this, now you can go," Diandra said.

"Y'all are just too nice, I can't stand it!" Starla said.

She joyfully linked arms with her new friend. When they were out of sight, the others sighed in relief.

"Jesus, if I'd known that all I needed to do was kick in a few bucks, I'd have paid someone to take her dancing three days ago!" Diandra laughed.

The crew played cards in the lobby throughout the evening. It was Ox who eventually brought up the Saber Air flight attendant's comments about the possibility of their sister airline running scheduled flights.

"It makes me nervous. Flint owns that company all by himself. No partners, no one else involved," he said. "Other people have money in our outfit, but he has controlling interest. He's got enough power here to siphon off Equity business to Saber and run us into the ground if he wants to. No other investors in the company would have the power to stop him."

"I don't know," Diandra responded. "I've seen other investors come and go in the years I've been here. Let's not get too worked up just yet."

They were still involved in an intense round of Uno when Starla returned a few hours later, her new friend in tow.

"Y'all missed a beautiful night, it was so nice," she gushed. "We sat by a fountain drinking wine and having a fine old time, and all of a sudden, these two guys got into a fistfight right

next to us. It was unbelievable! And then the two of 'em pulled these knives out in front of us!"

Everyone dropped their Uno cards.

"Then, this other man came out of nowhere," she continued, "and pulled a gun out and stuck it right in one guy's face and broke the whole thing up. It was so great! I tell you, I felt so safe!"

"What?" the rest yelled in unison.

"Two guys in a knife fight, and another guy with a gun and you felt SAFE?" Diandra exclaimed.

"Oh yeah," Starla beamed.

Then, her smile drooped.

"It was great, but you know," she said, "we never did go dancing."

At noon the next day, May stood on the sidewalk in front of the hotel waiting to board the van to the airport. She thought of the coin she'd thrown in the Trevi Fountain as they passed the Coliseum and a series of ancient aqueducts. She hoped that the magic would work and that she'd return one day.

It sure wouldn't be the same, she thought, glancing at the faces of her co-workers. *Not without this group to enjoy it!*

Derrick met them at the Rome airport in a pleasant mood after his three days in Switzerland.

"Did you have a good time?" Diandra asked.

He grinned at her. "Yeah, it was great."

"Must have gotten some good nookie," Carly hissed to May. "I'm sure he'll be sharp today."

May grimaced as they walked off to find the plane. The DC-8 would be full, which was no surprise. Then, she saw the plane at the gate.

Well, well, 115, Louisa and Marta's decompression plane, she thought ruefully. Every flight attendant knew the call numbers the planes in Equity's small fleet.

The flight got off the ground without a hitch and, after a short fuel stop in Shannon, Ireland, continued to its final destination of Detroit, Michigan. It was nearly 10 p.m. local time as they approached the airport.

May and her co-workers wearily closed up the galleys, picked up the remaining trash, checked the passengers one last time, and made their way to their jumpseats. May shared the rear jumpseat with Patrick. She barely had enough time to strap in before she felt the sensation of the ground coming to meet the plane. Over the past year, she'd learned to sense that moment just before touchdown without having to look out the window. A split second later, a terrific bang rocked the airplane as they hit the runway.

"What the hell was that?" Patrick said.

She and Patrick both jumped from their seats and looked out the porthole. May's lower back hurt from the impact. They could see nothing out of the ordinary, and the plane taxied normally to the terminal.

Passengers turned and looked questioningly at them. Neither spoke Italian, so they gave the passengers reassuring looks. When no announcement came from the cockpit, May called Diandra up front.

"So, what exactly was that?" May asked.

"I don't know, but just sit tight and don't do anything," Diandra directed. "We're almost at the terminal."

Once again, there was no access to a jetway and the passengers disembarked via mobile stairs. After the last one departed, the flight attendants cornered Cliff.

"What happened?" May asked. "I almost broke my tailbone."

"Derrick brought the plane in at such a high angle that he smacked the tail on the runway!" Cliff answered in a low voice. "It's pretty easy to do on takeoff, especially with a heavy load, but you really have to work at it on landing. We're lucky the tail didn't break off."

May walked to the tarmac to get a breath of fresh air. Mechanics walked around the tail of the plane looking for damage. Curious, she walked around to check things out for herself. A mechanic peered at the tail. She stood next to him, following his gaze. She couldn't spot anything unusual, but it was dark outside and difficult to see. The mechanic pointed upward.

"It's kinda flat there where it should be kinda round," he said. "Right there, see? I guess it'll be okay, at least until you get to New York, and they can take another look at it. You're lucky you didn't break the plane in half. These old crates can take a pretty good beating, fortunately."

He shook his head and uttered one of those phrases airline people were so fond of.

"I guess any landing you walk away from is a good one, right?"

He laughed, slapped May on the back, and walked away.

"Right," she replied to no one in particular.

They prepared to ferry the empty plane to New York. Derrick was red-faced and silent as he re-boarded. No one said a word to him. Just before they closed the door to leave, a customs agent checking the plane hustled up the aisle.

"Don't leave until I get off," he chuckled.

He had something in his hand.

"What do you have there?" May asked.

"Someone smuggled a bird in."

He displayed an empty homemade wooden birdcage, small, brown, and very dirty.

"He probably has it stuffed in his coat pocket."

"Do you think you'll find him?" May asked.

"No, he's probably through customs by now," the agent said. "People do this stuff all the time to avoid quarantining their animals."

"Poor thing, I hope it lives."

"Yeah," the agent replied. "And I hope it isn't sick." He ducked out the door. "You folks have a good trip. Goodnight."

PART FOUR:
Expecting the Unexpected, Spring 1983

CHAPTER SEVENTEEN

May looked into Jessie's eyes, determining when she would make her move. They had discovered the basketball court a few blocks from their house some months earlier and now made good use of it. "I can't believe that I'll have been flying for a year next month," Jessie said.

She dribbled the basketball.

"It's two years for me," May answered, as she blocked.

Jessie made a quick dodge around her and sank a lay-up.

"Nice shot," May said.

Inside, she smarted a little that Jessie had gotten around her so easily. Jessie stopped to catch her breath.

"I was furloughed for January and February, but I don't have to count that, do I?" Jessie said.

May stood, dribbling the ball slowly. "I'll never tell."

"And I managed to get off reserve this month too, I can't believe that either!" Jessie said. "April and I'm not on reserve! You and I can finally get to work on ground school, and I can spend more time with Vic. I'd like to see if this relationship is going anywhere."

May grabbed the basketball and threw it at the backboard. The ball bounced off across the court.

"I think you two make a real cute couple, a flight attendant and a fireman," May said. "The two of you can save the world."

Jessie looked at her, no longer paying attention to the basketball.

"You still miss Jake, don't you? Even after two years."

May stared.

"More and more all the time," she admitted. "I didn't realize how good I had it until I dated a few jerks during the last two years."

"Why don't you try to get in touch with him?"

May shook her head.

"I don't know how," she said. "I told him how I needed to be free to see the world. We could never have a relationship with me gone so much. And he wanted out too, remember? Anyway, he's probably married by now. Some other smart girl had to have snapped him up."

"You don't know that."

"No, I don't," May said. "But something tells me that I won't get a second chance with him."

There was an awkward pause. "I looked at your line of flying and your schedule overlaps mine quite a bit," May told Jessie in an attempt to change the subject. "We should run into each other in San Juan this month. Of all the times that I've been there, I finally get to stay!"

Jessie nodded. "We do have to work through Chicago and Miami to get there."

"It's a long work day, but the layover is nice, so it's worth it. It's still pretty chilly here in April, and the weather will be great down there. And," May added, "the hotel is right on the beach."

"Spring break, here we come!" Jessie said gleefully.

Jessie ran for the basketball, scooped it up, and charged toward the basket.

A few days later, May finally touched down in San Juan. The hot and muggy air hit her full blast as she dragged her bag from the plane into the jetway. A fresh crew was approaching from the opposite direction to take the DC-8 to Miami. Spotting Jessie, she stopped for a short chat.

"How was your layover?" she asked.

"Really nice," Jessie answered with a smile. "A bunch of us went to the fort in old San Juan. There are some pretty good restaurants in that area, too, so make sure you check one out."

She glanced hastily toward the rest of her crew boarding the plane.

"I'd better go. See you in New York," Jessie said.

May and her co-workers went to dinner that night at a small seafood place close to the hotel, and afterwards decided to have a nightcap in the hotel bar. As they entered the lobby, their captain stopped them.

"I'm glad I caught you together," he said to the group, his face somber.

A chill shuddered through May.

"Our San Juan to Miami flight got hijacked to Cuba."

May's mind flew to her roommate.

"I don't know much yet, but I do know everyone is okay so far," the captain continued. "We should hear more by tomorrow. I've asked operations to call me with any news. That's the plane we're supposed to use tomorrow, so we could be delayed." He turned to leave. "Don't worry too much, I think things will be okay," he assured them. "It's probably another homesick person from the Mariel boat lift from a couple of years ago.

That's who hijacked that Eastern Airlines flight two weeks back. Maybe someone else is having second thoughts about his new life in America."

"It's not like they have a lot of options," May said. "You can't even make a phone call to Cuba."

"True," the captain said. "And a plane is quicker and safer than a crappy, leaky boat."

That night, May awoke in her bed, thinking about Jessie. *She's okay. I'm sure she's okay.* She tossed for a few more minutes and fell back to sleep. The following morning, she walked into the coffee shop at 7:30 a.m. and found most of the crew sitting there, just as anxious to find out more about the hijacking. May squeezed herself into a seat and ordered a cup of coffee.

"Do you know anything yet?" she asked the senior flight attendant.

The other woman almost responded when all eyes shifted to the captain striding across the room. He pulled a chair over, ordered coffee, and sat down.

"Here's what operations told me," he said with authority. "Right after takeoff for Miami, a middle-aged man locked himself in the can. He started passing notes under the bathroom door saying that he had a bomb in there and he would detonate it if he wasn't taken to Havana. The crew took him at his word, diverted the plane to Cuba, and the Cubans let them land. I thought that was pretty decent of them, considering we don't have any diplomatic relations there."

"What happened next?" the senior flight attendant asked. "What did the crew do?"

"The captain told the flight attendants to evacuate the passengers using the escape slides in case the guy really did have a bomb. Nobody got hurt in the evacuation, and the hijacker gave up to the Cuban officials, no struggle, no fuss."

The whole crew exhaled in relief.

"What about the plane?" May asked. "How soon is it coming? Are we getting a different one?"

"This is where things get interesting," the captain answered. "The plane was there on the ground all night because the mechanics at the Havana airport had no idea how to re-pack the escape slides. The crew couldn't take off without having working slides, and they couldn't call the company for re-packing instructions because there's no direct phone line between the U.S. and Cuba. So they patched a phone line through Czechoslovakia and linked that with the U.S." He laughed. "It would be a miracle if they got the freakin' instructions right, a bunch of Spanish-speaking Cubans, talking through Czechoslovakians to a bunch of good ol' boys in Tennessee. Yessiree, I bet that was something." A waiter arrived and set the captain's coffee in front of him. He took a long swallow. "When they were finally ready to go, they had the damnedest time getting everybody back on the plane. The passengers and flight attendants were all in the gift shop buying up Havana cigars and every t-shirt they could find with the word 'Cuba' on it!"

Eventually, they got the plane to Puerto Rico, and May and her crew flew home. May rushed home to see Jessie.

"Did you get one?" May shouted.

"One what?"

"T-shirt, of course!" May replied.

"Yes, I got a t-shirt," Jessie said. "Do you want to see it?"

May nodded eagerly.

"Of course I want to see it."

Jessie pulled out the bright orange shirt, the word "Cuba" in big, bold letters across the front.

"That's nice. Wish I had one," May said. "But seriously, you were really lucky things."

"It wasn't too bad," Jessie said casually. "The officials in Cuba were really nice. I think the hijacker just wanted to go home, but I didn't feel like he was actually dangerous. He didn't really have a bomb."

"Something to tell your grandchildren," May said.

That wasn't the end of the Cuba hijackings. A few days later, May and Louisa stood talking in the crew lounge waiting to work their separate trips to Puerto Rico and Los Angeles. Kathleen, who was flying with Louisa, entered the room, spotted them, and walked over quickly.

"Did you guys hear? Eastern just got hijacked to Cuba again."

"Again?" Louisa gasped. "That's three in the last ten days!"

"I've got to get off of this route," May muttered. "Maybe that's the last one. You know what they say, things always happen in threes."

The rest of her crew streamed in.

"I've got to go to my briefing," May said. "You two have a nice trip."

Her flights through Chicago and Miami were full but uneventful. Then they filled the DC-8 to capacity in Miami and took off for Puerto Rico. May was making it a point these days to look out the window just after takeoff. A gigantic piece of artwork was on display in the waters of Biscayne Bay, eleven little islands skirted in bright pink polypropylene material. The artists, Christo and Jean-Claude, called it "Surrounded Islands." May couldn't decide if it was art or an ecological disaster. She was sharing the jumpseat with Patrick, her old acquaintance from her Rome trip.

"What do you think? Do you like it?"

Patrick grimaced. "Not my color."

The plane arrived late in San Juan, and the new crew, which included Jessie, waited at the end of the jetway. They were working the flight back to Miami. Both crews stopped to talk and after some good-natured joking about the recent hijackings, they parted.

"Hey," May called after Jessie, "if you guys do get hijacked, get me a t-shirt this time, will you?"

Jessie turned and waved.

"Sure, no problem."

May went to the hotel for dinner and had a nice evening in San Juan. At 11 p.m., her phone rang. It was her senior flight attendant.

"Meet me out in the hall," she said and abruptly hung up.

May scrambled to the door and stepped out. The entire crew was in the hall, including the pilots.

"Another hijacking," the captain said simply.

"Jesus," May whispered.

They all thought about the jokes they'd made to the other crew in the jetway. May bit her tongue as she remembered her t-shirt comment.

"We won't know much for a while, so you might as well all go to bed. It'll probably be morning before I get more information. Goodnight, ladies and gentlemen."

The captain turned and walked to his room, and the others drifted away. May opened her door, climbed into bed, and tossed and turned all night. For the second time that month, May arrived early in the coffee shop and joined the rest of her crew. The co-pilot was there this time, filling everyone in.

"The hijacker was a woman," he said.

The rest of the crew bristled.

"Was she old or young?" the senior flight attendant asked.

"Young. According to the ticket agent, nice, well-educated, and normal. A little on the Bohemian side. Absolutely no indications of her intentions. Once they reached cruising altitude, she went to the senior flight attendant with a flare gun in her hand, and said 'Take me to Havana.' The officials were great again and let the plane land. Then, the passengers just walked down the jetway."

"What happened to the hijacker?" May asked.

"She turned herself over to the officials, no struggle. The bottom line is, the passengers and crew are all fine. They're all going on to Miami and Chicago."

May suddenly laughed out loud. The others turned, staring at her.

"One of my roommates is on that crew. This is the second time she's been hijacked this month!"

There was silence until the senior flight attendant broke it.

"She could qualify for the Guinness Book of World Records. You should tell her to check that out."

May couldn't wait to get home and talk to Jessie.

"Hey!" May yelled as she pushed open the front door.

Jessie was on the phone in the kitchen. She finished her conversation and hung up. May gave her a hug.

"Everybody keeps calling me. They want to know all the hijacking details. I must have told the story a million times so far."

"You are a big star, after all," May laughed, "being hijacked twice in one month. Can you tell the story one more time?"

"The passengers were all on board, we took off, you know, all the usual stuff. We got to cruising altitude and this woman wearing a turban comes up to Mayalyn, our senior," Jessie said. "Have you flown with her? Anyway, this woman comes to the galley and mumbles something, and sweet Mayalyn leans over and says, 'What, hon?' The lady pulled out a flare gun and stuck it in her ribs and said she wanted to go to Havana."

"Jesus," May said.

"She made Mayalyn sit with her on the front jumpseat the whole way to Havana as a hostage. They were sitting there a long time, and Mayalyn really needed to use the bathroom. The hijacker wouldn't let her go, so Mayalyn got her a replacement hostage while she used the can. So, who does she pick? Liz Wilson."

"No! I forgot you were flying with her this month," May said. "She's crazy! I was on a layover with her in L.A. once. A bunch of us rented a car and went to Disneyland. She spent the whole time mooning people out the back window."

Jessie nodded. "She was not happy. She kept yelling at Mayalyn through the bathroom door that she would never do her another favor because this one used them all up. It was kind of funny, and you could see that the hijacker didn't know what to do at all. I was afraid she'd shoot Liz just to shut her up."

"You know," May mused, "Liz told us on that Disney trip that she'd been in a bad accident once, and that she has a plate in her head. Maybe that's why she's so goofy."

"Could be. Could be. Anyway, we got to the airport and the passengers got off and, of course, went to the gift shop."

"T-shirt?" May said hopefully.

Jessie shook her head. "Eastern Airlines cleaned them all out. The funniest thing was seeing the Cuban officials. They spotted me and started laughing their asses off. They came up, shook my hand, and gave me a big welcome back for my second visit."

May shook her head and smiled. "The hijacking score is tied at two a piece, between us and Eastern," May said. "I wonder how long this will go on."

A few days later, May was sitting in the kitchen when Louisa and Marta returned from their Los Angeles flight.

"There's been another one!" Marta yelled as they walked through the door. "And Jessie wasn't on it!"

"That's a relief. What happened this time?" May asked.

"A guy smuggled a liquid on board that he said was flammable. He threatened to ignite it if the plane didn't go to Cuba," Marta said.

"These hijackers are original," May said dryly. "No two of them have used the same method."

"Things turned out okay again," Marta commented. "I think everybody has gotten the routine down. I wonder when the Cuban government is going to tire of this and turned the planes away."

"I don't know," May answered, "But I just did my schedule for next month, and I bid to do those trips again. That schedule is the only one that gives me the time off and extra money I need for ground school."

"Cheer up," Marta answered. "Maybe the Cubans will have more t-shirts in the gift shop by then!"

The hijackings ended as abruptly as they'd begun. Perhaps because of improvements in security, or because everyone who wanted to go to Cuba made it there. Whatever the reason, the hijacking craze was over. May never got a t-shirt.

CHAPTER EIGHTEEN

"Hi, everybody!!" May and Jessie called in unison to greet their crew.

"So you're filling in for our guys who are on vacation this week," said Olivia, the senior flight attendant. "It'll be great to fly together again, May."

"Jessie and I are trying to fly as much as we can," May replied. "We're working on our pilot's license and need extra money."

May had flown with Olivia several times and liked the blonde, green-eyed 26-year-old. Olivia was dating Les, the captain piloting their evening flight to San Juan. He was several years older than Olivia, but they made a good couple. They liked to have fun, and their personalities complemented each other.

The flight from New York to Puerto Rico was routine. Passengers disembarked on arrival, and the crew waited while the airplane was serviced for the return flight. Boarding went smoothly. The passengers settled in their seats. Olivia stepped from the cockpit. She gathered the other flight attendants.

"Someone just phoned in a bomb threat for this flight."

"Jesus, Mary, and Joseph," Jessie groaned. "I swear this place is just jinxed. This airport has got to be on some ancient Indian burial ground."

The captain announced a delay without mentioning the bomb threat and directed the passengers to empty the plane. After the last one disembarked, he joined the crew.

"Ground personnel said they'd appreciate help searching for the bomb. Nobody is required to stay and search, but you can, if you want to."

Les returned to the cockpit. The flight attendants discussed the situation.

"You heard the captain," Olivia said. "Nobody has to stay and help."

Two new flight attendants, one man and one woman, (with barely two weeks experience between them) started toward the jetway.

"We need to do something in the terminal," the young man said nervously. "We'll be right back."

The rest elected to stay and help. Les got on the P.A. He offered advice about working together and being systematic.

"Be sure you check all of the catering in the galleys," he added. "That would be a good place for a bomb."

May and Jessie popped their heads from the rear galley, where they were already checking the supplies. From the cockpit door, Les gave a quick thumbs up as they inspected containers of food. Every corner of the cabin was thoroughly checked. Their searches turned up nothing, not in the airplane cabin nor in the belly of the plane. The new departure time grew close.

"Another hoax," May said to Olivia.

Olivia nodded, glancing at her watch. "Looks like they're about to re-board the passengers."

A customer service agent entered the aircraft, stopped briefly in the cockpit, then hurried away. Les stepped out.

"Someone just phoned in another threat. Said that the bomb will go off an hour from right now. They're a little more concerned here on the ground at this point. They want to check the plane more thoroughly. They want the airplane at the end of the field so they check it inch by inch. You guys don't need to stay onboard. Anybody that wants to go can go."

Most of the flight attendant crew exited the plane this time. The pilots, Olivia, May, and Jessie stayed behind.

"What are you two sticking around for?" Olivia asked her fellow flight attendants.

"I don't know," May answered. "Curiosity, I guess."

"I want to see how they search the plane," Jessie said,

The aircraft was pushed back from the gate, and they taxied out. The three young women squeezed into the two cockpit jumpseats behind the pilots. May couldn't be sure which direction led to the terminal once they lost sight of the lights. From her vantage point, it was nearly impossible to see anything behind them. May tapped Les lightly on the shoulder.

"You guys ever think about getting rearview mirrors for this thing?"

Les turned, smiled, and then returned to his task. Once they reached their destination, the engines were shut down and the inside of the airplane went dark. The girls walked into the cabin. May reached for one of the emergency flashlights, hesitating before pulling it from its bracket.

Olivia knew exactly what she was thinking. The senior flight attendant even laughed a little.

"Yes, May, this does qualify as an emergency. You are allowed to use the flashlight!" she said.

May smiled sheepishly. Every bit of emergency equipment on the aircraft was sealed, even the flashlights. If a seal was broken, the reason for its use needed to be documented. She pulled the light loose and it came on automatically, as it was supposed to.

They gathered a few soft drinks from the galley and returned to the cockpit. Minutes ticked by. There were no mobile stairs attached to the doors at either end of the plane, so there was no escape unless they popped the emergency slides.

It suddenly struck May.

This was her second bomb scare. It was an interesting comparison, this bomb scare and the one that occurred on her very first flight. She'd changed enormously since then. She thought of her apprehension that day, her first day on the job, having to deal with the prospect of a bomb on board a plane filled with hundreds of people. She'd been so green that day, green and afraid, just like the two new people on her present flight. She thought of her many experiences over the last few years, more situations than most people would deal with in a lifetime.

I've matured some, I guess, she thought.

Bomb sniffing dogs went through the passenger baggage in the belly of the plane. They found nothing.

"Looks like we're safe, boys and girls," Les declared. "We can saddle up and head back."

With security measures completed, the company wanted the plane in the air as soon as possible. Equity decided to have the DC-8 taxi back to the gate.

"Les," Jessie said to the captain as the plane moved toward the terminal, "we still have about ten minutes left until the bomb is supposed to blow, right?"

"Right."

"Aren't we going to get back just in time? I mean… if there is a bomb, and they didn't find it, won't we get back just in time to blow up on the gate in the terminal?"

He turned and faced her.

"Yeah, I guess so," he grinned. "So, we all agree that this is not a genius move on the company's part? Here's what we'll do. I'll park, and I think we'll all get off, stretch our legs and wait until zero hour passes before we board passengers. The hell with what the company wants."

He winked.

"One of the perks of being in command of the ship," he said.

With just two minutes to spare, the crew walked down the jetway and into the terminal. They walked quickly from the gate and joined the rest of the flight attendants sitting some distance away. May glanced at her watch and waited for the final moments to pass. The crew held their collective breath for a split second.

Nothing. No explosion, nothing.

A few passengers disappeared during the delay, perhaps discovering the real reason that they didn't take off on time. But for the most part they'd stayed, confident that everything would be okay.

"You've got to hand it to these people," Olivia said as they reboarded. "The common man. Takes some licks but always bravely returns."

"Amen," May said.

They loaded up and flew into the night.

CHAPTER NINETEEN

"These flying schedules are getting worse and worse," May said in disgust as she threw down the bid sheet. "And it's summer! I've got a really bad feeling with the way these schedules have been looking."

Jessie winced. "I know. More and more of the charters are going to Saber Air this summer," she said. "The latest scuttlebutt I heard is that Flint wants us to be all scheduled flying and Saber will be all charter."

"The rumors are really flying," May said. "Saber flys charters all over Central America! It scares me more and more that Flint will run Equity into the ground and keep Saber."

Jessie nodded forlornly. "That would make sense for him," she said. "We work a lot of hours with our crappy contract, but those guys get worked to death since they're non-union. He could take all of the business over there, shut us down, and just have one non-union carrier."

"Well, I hope I get this one schedule I'm bidding on," May said. "It has a trip to Brussels, a charter to Frankfurt and Lisbon, and the rest of the month is Puerto Rico layovers. And a Zurich trip that carries over next month."

She turned to Jessie. She wanted to forget the office politics for a while.

"By the way, do you want to study for our ground school test some more?" May asked.

For weeks, May and Jessie had attended a day-long class each Saturday, learning about the forces and systems that allow airplanes to fly. Pilots needed to understand navigation, safety, and the rules and regulations of operating an aircraft, as well as all types of weather and a plane's performance in those conditions. It was a huge amount of information to absorb, but studying with each other made the task more manageable. They would have to pass a rigorous test as part of the requirements for a pilot's license.

"Yeah," Jessie answered. "We need to pass that test. Then, we can concentrate on flying lessons."

"As soon as I find out whether I've passed, I'm starting... AGAIN!" May said. "I've been down this road so many times, so many starts and stops. Well, you know what? The weather is nice and I've got a little money put aside."

Several days later, May and Jessie dragging their suitcases up the steps to the beach house after their latest flight. Louisa opened the front door and popped her head out.

"How was your trip?" she asked.

Louisa ushered them inside.

"Great," May said sarcastically. "I got sick in Lisbon and stayed that way all the way to Frankfurt. My senior dragged me out to this really great seafood place in Lisbon. It was spectacular. So was the food. I coughed and hacked so badly that three waiters and the maître d' ran up with glasses of water. And then on the way back to the hotel we saw two guys having a knife fight in the street."

May sneezed. Louisa took May's suitcase.

"So much for your best trip this month," Louisa said. "Don't the rest of your trips layover in San Juan?"

May blew her nose. "All except the last one," she said. "I hope the warm tropical air will do me good!"

The senior flight attendant on the flight to Puerto Rico was Nancy: blonde, forty, and a 20-year veteran. She looked like someone's mom but acted like a teenager. She'd buddy-bid to fly with her best friend, Shelly, a 30-year-old brunette and also a free spirit. In addition to May and Jessie, the crew included a dark-eyed brunette named Chloe. She'd been raised in Maine by French-Canadian parents and spoke fluent French. The plane landed in San Juan in the early evening. After dropping their baggage at the hotel, the crew set out for a favorite restaurant of Shelly's located in Old San Juan.

"The food there is great," Shelly said. "Their chicken stew is better than sex."

"Have you told your husband that?" Nancy smirked.

"You just wait, you'll see."

It proved to be a lovely spot close to the thick-walled fortress that had protected the city from storms and pirates for centuries. The crew sat on an outdoor patio under palm trees and a starry sky, enjoying the meal. After dinner, they strolled around the fortress and hunted for a place with after-dinner drinks.

The club they chose was crowded, making it difficult to find seats together. As the crew juggled chairs around a vacated table, they failed to notice the tall, dark-haired young man at the bar observing them. They'd nearly finished their drinks and were discussing getting a taxi when he made his move. The attractive stranger followed the crew to the door, stopped them, and introduced himself. His name was Jason. He was nice, extremely polite, and offered to give some of them a lift to the hotel in his car.

"You can't all fit into one taxi," he said earnestly. "I'll gladly take you."

Nancy, Shelly, and Chloe accepted his offer. May, Jessie, and the pilots took a taxi.

"He seems nice enough," May said quietly to Jessie, "but he is a total stranger."

She leaned over the seat to speak to the driver.

"Follow him to the hotel and don't let that car out of your sight."

They arrived without incident. Nancy, Shelly, and Chloe invited the handsome stranger to join them for another drink in the hotel bar. Jessie decided to tag along with them, but May declined.

"I'm so tired, you guys. Have fun and I'll see you in the morning."

The tropical heat of the sun pouring through the hotel room windows when she awoke the next day. She donned her bathing suit, threw shorts and a t-shirt on over it, and walked to the beach. The others were already there. They were teasing Chloe.

"Did someone make a love connection?" May asked mischievously. "Fill me in."

"He's an FBI agent," Chloe said coyly. "And he's really nice. We're going to get together on our next trip."

"Wow, that's great! If it works out, you can see him on the rest of our trips this month."

"I know, I know."

Chloe was smitten. Three days later, they returned to San Juan on another flight, but with a few changes to the crew. One of the scheduled flight attendants had traded her trip with a girl named Emily. Emily was having a hot and heavy romance with a pilot named Ricardo, the captain working the San Juan flight.

Emily had traded her trip for this one so that they would be able to spend time together. Emily was attractive in a stern way. She was tall, pale, wore her light brown hair in tight curls, and her makeup included heavy mascara that set off her piercing green eyes.

Ricardo was the polar opposite. He was Spanish, but just wasn't quite the image of the Latin lover he wanted to be. So he helped himself along. He was short, but wore shoes with elevated heels. He was going gray, so he dyed his hair black. A little too black. He didn't get the shade quite right and it had a purplish tinge. His too-white teeth were false. Yet, in spite of his appearance, he managed to find attractive girlfriends. He was seeing Emily now, but years before he'd dated Nancy.

The crew checked into the high-rise hotel, picked up their room keys, and took the elevator to their floor. Usually, crews were assigned to rooms overlooking the parking lot, but every once in a while, someone got lucky and got a room with an ocean view.

As luck would have it, both Nancy and Ricardo got ocean-side rooms right next to each other. Nancy dropped her bags inside and got an idea. She walked across the hall to Chloe's room and knocked on the door. Jason opened it. He'd met Chloe in the hotel lobby and accompanied her to her room.

"I want you two to have my room. What do you think?" Nancy said.

"Thanks, Nancy," Chloe answered. "That's really nice of you."

"You two have a nice time," Nancy answered as they swapped room keys.

With much of the crew paired up, May and Jessie ate dinner together in the hotel restaurant.

"It's all couples on this trip," Jessie complained.

Jessie had recently broken up with Vic, her fireman boyfriend.

"What is it with us anyway? It never seems to work out for us," she lamented. "You go out on a few dates and then break it off and me, I can't figure out what I do wrong, but you're still not over Jake. How long are you going to pine away?"

"You're always bringing this up," May snapped. "I don't know, and I'm not pining. I'm choosy."

Jessie finished her dessert.

"Do you want to take a quick walk on the beach?" May asked. "Fresh air before bed always makes me sleep better."

The girls paid for their meal and strolled out on the sand as the sun was setting. The summer air was warm, but a light breeze made the evening comfortable. May took off her sandals and walked in the surf.

"You're right about me, I suppose," she told Jessie. "About how I feel about Jake. What really happened between you and Vic, anyway?"

Jessie pointed to a crab that had popped out of a hole in the sand and scurried away.

"I don't really know what I do wrong," Jessie answered. "I like them well enough in the beginning and then I lose interest."

"I think you haven't met the right one yet. And maybe you're a closet romantic. Like you want a prince to rescue you."

"You mean like that guy up there?"

Jessie gestured into the distance, toward their hotel.

"Huh?" May said.

"There's a guy, way up, look. He must be twelve stories up."

"What the hell is he doing?" May exclaimed.

Jessie squinted. It was nearly dark and difficult to see.

"I don't know, but he's only wearing his underwear," she announced.

"He's climbing over the balcony!" May cried in disbelief. "Omigod! He's a thief or a murderer or something! Come on!"

The two ran down the beach to the hotel, through the lobby, and to the front desk. Breathless, they described what they'd seen to the desk clerk.

"*Dios mío,*" he replied.

The clerk called for hotel security. The girls waited anxiously by the desk while the security guard investigated. After what seemed like an eternity, he returned.

"I checked several floors, ladies. I saw nothing. Everything is quiet. Are you sure you didn't just see someone enjoying the sunset from their balcony? It is quite dark now."

"That guy jumped from one balcony to another twelve floors up!" Jessie insisted.

"I will patrol the floors all night tonight," he responded reassuringly. "If anyone is there, I will find him. Please do not worry, ladies. Sleep peacefully tonight."

The girls thanked him and walked to the elevator. May pushed the number for their floor.

"I don't know how peacefully I'm going to sleep," Jessie said warily. "I know what I saw."

They headed to their rooms and promised to return to the beach in the morning. By the time Jessie and May reached the sand to fulfill that promise, Nancy, Shelly, and Chloe had gathered and were laughing loudly. May and Jessie approached them. The two threw their towels beside the other girls and flopped on top.

"What's so funny?" May asked.

Nancy was beside herself, tears of laughter running down her face.

"You're not going to believe this," she said.

Jessie rubbed her hands together. "Oh boy, this sounds like it's going to be good," she said, making herself comfortable.

"You guys know that I switched rooms with Chloe and that Jason came to stay with her last night."

"Yeah, sure," Jessie answered.

"And you know Ricardo's room was next door to that room."

"Right," the others said.

"He had no idea that Chloe and I switched."

"Is Emily staying in his room with him?" May asked.

Nancy's face contorted again in laughter.

"She couldn't have been," she said, "not with what he did."

"Why? What did he do?" Jessie asked.

"Our rooms are all on the twelfth floor, right?" Nancy said. "That idiot climbed over his balcony railing to get to what he thought was my balcony? Then he was stretching and straining, trying to look inside the room."

"My God!" May gasped. "The guy we saw from the beach!"

"I guess he still wants you, Nancy," Shelly said.

"Nostalgia for the good old days?" May suggested. "What did he do when he saw Chloe and Jason?"

This time, Chloe erupted in laughter.

"Jason saw him first," she said. "He caught a glimpse in the mirror of this middle-aged guy in his underwear hanging over the balcony and he thought he must be either a burglar or a psycho."

"He was in his underwear! I knew it!" Jessie shouted.

"Shh! Let me finish," Chloe said. "So Jason jumps out of bed, grabs his .357 magnum. He is an FBI agent after all. He runs to the balcony. Poor Ricardo sees Jason with his gun and absolutely freaks out. He must have realized that he was about to get his ass shot off! He flew over that balcony like Superman to get back to his own room."

The mental image of Ricardo risking his neck to spy on his old girlfriend only to be met by a man with a giant firearm was too much. May and Jessie also collapsed into the sand, rolling with laughter. Everyone looked up to see Jason approaching from the direction of the hotel.

"I didn't know what was happening," he said in his soft, Hispanic accent. "All I know is that I saw this guy looking in the window, so I grabbed my weapon and went after him."

He was almost apologetic.

"I don't think he'll mention it to anyone," Nancy reassured him. "Especially to Emily."

"But aren't you curious why he did it, Nancy?" May asked.

Nancy shook her head. "No, I don't think so. Some questions are best left unanswered."

The girls spent the rest of the afternoon enjoying the sun and buying the occasional refreshment from the vendors hawking their wares on the beach.

"Coca cola, Pexi cola, Sebben up, Buuuuudwizer!" called one as he walked by with a cooler full of beverages.

Another passed with delicious slabs of pineapple.

"Very, very, sweet pineapple!" he chanted in a singsong voice. "You don't like, you don't pay!"

A young male windsurfing instructor sat nearby under a large umbrella. Business was slow, so he allowed the girls to try free of charge. May was able to stand up on the board, but kept pulling it over on herself. After several attempts, she gave up and sat reflectively on the beach.

"I don't think we have enough trips left this month for me to get this," she said ruefully.

The afternoon disappeared. The girls ran to their rooms, threw on their uniforms, and met the rest of the crew in the hotel lobby. Nancy, Shelly, Chloe, May, and Jessie talked among themselves as they rode the van to the airport. Emily did not join in the conversation. Ricardo sat wordlessly, not daring to glance their way.

Chloe flew the same route the next month so that she could continue to see Jason. They remained involved for some time. A few months later, May ran into Nancy in the crew lounge and asked if she knew how Chloe and Jason were getting along. Nancy told her a strange story.

"They got really close, you know, got along fine. Chloe wanted Jason to meet her family in Maine," she said. "They had everything planned when he disappeared."

May was startled. "What do you mean, disappeared?"

"Disappeared without a trace. Chloe tried to find him but couldn't. He never called her, and she never saw or heard from him again. It was as if he'd fallen off the face of the earth. You know what's really creepy? She got in touch with the FBI. They've never heard of Jason."

May was dumbfounded. "How is Chloe?"

"Crushed, of course. Distraught."

May mulled over the information.

"What do you think?" May asked. "I mean, who do you think he was?"

"Who knows? A criminal, drug dealer, undercover agent? Maybe he was a psycho. Who knows. Whatever he was, he was nice."

They hugged and parted to head towards their separate airplanes.

Never get in a car with a stranger, May thought as she made her way to the plane.

CHAPTER TWENTY

"Last trip of the month together. And we're the only two females on this crew, can you believe it?"

Jessie held up an imaginary magazine, pretending to read the title of an article, as they stood in a quiet part of the plane together.

"I flew to Zurich with an all guy crew," Jessie laughed. "Sounds like a movie title."

"All guy or all gay?" May remarked.

"I heard that! Shame! Shame on you!" Sam said.

May and Sam had flown several trips together. May stuck her tongue out at him.

"Don't flaunt it unless you mean to use it, honey."

"You wish," May said. "Hey, work the beverage cart with me?"

"Yes, yes," Sam said. "You know I'd do anything for you."

"Tell me, Sam," May started. "Why are so many gay guys charming, witty, and funny?"

"You left out handsome."

"Did I? You notice I left out modest, too?"

"Ouch!"

Jessie broke in. "Get going guys, the food is ready."

Sam chuckled. "Let's go, May. First one to hit a passenger in the head with the cart has to buy at the bar."

"You're a sick man, Sam."

After the flight, most of the crew, including May and Jessie, met for dinner at a small restaurant close to their Zurich hotel.

"Does anyone know where Sam went?" May asked, scanning the area for her friend.

"I think he was meeting someone," one of the others answered. "Had a hot date."

"Oh," she answered, trying to hide her disappointment.

Later, upon returning to their hotel, May and Jessie spied Sam stepping into the elevator with an attractive, well-dressed young man.

"Must be the hot date," May whispered to Jessie. "He's cute! I'll have to ask Sam about him tomorrow."

The next day's flight to New York was full. The crew had no time to talk and relax until after the meal service. As May and Jessie prepared to eat their dinner, they overheard Sam being teased by two of their male co-workers.

"Better sit down, take it easy now Sam. You had a rough night," one joked. "Legs are probably tired."

The two girls giggled as Sam relayed his considerable sexual exploits in his usual humorous way.

"You think he remembers that we're here and we can hear everything he's saying?" Jessie whispered.

May chuckled. "I don't think it matters."

May never considered herself sheltered, but since joining Equity Air, she had spent a lot of time in different countries and with people of different backgrounds and experiences. She made a lot of gay friends at the airline. She didn't really think about their lifestyles until some discussion after first aid training made her aware of some dangers she hadn't known about.

*****

Some time later, the tires of May's old Buick squealed as she rounded the turn into the employee entrance at Kennedy Airport.

"Take it easy, will you?" Jessie shouted. "I want to get there alive!"

Jessie hit the inside of the passenger door. Louisa flung into Marta in the back seat and hissed something in German.

"I think she's swearing at you," Jessie said.

"We absolutely can't be late!" May hollered. "This is Doris Schultz teaching, remember? What do you think she'll do to us if we're late?"

"What do you think she'll do if we're dead?"

"It doesn't matter, we're here. Quick! Run! We can just make it!"

They'd reached the annual day of training, when crew members brushed up on their safety skills. Essentially, all flight attendants had to re-qualify for their jobs each year. This meant practicing— opening aircraft doors again, going over ditching procedures, and all the fun stuff they never really wanted to have to do. Equity didn't send their flight attendants back to Tennessee for recurrent training. They borrowed facilities and equipment at Kennedy.

Any flight attendant who failed was immediately taken off flight status. This was May's second recurrent training, but that didn't ease the anxiety about meeting Doris Schultz's tough standards. She, Louisa, Jessie, and Marta had studied earnestly before the big day.

Each year, special emphasis was placed on one responsibility, a topic receiving extra attention based on events that had taken place within the airline industry that year. This year, they were spending extra time on first aid. All four girls successfully renewed their CPR certification, as did the whole class. Afterward, Doris and the visiting medical technicians took questions from the group. The questions ran the gambit from heart attacks to broken eardrums. Then, the conversation took a peculiar turn. Several flight attendants were asking questions about drug use, its effects on the immune system, and illegal drugs in particular. May noticed a pattern to the questioning.

"Why are all the men asking about this stuff?" she said to Marta in a low voice.

Baffled, Marta replied, "I don't know."

The four roommates discussed it as they drove home.

"There have been stories in the news lately about a new disease, one that attacks the immune system," Marta said. "It's hitting gay men particularly hard. I read that the medical community thinks that maybe the problems are coming from a lifestyle that abuses the body. You know, too much drugs and too much sex. And most of our male co-workers, our friends, are gay. They must be scared."

In the months and years that followed, May lost many of her friends in the AIDS epidemic, including her good friend Sam. She thought about him often, especially of that trip to Zurich. Sam's dating life had offered a window allowing her to imagine how the disease spread around the world.

But in the end, none of that changed the fact that these smart, personable, and hard-working men were her friends.

CHAPTER TWENTY-ONE

September morning sun brightened the kitchen as May and Jessie sat at the table drinking coffee. May bit into a whole wheat bagel liberally slathered with cream cheese. She smacked her lips in satisfaction.

"I won't be living New York forever, and the thing I'll miss the most will be the bagels," she said.

"What do you mean?" Jessie sniffed. "You can get bagels anywhere."

"Not like these," May said. "You only get the really good ones here."

May eagerly looked at her watch.

"I've got to leave for my flying lesson," May said. "What time are you going to yours?"

"This afternoon," Jessie said, "so get the instructor warmed up for me. What do you think of him?"

"He's kind of all over the place," May said. "It's like he's not starting at a beginning point with a skill and teaching it all the way through."

Jessie nodded. "I've noticed that. I've had three lessons. He needs to pick a skill, take us through it step-by-step, and have us practice."

May put her dishes in the sink and headed for the door.

"Let's see what happens today. I'll see you later," she said.

At the small municipal airport on Long Island, May found her instructor waiting near the Cessna 152, a two-seat plane often used for pilot training. May did the required walk-around safety check using the checklist, then climbed inside with the instructor. He was about thirty, nice-looking, rather quiet, and all business. May made several efforts at friendly conversation, but so far was unsuccessful at getting him to talk.

Her instructor allowed her to man the controls on takeoff. The small plane sped down the runway, then climbed into the sky, heading towards the beach. It was a beautiful day, not a cloud in the sky. The brilliant sun reflected off a long stretch of sand. May admired the scenery before she turned her attention to the control panel. The steady hum of the engine suddenly hushed. There was only a muffled whoomp, whoomp, whoomp, of the propeller. May froze.

"We have an emergency," her instructor said staidly.

May waited for him to take control of the situation, but he did nothing. The airplane headed towards the shoreline.

"What are we going to do?" she asked nervously.

The propeller moved slower and slower.

Still, her instructor sat there. He said nothing and made no effort. May's heart dropped. The propeller finally stopped dead in the air. They accelerated on their plunge downward.

At last, when May thought the end was near, he scrambled. He fumbled with something on the floor by his feet, altered the fuel mixture, and ground on the ignition switch for several seconds. The engine finally sprung to life.

The plane recovered quickly, but May sat silently as they gained altitude. Eventually, their time was up, and they turned back to the airport. May found her voice.

"What happened?" she asked, her voice unsteady.

Her instructor shrugged.

"I wanted you to deal with an emergency, so I closed the fuel shut-off valve."

He motioned to a small lever on the floor between them. May said nothing, digging her fingernails into her palms.

"You have to be able to handle emergency situations," he said with an edge in his voice that implied she had failed his test. "There's another airport pretty close, so if we got into trouble I knew we could land."

Internally, May's simmer headed to boil as she flew the plane.

"I didn't think the propeller would stop," her instructor said. "That surprised me."

"Me, too," she said tersely.

May handled the controls until they reached the field. The instructor took over as they entered the airport traffic pattern. After they touched down, she took the controls once more and taxied the plane to the hangar. Still stunned, May climbed into her Buick and drove home.

May soothed her nerves by half-watching the news, drinking a soda, and eating another bagel in the empty house. Jessie walked in.

"You weren't kidding," Jessie.

May didn't answer.

"About the bagels?" Jessie said.

Jessie's face turned serious.

"What's the matter?" Jessie asked.

"How was your lesson today?" May inquired.

"Boring. He let me take off, fly up the beach for a while, and then we flew back."

"Is that it?" May asked.

"Yeah, why? Did you do something else?"

"Oh, yeah," May huffed.

May relayed the events of her lesson.

"You know, it would have been fine if it was a while from now, we'd already gone over emergency procedures," May said. "Shouldn't an instructor teach you… oh say…"

The simmer May had stifled all day finally bubbled over.

"HOW EVERYTHING ON THE PLANE WORKS first?" May hollered. "He hasn't even let me try to LAND the thing yet! I wanted to throw that bastard out of the plane!"

May snapped off the television.

"I've been thinking about this all day, Jessie," she said. "I'm not going back. That guy will get me killed."

"Are you sure that's what you want to do?" Jessie asked. "We've gotten so far—"

"Hell, yes!" May said. "There are other places. I can go to my airport in Connecticut. I can do that and keep my hand in the game until I find something closer."

Jessie frowned. "I wonder if he planned on doing that to me today, too. Maybe he saw your reaction and thought better of it. Maybe we can both do better somewhere else."

May sat, hiding her head in her hands in defeat. "Starting over AGAIN!" she exclaimed. She reflected before she continued. "I don't know Jessie, it's more than just this," May said. "Flying isn't as fun as it was, especially at work. "Saber gets all the good flying and better equipment. Have you been on that unstretched version of the DC-8? That model predates the longer version by years! It's antiquated even by Equity's standards. They insist it's airworthy, but the pilots said they've got more alarms ringing in the cockpit than they get in the flight simulator."

Jessie's jaw tightened. "I'm getting worried, too. Did you hear that two more of our newer stretch DC-8s went to Saber?"

"I didn't know that," May said quietly.

Neither girl said much.

"This is the downhill slide, kiddo," May said at last. "I don't think Equity will bounce back."

A similar conversation happened with May's sister during her next visit home. May pulled into her parents' driveway late one afternoon. She released a huge sigh of relief as she turned the engine off.

This old beater made it home again, she thought.

The 16-year-old car was overheating more frequently these days, especially when she hit traffic. Fortunately, today she'd sailed along without a problem. Lynn sat on the front porch reading a book. She had set it aside when she saw May's car in the driveway. The sisters met on the stoop and hugged.

"How long are you staying?" Lynn asked.

She helped May get her suitcase up the steps.

"A few days," May said. "I wanted to see you before you leave for Veterinary School. That's a lot of work, but I know it's what you've always wanted."

"Thanks. I'm glad you're home. How are you? Is work getting any better?"

"No. It just gets worse. The good flying has all but disappeared, along with more of our planes. Everything goes to Saber now. With the economy improving, there are rumblings about the major carriers hiring again," May said. "They've learned how to compete with the upstarts. If Equity disappears, it's because the owner wants it that way."

"Well, maybe this will be good news," Lynn replied. "You got some mail. Mom put it your room. Let's take your stuff up."

They lugged the suitcase up the stairs. Lynn placed it beside May's childhood bed as May reached for the business letters on the nightstand. She thumbed through them. Each one had the return address of a different major commercial carrier.

"Eastern, Northwest, American, United," she read aloud.

She ripped them open. One after one, an application fell from each. She studied the front of the envelopes, confirming that they were addressed to her at her parents' home.

"I haven't lived here for three years," May mused.

"It looks like the rumors are true. The big airlines are hiring again," Lynn said. "Can I see an application?"

"Sure."

Lynn pulled the contents from the American envelope. She glanced at May.

"This one asks if you can come for an interview."

"What?"

May snatched the paper from her sister's hand. She scanned it.

"It's in a couple of weeks!" May exclaimed.

"Are you going?" Lynn asked.

May nodded slowly. "Of course! My dream was to work for a big airline. I have talked with friends at United, and the flying is so different. You always know where you're going, and if a plane breaks, they can replace it right away. You're not gone for two weeks at a time. Your trip lasts for a few days, and then you're home for a few days. You can have a life and even a relationship."

She responded to all four of the airlines, hoping something would pan out.

PART FIVE:
Change is the Only Constant,
Fall 1983

CHAPTER TWENTY-TWO

May, Marta, Louisa, and Jessie sat quietly around their kitchen table on a mid-October morning, sipping coffee.

"I can't believe it's actually pink," Jessie said, reading her furlough notice. "You think they could at least have made it another color. Did they really have to give us a pink slip?"

"What difference does it make?" Marta said forlornly. "We're still out of a job."

"Maybe it won't last long," Louisa said.

"People can get a seat at a real airline now that's just as cheap as the upstarts," May said. "It's here to stay."

"Let's face it," Jessie said. "We can't afford this house anymore. We live month-to-month, check-to-check. We've got to make plans."

"We're all going to interviews," May said.

"My brother and sister-in-law have an extra room," Marta said quietly. "I can stay with them in New Jersey until I get on my feet."

On the other side of the table, Louisa squirmed.

"What is it, Louisa?" May asked.

"I didn't want to say anything, but..."

"Go ahead," May said.

"I heard from Northeast," Louisa said. "I go for a physical next week. I start training in November."

The girls jumped up, piling into a group hug.

"You're squashing me!" Louisa laughed. "Anyone else heard anything?"

May groaned. "My interview with American Airlines was a disaster. It was eight in the morning after I had worked a trip to Europe. I couldn't get an intelligent answer from my jet-lagged brain."

"Someone else has to have good news," Louisa said.

"Okay," Jessie replied. "You're not going to like this... but I applied to Saber."

The others silenced and dropped back into their chairs.

"Do you want to repeat that?" Marta asked.

"I haven't flown as long as the rest of you," Jessie said, "and I'm not ready to give this up yet. I like this wacky charter stuff."

May rubbed her forehead. "But… do you have to go THERE? Who knows what really goes on there. Do those planes really only carry passengers? Are you going to trust your life to a thug like Flint?"

"Maybe it won't be that bad," Jessie said. "Lots of people work there. Heck, if it turns out to be that bad, I'll quit."

"I hope you know what you're doing," Marta said.

When May didn't hear from any of her applications, she moved home when her money ran out. With no job and no savings, she had no choice. She hated it. To make herself feel useful, she would do random yardwork or surprise the family with dinner. In November, while Louisa was training for Northwest, May grabbed a rake and decided to battle the fallen leaves. The wind insisted on blowing them away before she could bag them.

"Little bastards," she swore.

She chased them across the yard. The mailman pulled in the driveway, shoved a pile of letters into the box, and sped off. May dropped the rake and headed to the mailbox. She fumbled through the letters. She hoped to find one from United Airlines.

Nothing.

Her mother approached from the house. A tear formed in May's eye, and she wiped it, a feeble attempt to hide her emotions from her mom.

"No news?" Mom asked.

May shook her head. "Nothing," she replied. "I don't get it. The group interview went well in Chicago. So did the individual interview. They asked for copies of good letters from passengers at Equity. They said they'd let me know in two weeks. It's been more than two weeks."

Her mother hugged her.

"I didn'r come out for the mail," her mom said. "I knew you'd get that. I came out to tell you that Debi called from Chicago," her mom said. "She wants you to call her back."

"Debi? She works for United."

"Maybe you should ask her what you should do."

"I suppose it couldn't hurt," May said. "Maybe she can find out something."

She phoned Debi right away. They'd been friends since college, and Debi was the first person she knew to get a flying job. She was hired by United Airlines just before deregulation and spent a painful period on furlough when the major carriers were hurting the most.

"Something doesn't sound right," Debi said. "They wouldn't ask for all of those letters if they didn't want you. I'll check around and get back to you."

"Okay," May said weakly. "I need to know one way or the other."

Debi called mid-morning the following day.

"May!" Debi said with an exuberance in her voice May didn't expect. "They have been trying to get in touch with you! They lost your number and address! I gave them the right number, so good luck."

May was speechless. She'd barely gotten off the phone with Debi when it rang again.

"Hi, May," a friendly female voice said on the other end of the line. "This is United Airlines calling to offer you a position…"

May couldn't say yes fast enough.

"Wonderful," the voice said. "We'll send you more information and we look forward to seeing you in January."

May set down the receiver, overwhelmed.

Luck is just everything, she thought as she paced the room. *How can I possibly be this lucky?*

She stopped. "I owe my new job to Debi."

First, she called Debi with the good news. Then, she called her pals from Equity.

CHAPTER TWENTY-THREE

May stomped the December snow from her boots and entered the familiar operations office. Ahead of her, Marta was signing in for the same Equity flight. The two hugged.

"Can you believe they called us back for Christmas?" Marta said.

"Yeah, I can believe it. It's always been the only holiday I never wanted to miss," May grumbled. "We'll get back late Christmas Eve if everything goes right, so keep your fingers crossed."

"When do you start training for United?" Marta asked.

"In a few weeks," May answered. "I took a leave of absence from Equity. I'm not giving up my seniority number until I've got United Airlines wings pinned on my chest."

"Did Equity give you a hard time?"

"Not at all. So many people are still furloughed, they didn't care. Any luck with interviews yet?"

"No, but I haven't been looking that hard," Marta said. "It's been nice spending time with my brother and his kids. I'll have to start looking soon. Have you heard from Jessie?"

May shook her head. "She called right before she left for training in Miami. We probably won't hear a thing until she's done. I hope she'll be happy."

The Christmas travel season kept May busy until her training with United. Once on leave from Equity, she spent six cold weeks in Chicago working like crazy to get through United's rigorous training program. She forged the same close bonds with her new classmates that she'd made with her Equity friends years before. Graduation took place in the middle of March, followed by two weeks of free time to find an apartment in her new home base of Chicago. Her first flight was scheduled April first.

Events moved so quickly that it wasn't until she finished training and was on a return flight to Connecticut that she could take stock of all that had happened. She stared out the window of the plane as the Midwest passed beneath her.

It's time to leave. It's really time for me to leave Equity. Time to go to a major airline like I always wanted.

The phrase repeated in her mind as she realized just how difficult it would be to leave Equity. In so many ways, the last three years were a blur, so much of it had taken place at 600-miles-an-hour, six miles above the Earth. Rome, Scotland, Brussels, San Juan. The all-night crossings of the Atlantic, the wacky mishaps, that crazy Rose Bowl trip, her friends.

She loved her friends dearly. She knew where she was going it would never be the same.

PART SIX:
All Those People ...
June 1984

CHAPTER TWENTY-FOUR

May sat in the kitchen of her Chicago apartment staring intently at the phone. She was on reserve all month and currently on call waiting to be assigned a flight. The end of her call period was approaching, and she wished that if she were going to be assigned a flight that it would happen soon.

Roommates all working and me here all alone. Come on, United, she thought, *Call me now!*

The phone jangled, and May nearly fell out of her chair.

Wow, I must be clairvoyant!

She fumbled with the receiver before answering with a loud, "Hello!"

"Hello yourself!" Marta answered on the other end of the line. "How's the Windy City?"

"Oh... Hi! I thought you were United!" May said. "I'm waiting for a trip. I've been sitting here on call for hours and I wish they'd hurry up. It's so great to hear your voice! The Windy City? Well, it's nowhere near as crazy as Equity, and I miss that, but the working conditions are great and the pay is a whole lot better."

May heard Marta sigh. "I'll bet it is," Marta said. "Are you glad you did it?"

"Yeah. It was really hard to resign, but I'm glad I did," May said. "Once I'm off reserve, I might actually have a personal life. How is it there?"

"Equity is on its last legs," Marta said. "They owe money everywhere and aren't paying anyone, including me. They can't even buy food for flights anymore."

"That's awful."

"But..." Marta said. "Guess what?"

"What?"

"I have a second interview with United next week," Marta said.

"That's great!" May shouted. "I know you'll get hired. Make sure they have your right address and phone number!"

They laughed.

"Have you heard from Jessie lately?" Marta asked.

"A few weeks ago. She's doing lots of charters. Some of them are to odd places," May said.

"Like?" Marta replied.

"Central America… Nicaragua, Honduras, places like that. Places with political problems. Insurgents, guerrillas, drug smugglers. And the Middle East… Egypt and Sinai, I think."

"That sounds scary," Marta said.

"She's flying to the places I worry about," May said. "She said she doesn't get any sleep, but she loves it."

"You got out at the right time," Marta said.

"I think things are coming together for everybody," May said. "Louisa is happy at Northwest. I'm happy here. Jessie says she is happy at Saber. Kathleen met a fabulous guy in San Francisco and is moving there. As soon as you get hired at United, I'll be able to rest easy."

"I'll do my best," Marta said with a chuckle. "I'll give you a call when I'm in Chicago next week."

"You better, talk to you soon."

May stared at the phone for another half an hour. It was late afternoon and an hour later in Connecticut than in Chicago, but she knew that Orrie and Hoot would still be at the airport. So, she figured she'd give her old friends and mentors a call. Orrie answered the phone.

"Well, how's our girl doing?" he asked. "You run into Al Capone out there yet?"

May laughed. "No, Orrie, not yet," she said. "Do you have a few minutes to talk?"

"Sure, Hoot's up with a bunch of victims now, and I'm takin' a break. What's on your mind?"

May hesitated.

"I'm worried about a friend," she admitted. "One of my old roommates took a job with Saber, and they've got her flying to Nicaragua, Honduras, and the Middle East. Should I be worried?"

There was a long pause on the other end of the line. May imagined Orrie scratching his head, then his chin.

"That doesn't sound good, considering old Skin Flint," he finally replied. "Your friend is a big girl, and she knows the score, right?"

"Yes."

"Well then, she has to make her own decisions," Orrie said. "I've been flying a lot of years, and I've done pretty well, because I always did what my gut told me to do."

"Does your gut say anything about this?"

"For her to get the hell out of there," he said. "Sorry, kiddo. That's probably not what you want to hear."

"That's okay, Orrie. I appreciate the honesty. You're right," May said. "She's a big girl, and right now she says she's happy. I have to respect that."

She glanced at the clock on the kitchen wall.

"I'd better go. I'm on call. United could still give me a trip. Tell Hoot I asked about him."

"Will do, and be good out there!"

May hung up. She usually felt good after talking to Orrie but not this time.

CHAPTER TWENTY-FIVE

May looked through flight schedules, her cheerful mood reflecting the fact that on this cold, late October evening, she'd completed her six-month probationary period with United and was no longer on reserve. She found herself adjusting well to life in Chicago and had even resumed her flying lessons at a nearby small airport. She had even made her first solo cross-country flight.

United continued to do well financially. Not only had the company expanded its route system, but they planned to hire hundreds of new flight attendants. May had enough seniority to hold a scheduled line of flying, but she still needed to bid for it. May had nearly completed her bids when the phone rang.

"Hi!" May answered happily. "How are things in our nation's capital?"

Marta had gotten a job with United, which was good because last month Equity finally folded. United's prosperity meant that flight attendants were needed at many of its bases, so Marta was sent to Washington, D.C. May was disappointed that Marta couldn't remain in Chicago, but the two kept in touch. On the other end of the long-distance line, Marta spoke in a whisper. May knew instantly that something was very wrong, but she couldn't understand anything Marta said.

"What is it, Marta?" May asked. "What's wrong?"

"Have you seen the news today?"

"No, I've been wrapped up with my bids," May said. "What happened?"

Marta's voice shook. "Saber had a crash. In Goose Bay. Canada. Fuel stop. They got their fuel, but when they took off, they got maybe five hundred feet in the air and then crashed."

May shivered.

"Was all of this on the news? What time did it happen?" May asked as more questions flooded her mind. "Do you know more details? How many people were on it? What about the crew?"

"I only know what's on the news," Marta said. "I've been on the phone with Equity people a lot since they owe me money."

May's head swam.

"May… May…" Marta's voice choked. "Everyone was kil—"

"NO!, NO! NO! NO! Don't say it, Marta," May screamed. "Please don't say it!"

"Jessie… Jessie was on the plane."

May gripped the phone. Marta sobbed.

"The news said… it was raining," Marta managed to get out. "Maybe… icing, I don't know."

May's throat tightened.

"The pilots," May said in her own whisper. "They will find out more."

"Yeah," Marta answered. "I called Benny."

"I'll call Olivia, she's still with Les," May said.

There was a long silence.

"May, I've got to go. I've got an early trip," Marta's voice broke again. "Somehow I've got to pull myself together."

May hung up the phone and turned on the television. Tears streamed down her face as she stared at the TV, weeping, waiting, for hours. Once they heard more details, many from the old Equity crew members made arrangements to visit Boston for Jessie's memorial service. United allowed May a few extra days off. Jessie's sister and younger brother organized the service. They were the only family present. The dozens (attending the funeral) were flight attendants and pilots from Equity and Saber Air.

After the service, May stopped in Connecticut to spend a day with her family. She had some time before her flight to Chicago. She paced restlessly around her old bedroom. Her sister knocked quietly.

"Can I come in?" she asked.

"Sure," May answered.

"How are you doing?"

"I always had a bad feeling about that company. Call it intuition or whatever you want," May said. "Flint couldn't have a conscience working people the way he did. What other kinds of things was he willing to do to make a buck?"

"How do you feel about flying now?" Lynn asked. "Do you still want to do this job?"

"I'm not scared to do the job, if that's what you mean," May answered. "But my heart isn't in it. Loosing Jessie took something and I don't know if I can get it back."

Lynn put her arm around May.

"I can't imagine losing a friend like that," her sister said. "You guys had so much in common. I think I know someone who might understand." Lynn hesitated. "I don't know if I should tell you this or not," she finally said. "Jake is home from Alaska. I ran into him at the grocery store. He asked how you were doing."

May didn't say anything for a minute. "I don't know if that is good or bad. Does he know that I'm here now?"

"No," Lynn said. "I thought you could approach him when you're ready."

May's eyes teared up.

"I almost forgot… I came up to tell you," Lynn said, "Mom's making meatloaf."

May smiled through her tears. "Comfort food always helps."

May didn't reach out to Jake, and she didn't get any of the answers about the crash that she craved. She also didn't find any certainty about what flying meant to her now. But she had to go back to Chicago, especially if she hadn't drawn up another plan. She didn't talk to anyone from Equity until she ran into Marta four weeks later in the terminal in Chicago.

"I've heard some things," Marta said. "Officials in Goose Bay say it wasn't icing at all. It's a big controversy."

"What do you mean?" May asked.

"The plane was a military charter of 250 soldiers returning from the Egyptian desert. We've both done military flights before. We know the soldiers come with weapons."

"Stowed in the belly of the plane," May replied.

"People think they were carrying ammunition that exploded somehow." Marta paused. "Les and some other pilots are speculating. Maybe Flint was smuggling weapons they shouldn't have been transporting. Missiles or something. At the crash site, some military guys loaded a bunch of big boxes from the plane into a truck and drove away." Marta paused again. "Their last stop was supposed to be Central America."

May gasped. She remembered her flight to Germany a few years earlier and the attempt to transfer crates from a Saber jet to theirs. The two flight attendants stood silently. Passengers hurried past them in the terminal.

May finally spoke. "Did you notice… the plane was 115?"

Marta nodded. "All of those lives, all of those people, and Jessie."

"All of those people," May repeated, "and Jessie."

CHAPTER TWENTY-SIX

May slammed the truck door shut and wheeled her bag down her parent's driveway. Rows of daffodils bobbed in the afternoon breeze. May's mother stood from tending her flowers.

"Where is your car?" her mother asked.

"The old heap finally gave out," May said. "It was burning tons of oil and was overheating non-stop. I closed the car door one day, and the other skirt guard fell off. So I got a little truck?"

"Nice, very nice."

"I got an auto loan through the company credit union. I'll be paying on it forever, but I had to do it. It was a long drive from Chicago, but I wanted to break it in with a long road trip." May stopped to smell the daffodils. "These are so pretty. How many different varieties did you plant?"

"Too many," her mother answered. "How long can you stay?"

"A few days. I..."

Another vehicle came down the long driveway. A dark green Jeep that she did not recognize parked beside her truck. Jake stepped out, tall and lean. His appearance was more rugged, his face a little weathered, and, despite it, May thought him more handsome. The time in Alaska had matured him. A flush went through her.

"Well, hey," she stammered, approaching him. "It's been a long time."

Her mother turned and went into the house.

"How have you been?" he asked.

She extended her hand to shake his, a formal gesture that felt silly. As his hand touched hers, she drew closer and gave him a quick hug. His body was firm and strong, as she keenly remembered, and she found herself wanting to stay in his arms. She backed away.

"I heard that you've been around for a couple of months," May said. "Your family must be glad for that."

"Yeah, I've been traveling between here and Colorado quite a bit," Jake said. "A few friends and I are working on getting a business off the ground. My sister and brother have been running the outdoor equipment business pretty well so it's time to expand. How are you?"

May shrugged. "Okay. United is a nice company to work for. I finally got that job with a big airline."

"That's great. It's what you wanted."

"Yeah. It's what I wanted." She walked over to her truck and leaned against it.

Jake followed. "Your sister told me about your friend. I'm so sorry. She told me how close you two were and how much you had in common."

May's head dropped. "I can't seem to get myself past it. I've been moping for months. You know how much I've always loved airplanes. I wanted to learn to fly for as long as I can remember. I was so close to getting my license," May said. "I was getting ready for my flight exam. When she died, I stopped going. I feel guilty I'm doing it and she can't. She loved flying just as much as I did."

"Look," he said. "You two were great friends, right?"

"Yes."

He put both hands on her shoulders.

"If it had been you and not her, would you have wanted her to give up her dream?" he asked.

"No, of course not," May said. "Actually, I'd be really pissed if she did."

"Right," Jake said. "And if she were here right now, what would she say to you?"

May laughed. "She'd be pissed at me. I can hear her. "Hey jackass, stop wasting time and get your license!'"

Jake put his arms around her and held her close.

"What kind of business are you trying to get off the ground?" she asked.

"Well, when I was in Alaska for all that time, I discovered that it's pretty hard to get around. Unless you can fly, of course."

May stood bolt-upright and stared at him.

"I got my pilot's license a few years ago," he said.

Her mouth dropped open.

"A friend of mine in Alaska was looking for partners to buy a small airport a few hours from Denver. The location is great. Lots of skiers, vacationers, skydivers, you name it. It's ours now. We've got plenty of work to do if we're going to make a go of it."

May couldn't utter a word.

"We're going to need good people. As a matter of fact, I've been talking to those two buddies of yours out at your old airport. I think I've got them convinced to get a skydiving business going." He laughed. "Your buddy Hoot said, how did he put it? He's more than happy to take people up that want to hurl their asses into space, as long as the pay is good and the scenery is nice."

She gazed at him.

"Say something!" Jake laughed.

"I can't. I just... I can't believe you!"

"May, I was hoping I'd catch you. I needed to see if there was anything still alive between you and me. I've thought about you so much these past few years, and I know how I feel. So, can we talk?"

She walked over to his Jeep and looked inside. "Is it four-wheel drive?" she asked.

"What? Yes, it's four-wheel drive!"

"That's good. Four-wheel drive is good to have in Colorado. My truck is four-wheel drive."

Jake looked at her, exasperated, as she continued to walk around the Jeep.

"I have a good work schedule now. I know when my days off will be, so I can plan things like appointments and flying lessons."

Jake stared at her.

"United has a big base in Denver," she said.

She rubbed away a small smudge on the hood of the Jeep and then turned to him.

"It's open right now to anyone that wants to transfer there. It will be open for the next few months."

She walked to Jake, gazing deeply into his eyes. She put her arms around his neck.

"I never stopped thinking about you either," May said. "And I'll need a nice little airport where I can finally get my pilot's license."

ABOUT THE AUTHOR

DAWN O'HARRA worked as a flight attendant for a small carrier and later moved to United. Any Landing is based on her experiences in the airline industry. She has her pilot's license, lives in the Pocono Mountains of Pennsylvania, and spent the bulk of her professional life as a science teacher.

For travel memoir and how-to on the ground...

Motorhome Gypsies

Practical RV Living Advice & Real World Adventures

by Rachel Thompson & Lisa Cross

Before #RVLiving and #VanLife exploded from the fringes to the mainstream, Rachel Thompson and Lisa Cross packed up their worldly possessions and let the lease on their apartment lapse. They purchased their first motorhome and set out to travel the country, both for the experience and in search of the next place they wanted to call home.

Now, 15 years later, Rachel and Lisa still embrace RV living, and a life as "motorhome gypsies" as they say in the subculture. They have compiled their wisdom, their advice, their good times and even their mistakes into this 200-page volume that is part memoir, part travel writing and part how-to.

Whether you are merely curious about the lifestyle or preparing a bug-out vehicle, this book provides practical guidance that you need to read before you commit. Don't waste your money or lose your sanity because of things you don't know about motorhome life.

For more historical fiction from the latter half of the 20th Century...

The Death of Big Butch
by Larry Sceurman

May, 1974.
Jimmy Washburn, young family man, loses a good friend to a heart attack when only 27. The death teaches Jimmy about his community, friendship, and responsibility just in time for the birth of his second child. This debut novella from Larry Sceurman captures small-town Americana with humor and poignancy.

Purchase our titles on our website, online or ask for them at your favorite bookseller.

Looking for a Romantic Comedy?...

TRAPPED

What If Skunks Were Matchmakers

by Seneca Blue

Edna Gardner, who goes by Ed, is over-educated and under-employed, approaching 40 and overweight. She hasn't had a date in several presidential administrations, works several part-time jobs (professor, graphic designer, photographer and journalist among them), and has resigned herself to a future with her drunken sister, Gertrude, as a roommate in the dying steel town where they were born.

Her life consists of one comedic tragedy after another, until the day skunks invade her backyard.

Then, she hires Clint Anderson to trap her skunks, and he revives her interest in men, builds her confidence and shows her that maybe she can fall in love.

Purchase our titles on our website, online or ask for them at your favorite bookseller.